All the Little Lies

Curran has worked as a teacher, an actor and scriptwriter,
w reviews fiction for various publications and blogs. She
lished short story writer and her most recent, *The Thought*
was shortlisted for the 2017 CWA Margery Allingham
tory Competition. An early draft of her debut novel,
Mindsight, was shortlisted for the Yeovil Literary Prize in 2013.
All the Little Lies is her fourth novel.

@Christi_Curran

Also by Chris Curran

Mindsight
Her Turn to Cry
Her Deadly Secret

CHRIS CURRAN

ALL THE LITTLE LIES

KILLER
READS

A division of HarperCollins*Publishers*
www.harpercollins.co.uk

KillerReads
an imprint of HarperCollins*Publishers* Ltd
1 London Bridge Street
London SE1 9GF

www.harpercollins.co.uk

This paperback edition 2019

First published by HarperCollins*Publishers* Ltd 2019

A catalogue record for this book
is available from the British Library

ISBN: 978-0-00-833634-9

Set in Minion by
Palimpsest Book Production Limited, Falkirk, Stirlingshire

Printed and bound in the UK by CPI Group (UK) Ltd, Croydon CR0 4YY

MIX
Paper from
responsible sources
FSC™ C007454

For Emma and Neil with much love.

CHAPTER ONE

Eve

She had to go. And quickly. Before they woke up. But still Eve stood by her daughter's cradle, looking down at her in the glow of the night light, longing to stroke the warm little head once more. To run her finger down Ivy's fat cheek and across her tiny damp mouth. The baby snuffled and shifted, and Eve held her breath. It was midwinter and still dark outside, but morning was on its way. She had to go now or it would be too late.

She crept barefoot past the bedroom where her husband was sleeping, but didn't look in. The baby monitor would wake him when Ivy cried. Since her birth he had done as much for her as Eve had. And managed it better. He often did the first morning feed and there was breast milk in the fridge and stored in the freezer too.

She had left a note on the kitchen table. There was nothing more to do.

Her clothes and trainers were in a plastic carrier in the cupboard under the stairs. She threw them on and shoved her dressing gown inside. With any luck Alex would see it wasn't hanging on the back of the bedroom door when he woke and

1

assume she was with the baby or downstairs. It might give her a bit more time.

For once she was thankful they had no driveway or garage and it was nearly impossible to park outside their house. So Alex must have thought the car was down at the other end of the road when he got home. It was actually a few streets away.

Everything was so still and silent in the early morning chill that she was aware of her own footsteps even though she was wearing soft-soled trainers. The icy air bit into her lungs. Plumes of white steamed out as she breathed and the atmosphere had that heavy feeling that means snow is not far off.

There was a forlorn-looking Christmas tree in the window of one house and a string of lights twinkling from the gables of another. It was still officially the Christmas season. Today was the sixth of January – Twelfth Night – and the Eliot poem about the three wise men came into her head. Something about a journey, a long cold journey.

In the glimmer of the street lights the pavement had a frosty glitter and she told herself to concentrate. It wouldn't do to fall.

Once, she thought she heard footsteps behind her and stopped, holding her breath. The footsteps stopped too, and she looked back down the street. There was a shape, totally still, under a tree at the end. It could be a figure, but might just be a shadow. And she needed to hurry.

The car windows were thick with white and she used the de-icer and scraper as quietly as she could. The rucksack she'd packed with a few essentials was already in the boot, so all she had to do was to climb in and start the engine. But when it was humming she sat for a moment breathing heavily.

And asking herself if she really wanted to go through with this.

Three Months Earlier

It was a relief to see Suzanne's name pop up on her phone. She would want to talk about work and Eve always enjoyed that. It felt so strange to be at home in October instead of teaching. She was even missing the staff meetings. Suzanne had taken over as head of the art department and she rang once a week or so to talk things through, although they both knew she was perfectly able to cope on her own. Suzanne probably realized how much Eve needed to feel she was still part of school life. And it was good to talk about something other than her pregnancy.

'Hi, Suzanne. How's it going?'

'Fine. And you? Alex still driving you mad?'

Eve felt a flush of guilt. What had she said? It was true she was fed up with Alex treating her like an invalid, fussing over everything from how much she slept to her diet, but she must have told Suzanne more than she meant. She tried to make her voice light. 'No, he's fine. It's my mum who's the real worrier. Anyway what's up?'

They spent a few minutes discussing the new exam syllabus. Then Suzanne said, her voice rising a little, 'What did you think of the link I sent you?'

'I haven't checked my phone recently.'

'It's nothing urgent. Just made me think of you.'

When they'd said their goodbyes Eve looked for the message. It was brief:

Have a look at this. Any connection?

Apart from that there was just a link to a newspaper story:

LOST ARTWORKS RESURFACE AT BALTIC GALLERY

Newcastle's Baltic Gallery has a new exhibition of paintings by artist, Stella Carr. If you haven't heard of her it's not because she's a new talent, but because soon after making a brief splash in the art world in 1986 she disappeared from sight and died tragically (and somewhat mysteriously) a year later at the early age of twenty-one. If she hadn't done so it's likely she could have been one of the leading lights in the BritArt scene of the late 80s, early 90s.

At the time of her death it seemed that the handful of her pictures seen in an exhibition of promising young artists, at London's Houghton Gallery, were all Stella had left behind.

Seeing the name of the gallery made Eve pause. Her father had been a partner there. She couldn't remember mentioning it to Suzanne, but if she had that might explain why she'd sent the link. He'd certainly be interested because he would have been there at the time of Stella's exhibition. She carried on reading.

The ever-fickle art world moved on and Carr was forgotten. But with this new display it's clear that she was a considerable talent. While some of the paintings were in the Houghton exhibition, and others appeared soon after, a few have never been seen before. According to The Baltic they were her last completed works. They are giving away very little about how they came by these. All this paper could learn is that they are from a private collection.

Below the article were two of the paintings. One showed a terraced hillside covered in dark trees. It was called *Pines* and the second, *Mermaid*. This was particularly arresting. Instead of a fish's tail the mermaid's whole body was green and almost snake-like. Only the face – beautiful but secretive with floating hair – looked human.

She really liked the style. There was a freedom in the brush-strokes; a vitality about them that she loved.

There was a close-up of the signature, and Eve stopped scrolling to stare at it. It wasn't a name but a shooting star, just like the ones she used to love drawing when she was little. And something else stirred in her memory. Something that made her move on faster.

There was a third picture entitled *Maggie and Me* and this was lovely. Two young women, both very slender, one with a mass of brown hair and the other with a tumble of russet curls. They stood in a woodland glade. Trees heavy with leaves surrounded them. Their long skirts, one green, one dark blue, floated in the breeze. Strands of hair trailed across their faces.

At the bottom of the page she found a photograph. Not very clear, but Eve saw enough to make her catch her breath. This was what Stella Carr had really looked like. She was the one with the red hair, although here it was more ginger than russet and there was a scattering of freckles across the pale skin that the painting had omitted. She seemed to be not only slim, but small. And Eve could understand why Suzanne had sent the link now.

Stella Carr was extraordinarily similar to Eve herself. Not that Suzanne could have understood the significance – she knew nothing about Eve's origins.

But the photograph, the link with the gallery, and that tantalizing hint of memory were enough to tell Eve one thing.

This woman, Stella Carr, had to be her own birth mother.

At 4.30 it was still light outside. They'd been having an Indian summer, but as evening drew closer a chill wind had sprung up off the sea sending a few dead leaves rattling along the footpath. Eve pulled her jacket close to her throat, trying to control her breathing. She needed to deal with this as calmly as she could.

Her parents lived only a short distance away, down the hill in the Old Town of Hastings. She always used to walk there, but although it was tarmac or solid steps all the way, it was steep going. She had to agree with Alex that at seven months pregnant it wasn't worth the risk. And the climb back would be impossible.

When she was sitting in the car she took out her mobile to text Alex. He had been coming home earlier and earlier recently and he would panic if she wasn't there.

Just popping over to see Mum and Dad. Love you XXX.

After she'd sent it she shook her head at how different it sounded from the way she was feeling.

As she drove down towards the sea she shivered at the sight of the foam-topped waves speeding towards the beach and the bank of grey cloud on the horizon. Winter was coming. And her baby girl was due in the dead of winter. She had been looking forward to it so much. But now she was so disturbed she could hardly think let alone formulate the words she would need when she confronted her mum and dad.

They had lied to her.

All these years they had told her they knew nothing about her birth mother except that she was young and alone and couldn't look after a child.

Eve was in no doubt that Stella Carr was her mother. They were so alike that seeing the photograph was like looking in a mirror, but what clinched it was the mention of the Houghton Gallery, where Stella's only exhibition during her lifetime had been held. Eve's father, David, was a partner in the gallery throughout the 1980s. It didn't belong to him: his friend, Ben Houghton, was the money man. But it was David who knew about art and had *the eye* as he always said. He was the one who organized the exhibitions. So if Stella Carr had been part of one he must have known her.

Her parents moved to Hastings when they decided to start a family and bought a tiny gallery just off the seafront. Eve had never seen Houghton's, which had closed when she was very young, though she imagined it had been a lot more swish than the little Hastings shop. But her parents were happy with the move. Except they found they couldn't have children and so they adopted Eve. When she left home to go to university they had sold the family house and now lived above the shop (her dad hated her calling it that: 'It's a gallery not a shop, Eve,') in a cosy little flat.

The cobbled street outside the gallery was pedestrianized, so Eve had to park a few hundred yards away. As she came close to the shop her steps slowed and she hugged her jacket to her, dreading the next few minutes. She loved her parents so much, but this seemed to change everything. How could they have deceived her all her life?

Her dad was alone wrapping a picture on the small desk at the back of the gallery. He beamed at her. 'Eve, what a lovely surprise. Alex not with you?'

'No.' She couldn't even pretend to act normally.

'Everything all right, lovely?'

'I need to speak to you and Mum.'

He took off his glasses and rubbed his eyes in the way he always did when he was worried, and she bit back on the temptation to say everything was all right.

Because it wasn't.

One long look and he said, 'Your mum's upstairs. Ask her to put the kettle on and I'll be with you in a minute.'

He seemed about to reach for her, but she walked past him and through the door at the back that led to the stairs.

She couldn't avoid her mum's arms as she came out into the warm kitchen at the top. It was the same soft hug with a little squeeze at the end that Eve knew so well, but today it felt different. Counterfeit somehow. The way it had sometimes seemed to her when she was a teenager and she and Jill argued endlessly.

'Are you all right, darling? You look pale.'

Eve sat at the pine table. It had stood in the kitchen of their old house for as long as she could remember. 'I'm OK. I just need to speak to you and Dad. Together.'

Her mother thumped down opposite. 'What is it?' Her voice wavered. 'Not the baby?'

'No. It's fine. I'm fine.'

Jill moved to touch her hands across the table, but Eve sat back arms crossed.

'And there's nothing wrong between me and Alex either.'

She had printed out the article, and she pulled it from her bag to put in front of her mother. Jill looked down at the paper, her fingers plucking at one corner. Long after Eve knew she must have finished reading she stayed staring down, saying nothing.

Finally Eve could stand it no longer. 'Why didn't you tell me?' she said.

Footsteps sounded on the stairs and Jill turned as Eve's father came through the door. He looked from Eve to her mother. The silence felt heavy, but Eve didn't speak. Instead she pulled the article from Jill's fingers. Her mum gave a tiny cry as if it had hurt.

Eve thrust the paper at her dad. 'Why didn't you tell me?' she repeated.

It seemed to take only a glance for him to see what it was. A sigh. 'Let's have a cup of tea and talk this through properly, shall we?'

Before he'd finished Eve's mum stood and began to fill the kettle. Eve wanted to shout at them that she didn't need tea, she needed the truth. But when her dad sat next to her, turned his chair towards her and took her hands, she felt like throwing herself into his arms and asking him to tell her it was all a mistake. That nothing had changed.

As Jill took milk from the fridge, Eve watched her familiar figure. She was small and dumpy with a round face that still showed only a few wrinkles. Her curly hair was coloured the same soft brown it had always been, with just a hint of grey at the roots. But since her heart attack a few years ago she had begun to walk with a slight stoop. When she came to sit with them at the table again she lowered herself carefully.

Eve felt a twang of guilt for upsetting her, but she had to know. Eventually her mother met her eyes.

'We didn't mean to deceive you. Please believe that.' It was almost a whisper. She reached for her husband's hand and his fingers tightened on hers as he began to nod in time with her words. 'You always knew you were adopted. When you were tiny, we told you we loved being your parents and that you were the most wonderful gift we'd ever been given. That's the only truth that matters.'

Eve bit her lip so hard it hurt, fighting to keep the anger from her voice. 'You said you knew virtually nothing about my birth mother.' She felt the baby kick under her ribcage and rubbed her hand over the hard mound of her belly. *It's all right, my darling.* She had to keep calm.

Jill sighed and ran her fingers through her curls, and David said, 'We told you she was very young and couldn't look after a child. That she wanted you to have a family, the kind of life she could never give you. The only thing we didn't tell you was her name.'

Eve couldn't hold back a bitter laugh. 'You didn't think to mention you knew her?'

'What good would that have done? She was dead.'

'And you didn't tell me that either.' This was unbelievable.

Her mother's fingers were pressed to her mouth, muffling her words. 'When you were little it would only have upset you. And as you grew older you didn't seem interested in knowing anything more.'

Eve stood, pushing the chair back. Her dad stopped it from falling over. 'Of course I was interested, but you always made me feel you would be hurt if I tried to find my real parents.'

'Oh, Eve, don't say that.' Her mother's voice cracked and she pulled a tissue from the box on the table.

David's expression, when he looked at Eve, was one she remembered from when she misbehaved as a kid. 'Please, Eve. You're upsetting your mother and in your condition you mustn't get stressed.'

She felt suddenly exhausted, her knees so weak she could no longer stand. She dropped back onto her seat and her words came out on a huge sigh. 'Just tell me everything.'

Her dad went round the table to stand behind Jill, resting his hands on her shoulders. They both looked at Eve. 'Ben and I decided to mount a show of upcoming young artists and she was one of them. The best of the bunch. Then I found out she was pregnant. She was young, poor and alone. And I offered to help her. We couldn't believe our luck when we became your parents. Still don't.'

He dropped a kiss onto Jill's curls then turned away to switch on the kettle again, saying. 'Now whatever happened to that tea?'

Eve could hear the Scottish lilt that became stronger when he was stressed. Her mum wiped her eyes and blew her nose.

'So how did she die? I mean I could have inherited something.' She rubbed her bump again. 'My baby could have.'

Her mum spoke fast. 'No it was nothing like that. It was an accident.'

Eve coughed. Her voice threatened to wobble. 'What happened?' She touched the article. 'It says her death was tragic and mysterious.'

David came to sit beside her again, speaking softly. 'It was certainly tragic. She died in a fire.' He must have heard Eve gasp because he stopped. 'I'm sorry, darling.'

She had covered her eyes with her hands, but dropped them again. The images behind her lids were horrible. A deep breath. 'Go on. Tell me everything.'

He reached for her hand, squeezing gently. 'It was in Italy where she was staying. I can't remember how we found out officially.

But sometime later her friend sent us a note and the newspaper report.'

She managed to say, 'Who? Who was this friend?'

He stood again and went back to the kettle, tearing the cellophane from a new box of teabags. 'Just a girl she knew. I think they shared a place in London when they were at art school. Her work was in the exhibition too, but it was fairly mediocre if I recall and I know nothing else about her. She obviously didn't make it as an artist.'

'What about the letter?'

He turned to her mother who said, 'It was just a note. I'll have a look for it, but it was very brief. Didn't give much information. Nor did the newspaper.'

Her dad put a mug of tea in front of her. She took a huge gulp. The thought of her mother – that vibrant young girl in the photograph – burned to death was so horrible she was trembling. They all sat silently as they drank. It was as if they'd just suffered a bereavement.

After a while she took a deep breath and, looking from one of them to the other, asked the obvious question. 'So who was my father?'

Her mother screwed her tissue into a ball and shoved it up her sleeve. 'We never knew. A boyfriend she'd broken up with I suppose.'

Eve nodded, forcing herself not to say what she was thinking. *Or an older man? Maybe someone who was married?* She ran her finger down the article. In small print at the end it gave the dates of the Houghton Gallery exhibition. Eve was born close to nine months after the exhibition ended.

She looked up at her father. And that would be nine months after Stella met *him*.

CHAPTER TWO

Stella 1986

Stella was putting the finishing touches to a painting of her grandmother, standing close to the window to catch the last of the natural light. Her bedroom overlooked the tiny walled yard at the back of the house. Here in Marylebone they were surrounded by other Victorian terraces, so it wasn't the best place to paint especially on a dull March afternoon. She squinted at the photograph propped on the easel. She'd replaced the armchair her nana was sitting on in the photo and the striped wallpaper behind her with a riot of huge exotic flowers – a fantasy garden. Of course the portrait was a fantasy too. Nana didn't look like that anymore – she sat drooling in a chair in the nursing home – but this was how Stella wanted to remember her. She stroked the photo with one finger and swallowed on the lump in her throat.

Thank goodness for Maggie, thundering up the stairs even faster than usual. Stella put down her brush as her bedroom door burst open. 'Where's the fire?'

Maggie ignored her and threw herself on Stella's bed. 'Got anything decent to wear?' She laughed and before Stella could speak, 'Don't answer that. Come to my room and try something on.'

There was no point in arguing and anyway it would be too dark to carry on soon. 'Where are we going?' Since she'd come to live with Maggie – been taken under her wing was how Maggie described it – she'd had the kind of social life she'd only ever dreamed of.

Maggie's room was even untidier than Stella's and she flung open her bursting wardrobe and tossed a great pile of dresses onto the unmade bed. As Stella picked through them Maggie pulled off her own jeans and shirt and stood in her black bra and lacy knickers, one hand on her hip, studying Stella and shaking her head as she held dress after dress up to her shoulders. Stella knew her own figure wasn't bad. She and Maggie were pretty much the same size but she would never have Maggie's confidence. Came from always having had money she guessed. The best schools and all that. This house actually belonged to Maggie. Before coming to art school Stella had never known anyone who owned their own house and it was almost unbelievable that someone in her early twenties could do so.

'I can't choose until I know where we're going, *Margot*.' She grinned as she said it, knowing Maggie hated the name her parents had given her. Hated them too for that matter. She said her dad had only gifted her this house so he wouldn't feel bad about moving to the States with his new young wife. At least that was more than she'd had from her mother who, according to Maggie, had deserted them when she was a toddler. The fact that neither Maggie nor Stella – now her nana no longer recognized her – had any real family had helped their friendship develop.

Maggie threw a shoe in Stella's direction and plonked down among the pile of clothes, lighting a cigarette and talking through puffs. 'My man has invited us to a gallery opening. So pick something *tres* glam.'

The gallery was beautiful. All pale walls with black leather sofas. Waiters circulated carrying trays of champagne. Stella had never had it and wasn't sure she liked it, but Maggie swallowed hers in one gulp and grabbed another. Then Stella felt her stiffen beside her.

'Damn it, the old bitch is here.'

Following her gaze across the room Stella saw a tall, blonde woman in a slender black dress. Her hair gleamed under the lights, and just looking at her made Stella feel like a scruffy midget. This must be the wife of Maggie's current man, Ben. Maggie liked older men and was never bothered if they were married.

It had to be Ben who approached them. He took both Maggie's hands in his and kissed her cheek and from the way Maggie stroked his jacket and gazed up at him Stella could tell he was more than one of her flings – a lot more.

He was probably at least forty, but very handsome in a dark Irish kind of way. 'It's Maggie, isn't it?' he said, his eyes twinkling.

With a quick glance around, Maggie punched his arm. 'You never told me *she* would be here,' she hissed.

'Couldn't be helped, I'm afraid, but I doubt you'll be lonely.' He turned to Stella. 'And that goes for both of you.' He took her hand, and she felt herself flush, wishing she'd had time to wipe it on her dress because it felt sticky. He looked from her to Maggie. A flash of white teeth. 'Are you related?'

Maggie moved closer to him, touching his arm. Her voice turning gruff. 'Stella is my flatmate.'

'Ah, just alike in beauty then. So are you an artist too, Stella?'

'An art student, yes.'

'That's wonderful. Did Maggie tell you we're planning a small exhibition of young talented folk like yourselves? We've already snapped up a couple of Maggie's collages.'

Before she could answer he beckoned to another man who had been talking to an elderly couple nearby.

'You must meet my partner, David Ballantyne. He knows more about art than anyone in London.'

As the other man came over Ben said, 'David, meet two of the young talents for our new show.' Then he gave Maggie's bottom a pat and headed away.

David was a bit younger than Ben. Mid-thirties Stella guessed. He was nice-looking where Ben was handsome, with fair hair and glasses, but still looked good in his dinner jacket and black specs. His smile was friendly, but he seemed embarrassed to be stranded with them, especially with Maggie rather obviously scowling after Ben's retreating back.

'I'm sorry, I didn't catch your names,' he said, and Stella thought she detected a hint of a Scottish burr.

Maggie gave him her brilliant smile and held out her hand. 'Maggie de Santis.' She always pronounced her surname with an almost comical Italian accent. Despite hating her first name, and the parents who gave it to her, Maggie was very proud of the fact that her ancestors had been Italian aristocracy. She tossed back her shining chestnut hair. 'You and Ben chose two of my collages for the show.'

David's eyes crinkled as he turned to Stella with a laugh. 'Ah, that explains where I've seen you before. It's a very amusing picture, although not a good likeness if I may say so.'

The collage he must be talking about had lots of photos of Maggie's friends in the most bizarre poses and situations. Stella's face was right in the middle; she was wearing a bathroom plunger as a hat, decorated with a huge feathery-topped carrot. Her laugh came out too loud. She had no idea Maggie had got the picture into an exhibition.

Maggie smacked David's hand. 'Naughty boy. That was supposed to be a surprise.'

Stella could never believe how confident Maggie was with men who were so much older and more sophisticated. But then looking at the way David's face had flushed perhaps he wasn't so sophisticated after all.

His eyes were still on Stella. 'I don't remember seeing any of your work.'

'You haven't.' It sounded rude and she was very aware of her Geordie accent but he didn't seem bothered.

'Well why don't you bring some stuff in tomorrow for me to see?'

Someone waved from across the room, and he smiled and told them to enjoy the evening and was gone. Stella's heart was beating so fast she thought she might collapse. And when Maggie grabbed her arm she leaned in to her for support.

'Oh my god! Thank you so much.'

Maggie tapped her glass with her own. 'That's what friends are for. He'll love your stuff. And I wouldn't be surprised if he's taken a fancy to you, too.'

Stella told her not to be silly, but watching him smiling and chatting as he moved around the room she did think he looked rather lovely.

Eve

The doorbell to the flat shrilled into the silence. They all ignored it. Eve didn't take her eyes off David. Could he be her real father? Surely not. She knew how much he loved Jill. But no marriage was perfect and she guessed her parents' must have come under strain when they realized they couldn't have children of their own.

As if he knew what she was thinking David met her eyes and shook his head. His voice was suddenly old and weary. 'We were wrong to keep all this from you, but there never seemed to be a right time.'

The doorbell pierced the air again, a long ring, but Jill spoke over it. 'But we were all so happy, weren't we? How could that be wrong?'

Eve's phone began to buzz on the table – *Alex*. She had to answer.

'I'm outside. Got your message.' He must have come straight from the train.

'I thought we could drive home together. The light's not good at this time of night.'

She bit down on a spasm of annoyance. She was a better driver than Alex even with her bump. Why did he insist on treating her like an invalid?

'Stay there,' she said, 'I'll be down in a minute.'

Her father said, 'Eve, my darling …'

She shook her head and held up her hand to keep him from going on. 'It's all right, just leave me to think about it.' She shoved the article into her bag and turned to her mother. 'But please try to find that letter for me.'

As she was buttoning her jacket, Jill said, 'Why don't I come round tomorrow morning and we can talk this through? You can ask me anything you want then.'

Eve nodded. 'OK.' She must have said it more coldly than she meant because Jill's face crumpled.

'Eve, you must believe we've always done our best by you,' she said pulling at the curls on the nape of her neck.

It was a gesture so familiar that Eve felt a twist of pain deep inside. She said, 'I know you have,' and kissed her mother's cheek. 'I'll see you tomorrow.'

Alex talked about work on the drive home, but she was hardly listening. He was twenty years older than her and taught art history at University College London. It was how they had met. They hadn't got together until just before she graduated, and he never actually taught her. Her parents weren't too happy at the time. He'd been married before and Eve knew they were hoping she would come back to live with them for a while after she graduated, but there was never any chance of that. Although she couldn't have hoped for a better childhood, her teenage years had been difficult as she began to find their love stifling.

They'd grown to like Alex when they realized how happy he

17

made her, especially when he agreed with Eve that they would move to Hastings after her mother's heart attack.

As they pulled up outside the house he said, 'What's wrong?'

She wasn't ready to talk about it in the car, so she shook her head and, despite the baby bulk, got out quickly and had let herself in by the time he'd retrieved his briefcase from the back seat and locked the car.

Standing in the kitchen she could hear him take off his coat and walk in behind her. When she turned, his kiss was so warm and familiar she felt bad for shutting him out.

'Come on, Eve, tell me,' he said.

She took the scrunched-up article from her bag, then pulled him into the living room to make him sit on the sofa beside her. 'I found out today that my parents have been lying to me all my life.'

He took the article and glanced at her, expecting her to explain, but she tapped the paper and he fumbled in his pocket for his reading glasses. 'What is it?'

'Just read it, please, Alex. I'll go and dish the dinner up.'

She'd made a casserole in the slow cooker, so there was nothing much to do except to lay the table and put on some microwave rice. She expected Alex to come and talk to her when he'd finished reading, but he didn't, so she ladled out the food and called him. When she handed him his plate he didn't look at her.

'Alex? You realize who she is, don't you? And my parents lied to me about knowing her.'

He grabbed her hand and squeezed it. 'I'm sorry, sweetheart, that must have come as a real shock. I can understand you being upset, but I suppose they thought it was for the best.'

She knew her voice sounded bitter. 'Best for me or for them?'

'Well I'm sure it would have upset you to know your mother was dead. And when would be the right time to come out with something like that? Did they tell you what she died of?'

'Just that it was an accident.' She shuddered. 'She died in a fire – how awful.'

'Oh, no. Well, that would have been a difficult thing to tell a child.'

'And there's the suggestion that it was mysterious. Whatever that means.'

They were both silent, thinking about it, until Eve felt a kick from the baby that was so hard it made her cry out.

Alex said, 'All right?'

'Yeah. Just a kick.'

'All the same, you look exhausted. Maybe you should get an early night.'

She wanted to tell him to leave the worrying to her, but she knew how much this baby meant to him. It meant a lot to her too, of course. She was thirty-one and they'd tried for three years before she got pregnant. Although Alex looked wonderful for over fifty – his hair was still thick and there were no signs of grey – he'd been anxious that he might be too old for babies soon. And of course he'd already lost two children. His first wife had taken his son and daughter to Australia after the divorce and had apparently told them all sorts of lies about Alex, so they refused to see him. They were teenagers now, but he didn't even know how to contact them.

She touched the article. 'Have you noticed the date of the Houghton exhibition?'

'Yes, the year before you were born.'

'I looked it up. It was just over nine months before.'

Alex studied the report again, then put down his glasses. 'You're not thinking …?'

'It makes sense. Young artist trying to make it and an influential older man.'

Alex shook his head. 'No, I can't believe that of David.'

'He knew Stella at the time and if they did have an affair he could have been lying to Mum all these years as well as to me. Or maybe she decided to forgive and forget. Just glad to get a baby.'

'Eve, this is ridiculous. It's your parents we're talking about.'

'I wonder what he'll say if I ask for a DNA test?'

'You wouldn't do that, would you?'

She suddenly felt enormously weary. 'I don't know.' Alex was right that she needed to rest and she wanted to be alert when her mother came round tomorrow. She collected their dishes, tipped the remains in the bin and put the plates into the sink. 'I think I *will* go up now.' She kissed his hair, but stopped at the door. 'You know, after what I've learned about my parents today I don't feel I know them at all.'

She fell into a fitful sleep as soon as she was in bed. At one point, half-awake and not sure if she was dreaming, she thought she heard Alex talking to someone on the phone.

CHAPTER THREE

Stella

Stella had delivered two paintings to the Houghton Gallery. Holding them at arm's length, as if they were grubby or possibly dangerous, the glamorous receptionist had put them into a cupboard behind her desk and said Mr Ballantyne would call when he'd had a chance to see them. It was clear she didn't expect the news to be positive.

That was two days ago and, although Maggie told her she was stupid to be downcast, she kept expecting a request to remove her rubbish from the premises.

She had spent the morning at the Tate Gallery. She loved the place and at the moment they had a small exhibition of a group of artists who worked in the East End of London during the 1930s. One of them, George Grafton, was her favourite. Many of his paintings had been destroyed in the 1941 air raid in which he died: but some of his drawings had survived and she found copying them oddly soothing. She'd even started doing one or two of her own in his style. They were quite different from her usual stuff, but that was part of the pleasure. Made it more like playing than work.

It was a lovely afternoon and when she walked down the steps from the gallery there was the first hint of spring in the air. The Thames across the road glittered; each ripple sparkling as it caught the sunlight.

When she opened the front door, calling to Maggie as she did so, Ben waltzed out of the living room. Maggie was behind him looking furious, and Stella headed towards the stairs. Best to make herself scarce.

But Ben was looking at *her* with a broad smile. 'Ah, just the girl I want to see.'

She stopped and glanced at Maggie, but she muttered something and went into the kitchen closing the door behind her.

Ben said, 'David hasn't stopped raving about your work for two days. Wants to make it the centre of the exhibition. If he has anything to do with it you're going to be a star.'

Stella stopped halfway up the stairs. After what seemed an age she managed to say, 'Thank you. That's wonderful.'

Ben was rubbing his hands together. 'Now, I've got the car outside and Maggie tells me you have more work complete. So what do you say we load the boot and take it to the gallery now?' He bounded up past her, holding out his hand to take her drawing folder from her.

She hadn't made her bed this morning and there were clothes scattered on the floor and dirty cups on the bedside table and the window ledge.

With her folder under his arm, Ben headed straight for the picture of her nan on the easel, touching it with a fingertip to check it was dry. 'Right, we'll take this one and …' He turned to the canvases propped up by the wall. 'This and this and, yes, this too.'

In less than ten minutes they had carried them out to his car.

As she left the house she called, 'Goodbye,' to Maggie. There was no reply.

Eve

As soon as Alex left in the morning Eve went onto the Internet looking for more information about Stella. There were several reports on the Baltic exhibition, talking of her talent and the tragedy of her early death. Only one gave any details about that and as Eve read she felt something cold clench deep inside.

Stella's death was tragic. She had recently moved to Italy and was painting in a garden studio when it burned down. There were some suggestions that she was depressed at the time, but the Italian authorities eventually declared her death accidental.

Depressed at the time. Eve looked away from the screen and turned the phrase over in her mind. Where had those suggestions come from? The article was from *The Guardian,* so she found the contact details for the columnist and wrote a message.

I'm doing some research into the life and work of Stella Carr and wondered if you could tell me where the suggestions that she might have been depressed before her death came from.

She thought about it for a moment and added:

I'm working with Dr Alex Peyton and with David Ballantyne.

It was true, up to a point, and she hoped her own name, Eve Ballantyne, might help to give her enquiry more substance.

She couldn't stop that phrase *depressed at the time* from echoing in her head. Was it code for suicidal? Eve knew about depression. Her first year teaching art in a tough London comprehensive had been difficult. She had been trying to make a go of her own painting; working late into the night after she'd completed everything for school. Alex had been supportive, but eventually she had a breakdown. It was a nightmare that went on for months and, just as she was beginning to come back to herself, her mother's heart attack sent her back into turmoil. But that turned out for the best. They moved down to Hastings, she took a job in a local school and loved it. Nowadays she hardly painted.

What if she'd inherited a tendency to depression? She shook her head. Nothing good could come of thinking like that.

It didn't help that when her mum arrived at the house later that morning her first words were, 'Eve, you look exhausted.'

She forced herself not to say that it might be because of the shock she'd had yesterday. During her teenage years she had fought with Jill all the time and she still felt guilty about that.

As usual Jill headed for the kitchen, opening the lid of the cake tin she was carrying. 'I made a sponge.'

Eve had expected this and, although she was desperate to get down to talking about Stella, she had already percolated the coffee and put mugs and plates on the table. Her jaw tensed as she watched her mother cut the cake saying, 'What do you think? I thought it looked a bit dry.' Just like any normal day.

Eve nibbled at a few crumbs. 'It's fine. Lovely, as always. Now please, Mum, tell me everything.'

After what seemed an age Jill put her palms together and said, 'We're sorry for not being honest with you. We spent all last evening talking about it and your father seems to think the friend who let us know about Stella's death was the girl with her in the painting from the article – Maggie. He vaguely remembers her from the time of the Houghton exhibition and has an idea that Stella was sharing a house with her.'

This was something. 'What was her surname?'

'He can't remember. Only that she had some collages in the show. Apparently they weren't very good. Ben chose them and he wasn't the greatest judge of art.'

'Gallery owner was a strange choice of career for him then.'

'Dad says he liked the glamour of it. It actually belonged to his wife, Pamela. She had the money and was a bit of a socialite, enjoyed hosting openings and so on. Not something I was interested in. I hardly ever went there.'

Eve told herself to be patient. It wasn't easy. 'So you never met Stella?'

Her mother fitted the lid of the cake tin back on, pressing it carefully into place. Still smoothing her hands over it, she spoke without looking at Eve. 'Actually she stayed with us for a while before you were born.'

'What?' Eve plonked her mug down so hard the coffee splashed on her hand. She rubbed it off with the sleeve of her jumper, struggling to get the words out. 'Stella lived with you down here?' She was, what was the word? *Damn pregnancy for making her head so woolly.* Astounded, that was it, she was astounded. She'd assumed her mother had only met Stella when they picked up the baby (it was impossible to think of that child as herself).

'She didn't have anywhere else to go, you see. No family and I think she had to move out of the place where she was living.'

'With Maggie?'

'I suppose so. Although …'

'So it wasn't just Dad? *You* knew my birth mother too and you never told me.' It was little more than a gasp.

Jill moved back – away from her – and turned her mug round and round on the table looking at it with intense concentration. Her voice wobbled. 'We never set out to keep anything from you.'

'But you *did*. You *knew* her. You could have told me what she was like. You could have told me so many things. Even the fact that my mother was an artist might have made me try a bit harder with my own painting.' A chill shivered through her. 'Was she so horrible you thought it better I didn't know?'

Jill grabbed her hand. 'Of course she wasn't. Like we always said, she was a young girl in an impossible situation. And giving you to us was her way of doing the best she could for you.'

Eve looked into the hazel eyes she knew so well. The eyes that had comforted her when she was a little girl crying over a scraped knee or a bust-up with her friends. Eve's own eyes were a similar colour and she'd always been happy about that. It seemed to connect them.

'Please, Mum, tell me everything. I mean how did Dad even find out about her pregnancy if he hardly knew her?'

Her mother shook her head and took in a shuddering breath. 'I know what you're thinking, but there was nothing between them. He would never have done that to me. He's always been the kind of person people can talk to and she confided in him. She was alone and virtually penniless. She came to live here because she had nowhere else to go.'

This was unbelievable. 'You must have got to know her then.'

'Not really. She was very quiet and she wasn't here long.'

'And how did you first find out about her death?'

Her mother shook her head. 'I'm not sure. Through people in the art world I suppose. The note came later and even that was just a few lines. The truth is, and I'm sorry if this makes us sound callous, we knew Stella for such a short time and we began, very early on, to think of you as our own. We loved you so much right from the start that we didn't want to be reminded of how you came into our lives. But we've always been grateful to her.'

They didn't speak for a long while. Eve told herself nothing had really changed. She'd had a wonderful childhood; couldn't have chosen better parents. But why, oh why, hadn't they told her the truth? 'What about the note? Did you find it?'

Jill looked at her watch. She was always busy. If she wasn't helping David in the gallery, she was involved with various local groups and charities. She began rooting in her bag for her car keys. 'I'm sorry, no, but I'll search for it tonight.'

'What did it say about how she died?'

'Just that there was a fire.' The zip on her handbag seemed to be giving her trouble.

Eve took a breath. 'Only I read that there were suggestions she was depressed. Which might mean it was suicide. And then there was the comment about it being mysterious. What does that mean? That the fire might not have been accidental?'

Jill stopped. She sat down again and gripped Eve's hand. 'Oh, don't start thinking like that.' Her voice quavered. 'I promise I'll find the note and we'll answer as many of your questions as we can. But, darling, please concentrate on yourself and the baby for the moment. It's all in the past. Your health is the most important thing. Alex said you were exhausted last night.'

'You've spoken to him?'

'Dad rang him when you were asleep. Just to check you were all right.' Eve's face must have shown what she was feeling because Jill touched her cheek. 'Oh, I'm sorry, I've said something wrong.'

Eve tried to smile. 'No, it's fine.'

But it wasn't fine. Alex hadn't mentioned the call, and she didn't like the idea of them all discussing her behind her back. She followed Jill to the door and after they'd hugged she went into the front room, standing away from the window so she couldn't be seen, and watched her mother heading along the street to her car.

At the car door Jill turned to stare back at the house, her knuckles pressed against her lips. And the chill that had settled in Eve's stomach turned to ice.

Stella

Houghton's was closed, but Ben let them in through a side door. David appeared and helped take the pictures inside. He leaned one against the reception desk and spread the others out along the pale wall. For a few silent minutes he stood, arms folded, looking at them. Then said one word, 'Superb.' And finally Stella was able to breathe.

'Thank you,' was all she could say, and it seemed to make David aware of her for the first time.

He shook his head at her. 'No, thank *you*, Stella. These are beautiful. Fresh, original and so full of life. Just what we need as the centrepiece of the exhibition.'

Ben had disappeared into the office and came back with a bottle of champagne and three glasses. Stella stood in a daze as he popped the cork and poured the foaming wine into her glass. They clinked and Ben and David both kissed her on the cheek.

David raised his glass to her. 'Here's to our new star.' He laughed. 'I love the signature by the way.'

Stella grinned, too shocked to say anything. Her nan had always called her a little star and that's why she used the shooting star as her signature. Ben had obviously not noticed it because he bent down to study the bottom of one of the pictures. 'Ha!' His laugh was loud in the big empty space. 'A star for a star. Very clever. And I predict you will soon be stellar, Stella.' Another booming laugh.

Stella glanced at David, not sure why she felt embarrassed, but he just swallowed the last of his champagne and said, 'Well, I must get home, lots to do tomorrow. It's times like this when I wonder if we were right to move down to the coast.'

Ben laughed and slapped his back as he walked away. 'Don't say I didn't warn you,' but David gave a cheery wave.

Stella finished her wine, coughing slightly because it was so bubbly, and Ben went to fill her glass again. 'Thank you, but I'd better get away too. I'm going out tonight.' It wasn't true, but she knew she wouldn't feel comfortable alone in this big space with him. Silly really because he could obviously have his choice of women, so would hardly be bothered with an ordinary girl like her.

'I dragged you over here, so you must let me take you back.

Anyway I want to talk to Maggie.' He rubbed her shoulder. 'Think I annoyed her this afternoon.'

Stella had been so nervous on the way that she hadn't noticed how fast he drove, but in the car going back he obviously guessed she was worried and put his hand on her knee.

'Relax, it's quite safe.' She must have tensed because he gave her a little pat and said, 'I'll slow down.'

He began talking about her work. Full of enthusiasm. 'I've never seen David so excited. We see a big future for you, Stella. And we want to feature your picture on the cover of the catalogue.'

It was all so amazing she just sat staring out of the window seeing nothing but a blur. Finally she realized he was waiting for her to say something and she blurted out, 'Which picture?' flushing because that sounded stupid.

Another of his loud laughs, making her feel idiotic again. 'No, I mean your photograph. You'll be the perfect poster girl.' Another pat to her thigh. 'I'll be honest with you, we were going to use Maggie, but you're much the better artist.'

His large hand was still on her knee as they drew up outside the house and it was impossible to move without seeming rude. Still tongue-tied she could only manage a strangled, 'Thank you.' She put her hand on the door.

'And of course ...' he gave her thigh a little squeeze as he opened his own door, 'you just about beat Maggie in the looks stakes, too.'

Before she could get out he was round her side taking her hand to help her. She moved quickly away, planning to run straight up to her room with the excuse that she had to change for her imaginary night out.

But as she reached the gate he said, 'On second thought, I won't come in just now. Let her ladyship cool down.'

Then, before she could move, his hand was behind her head and he was kissing her hard on the lips. It only lasted a second then he turned away, heading back to the car as if nothing had happened.

In the driver's seat he rolled down the window and said, 'We need to do those photos ASAP. So I'll collect you in the morning and take you to the studio. Eight sharp.' That loud laugh again, echoing down the quiet evening street.

When he roared away Stella stood one hand still on the gate the other pressed to her lips. She was almost afraid to let go of the gate because her legs felt like jelly. What had just happened? And was it really true that her work was set to be a success? She couldn't think and told herself the only thing to do about that kiss was to pretend it had never happened.

But as she gave herself a little shake and opened the gate, she realized the curtain in Maggie's bedroom was pulled back and Maggie, her face a frozen white mask, was standing there staring down at her.

Eve

When Alex got home Eve was checking the cod roasting in the oven. It took her a while to straighten up nowadays and Alex laughed and came behind her to haul her upright. Then he lifted her hair and kissed the back of her neck. 'Sorry I'm late. They cancelled my usual train and the next one was a packed.' He opened the fridge and poured himself some milk, holding up the carton. 'Want some?'

She shook her head determined to get it out right away. 'You didn't tell me about Dad's call last night.'

He ran his fingers through his hair. 'Oh yes, I completely forgot in the rush this morning. He only wanted to check you were all right. I told him you were asleep and that was it.'

She wanted to say that she didn't like them discussing her as if she was a child who needed looking after, but the way she was feeling she knew it was likely to turn into an argument. Besides she had something more important to tell him.

It was difficult, but she forced herself to wait until they were eating. 'I've decided to go to Newcastle this week, to see that exhibition.'

Alex swallowed a mouthful of potato and took a drink of water. 'The train tickets will cost a fortune this late, if we can even get any, and I have work commitments.'

'You don't have to come and I was planning to drive.'

He put down his fork. 'You're joking. You shouldn't be driving or travelling distances. Certainly not on your own. You can access the pictures and all the information you need online.'

He reached out for her, but she crossed her arms. She'd been prepared for this. 'I have to see them as they really are, and I want to talk to someone at the Baltic about this collector. It could be someone who knew my mother. Someone who might know more about the circumstances of her death.'

Alex wiped his mouth. She'd obviously spoiled his appetite. 'If *The Guardian* couldn't get that information out of the gallery you're hardly likely to.'

'I'll tell them I'm her daughter.' Why was she feeling like a naughty child? She felt tears gather in her eyes and a pain stab inside her throat. Was his support too much to ask for? She ripped off a piece of kitchen roll and headed for the door pretending to blow her nose rather than wipe her eyes. Turning back to him she said, 'Well I'm going and that's it.' She just managed to stop herself from adding, 'So there.'

It was pathetic and she knew it, but she ran upstairs and locked herself in the bathroom, sitting on the toilet her arms wrapped round herself. *Damn, damn, damn. Damn her mum and dad, damn Alex and damn Stella Carr.* This ought to be the happiest time in her life, when she should be thinking about the future not the past. But she knew she wouldn't be able to rest until she found out all she could about her birth mother.

And about how she died.

CHAPTER FOUR

Eve

It was a long way to Newcastle and Eve would normally have insisted on at least sharing the driving, but this time she slept for much of the journey.

Alex had come upstairs while she sat miserably in the bathroom and tapped on the door.

'Eve, I'm so sorry. If it's that important to you, I'll cancel my appointments and come with you. Let's book a hotel for a couple of nights and I'll get in touch with the Baltic. As an art historian I should at least be able to arrange for us to meet a curator.'

He nudged her as they approached the city. It was already dark and her eyes were dazzled by the lights. 'We're nearly there. Our hotel is just across the river from the Baltic.'

She sat up and shook her head. They were approaching a steel bridge flanked by two others. On the right she recognized the Tyne Bridge. The river below them was a dark mirror gleaming with reflections of city lights.

When they stopped outside their hotel Eve looked across the water. The gallery was a great chunk of a building. Over the front

32

the massive words, **BALTIC FLOUR MILLS**, proclaimed its industrial past, but brightly lit glass sections at the top and sides relieved its bulk.

Eve stared hard at it almost imagining she could see the pictures inside. She'd hoped to have a look round as soon as they arrived, but the exhibition spaces must be closed by now. Alex had got them an appointment with one of the curators next morning.

Eve was still cloudy from sleep and struggled to listen as he carried on talking and pointing. 'That's the Millennium Bridge leading over to the Baltic. They call it the Blinking Eye.'

Eve could see how it had got its name. Hanging low over the water it really did look like the slender outline of the upper and lower lids of a wide open eye. Its two semicircles of light, the top lid lit up in blue and purple and the lower a curve of brilliant white, shone in the black glass of the river.

She smiled at Alex. 'You sound like a city guide.' When he looked down and she noticed his knuckles turn white on the wheel she realized her mistake, but said nothing. Alex had done his PhD at Newcastle University and it was where he had met, married and lived with his first wife, Beth. Where their children were born. Where their marriage fell apart before Beth took the children to Australia and broke contact.

'It's changed quite a bit since I was here,' was all he said as he pulled into the hotel car park and turned off the engine.

He took her hand to help her out and must have realized how wobbly she was because he pulled her close. She rested her head on his chest, wanting suddenly to cry. He was very warm and held her tightly, whispering, 'Was the journey all right? I know you hate being a passenger. And I'm not a patch on you for driving. Had a sticky moment on the M25 when that bloody Audi cut me up.'

She remembered jolting awake to see a silver flash speeding away from them and hearing Alex curse, but she had fallen asleep right after. Now she saw how anxious he must have been all these hours and one tear spilled onto her cheek. She wiped it away. 'You did brilliantly.'

He kissed her gently on the mouth and for the first time in weeks she felt a surge of desire.

'Let's check in,' she said.

When they got to their room she had to dash to the toilet. Nowadays she felt as if her bladder had shrunk to nothing. She came out to see Alex standing by the window looking over the river. It was a lovely view, but she pulled off her shoes and trousers and lay on the bed looking at him. He was tall and slim, and although he was twenty years older than her, he didn't look it. And there was something about his back, with his T-shirt all crumpled from the long drive, that was so vulnerable it made her want to cry again. He usually seemed so calm and composed that she still sometimes thought of him as a professor and herself as a student, but today she felt almost maternal. And guilty. She had been completely wrapped up in wanting to find out about Stella Carr and hadn't thought how coming here would stir up memories of his first marriage.

Without turning he said, 'Shall I make you some coffee?'

'I don't want anything but you right now.'

He came to her and they kissed and he held her very tightly. When he moved back to look at her, his eyes shone almost gold in the light from the bedside lamp. They made love then, slowly and in silence and when it was over they lay close together, their breath coming in matching rhythms.

The next thing she was aware of was Alex brushing her hair away from her face, and she realized he was dressed and that she had slept.

'I can't face going out to eat, can you?' he said. 'Room service is a bit pricey, but I could get a takeaway and sneak it in if you like.'

Eve was too sleepy to be hungry, but knew she should eat. 'A spicy pizza would be nice and some cold juice.'

He jumped up. 'Just what I fancy, but with a couple of beers instead of the juice.'

Alex put the TV on for her, but she grabbed the book she was reading from her bag.

It wasn't until she heard the music for the television news that she realized how long he'd been gone. A few minutes later he came in with a pizza box and a carrier bag. His hair was damp.

'There was a queue, then it started pouring with rain and I had to wait in a doorway.' He rubbed a hand over his face.

She pulled herself up straight in the bed. 'Alex, what's wrong.'

He had turned to the little table by the window and was unpacking the bag. 'Oh, nothing, except some boy racer nearly knocked me into the river. Just managed to jump out of his way and, more importantly, to save the food.' He faced her with a smile. 'No harm done. Now let's eat before you fall asleep again.'

Stella

The photo session turned out all right in the end. After Ben Houghton drove away and Stella saw Maggie staring down at her, she raced inside and up the stairs, but Maggie was in the bathroom. Stella tapped on the door.

'Maggie, are you all right?' There was no answer, so she went to the kitchen and made herself some beans on toast.

When the phone in the hall rang Maggie hurtled down wrapped in a towel. She leaned over and closed the kitchen door so that Stella couldn't hear what she was saying. Minutes later she was slamming out the front door.

Stella had been awake for hours when she heard a hoot from outside. As she opened the front door she felt a lurch of anxiety. What if Ben did something while they were alone in the car? But Maggie, looking straight ahead, was in the passenger seat.

Stella sat in the back of the car watching Maggie nuzzle at Ben as he drove with one hand on her knee. He looked back and winked at Stella, which made her face go red.

What he had said to her yesterday – what he had done – had obviously just been to make Maggie jealous. And it turned out that the photo session was for all the artists. The four others were men. Stella knew one of them, Baz, from college and the rest were all a similar age to her and Maggie. The photographer wasn't much older and he encouraged everyone to clown around as he took lots of snaps very quickly.

A few paintings had already been hung, and he was photographing one of the men in front of his work, when Maggie came and sat next to Stella on a black sofa.

'It's all right,' she said, 'I've got over it, so no need to avoid me. I know Ben only kissed you to annoy me.' She held up her wrist to show Stella a lovely gold bracelet he'd given her. The phone call the night before had been from him and he'd come back to take Maggie to dinner and a hotel for the night. 'We've been making plans,' she said with a secret smile.

Before Stella could ask anymore David Ballantyne arrived with sandwiches and bottles of beer, and they all went out into the courtyard. One of the men, James Stone, who had dark floppy hair and a silver earring, came to sit on the stone bench next to Stella. She liked him and as they ate and drank in the sunshine she felt as happy as she had ever been. A thought came into her head. *This is when my real life begins.*

When he stood to leave James nudged Stella with his knee. 'Coming?' But Maggie called out. 'Don't go, I need to talk to you.' So James waved and said, 'See you around then.'

Stella sighed and followed Maggie back into the gallery. She whispered, 'Don't you want to be alone with Ben?'

Maggie laughed. 'And miss the best bit. Look.' She was holding a small bag and pulled out the two dresses they had worn to the preview. 'Ben wanted a photo of me in something a bit more glamorous and we thought it might be nice to have one of the two of us together.'

When they'd changed, the photographer asked them to come back into the courtyard where he took several pictures. Then Ben appeared and said, 'Now a few of Maggie on her own, I think.'

Maggie was trying out various poses, some sexy, some sedate and some comical, and she and the photographer were soon laughing together, so Stella wandered back into the gallery. She was looking at a picture by James and was so absorbed that she gasped when she felt a hand on her shoulder.

It was David Ballantyne. 'Sorry. I thought you heard me,' he said. He gestured with his head and they moved over to a beautifully lit corner of the gallery where six canvases were leaning against the wall. Although only their backs were showing, Stella recognized them as hers.

'What do you think?' he said, and when she looked blank he smiled and added, 'I mean how's this corner for your work?' He gestured towards the rest of the room. 'It's visible from pretty much everywhere and people will be drawn over as soon as they come in.'

It was difficult to speak. 'It's wonderful. The light …' she couldn't go on. There was a pain in her throat as she struggled not to cry at the thought of her pictures on display in such a beautiful spot.

'You'll be the star of the show. No doubt about that.'

All she could say was, 'Thank you.'

He was looking away from her and fiddling with the frame of one of the canvases. 'I want you to know I think you're a rare talent and I'm very proud to have you in the exhibition.'

Stella was glad he left her then, muttering something about *work* and *busy*, because she had to move close to the wall to hide her tears. She was so thrilled that her heart seemed to throb. Was it possible to die of happiness?

She turned one of her pictures around. It was the first she'd done in London when she was feeling lost and homesick and was a fantasy version of the Tyne Bridge. She'd removed all the other bridges around it and painted it as if it was in the middle of jungle rather than in Newcastle. Was it really as good as David said?

'Put that back the way you found it, young lady.' Ben Houghton's voice boomed out, and she automatically did as she was told. He clapped her on the back and gave his huge laugh. 'Only joking, my darling. If anyone's entitled to handle it, I'd say it's you. Now will you step into my office for a moment?' He smiled down at her, raising one eyebrow.

CHAPTER FIVE

Eve

Alex had emailed the Baltic to say he was researching a book and wanted to include some details about Stella Carr. He had kept it as vague as possible.

They arrived with an hour to spare. It was cold and drizzly but, despite the gloom outside, the gallery was full of light and space. When they left the glass elevator on the third floor, Alex wandered straight into the exhibition. Eve stood at the entrance reading the information on the partition.

The Baltic is especially glad to welcome the works of Stella Carr because she was born in Newcastle in 1966. The Tyne Bridge is clearly recognizable in one of her earliest paintings.

Nothing is known about her father, and her mother, Karen, died when Stella was only nine years old. From then on she lived with her grandmother. She attended Newcastle's Bath Lane College of Art until she won a scholarship to St Martins in London.

Eve looked over towards Alex. So Stella was actually from Newcastle. Alex was a student here during the Eighties and later taught at the university. She wondered if anyone he knew from that time had ever come across Stella.

She read on:

> *The painting, Nana, shows Stella's grandmother when she was in a nursing home suffering from dementia.*
>
> *Stella's only exhibition during her lifetime was at the Houghton Gallery in 1986. Five of her paintings were sold, but Stella refused to part with Nana. She moved to Italy the following year and was tragically killed when a fire destroyed her studio. Some of the paintings in our exhibition are from the original London show, but a number were produced during her final weeks in Italy. These have never been shown before. They survived because the studio was too small to store her finished works and they were kept in the main house.*

So the studio was separate from the house. Surely that would have made it easier to escape from. She wondered what it was like. Needed to find out.

She walked into the exhibition space, her breath caught, and she couldn't move. It was like being inside a kaleidoscope, not just because the colours were so vivid, but because she felt as if they were whirling around her as she tried, and failed, to focus on any single painting.

She walked to the glass case in the middle of the room where the catalogue for the Houghton exhibition was displayed. The photo of Stella that she'd seen on the Internet was on the front cover. A second copy of the catalogue was open at a two-page spread. On one side was Stella with another small and slender young woman. It was obviously the photograph that had inspired the painting of *Maggie and Me* that Eve had seen in the original article. They were wearing the green and blue dresses in what looked like a courtyard with white walls. The caption under the photograph read:

Stella Carr and Maggie de Santis.

So this was the friend she had lived with.

On the opposite page were four smaller pictures of the other artists: all young men. Eve took out her notebook and wrote down their names. Then began to walk around the room. The first painting was *Nana* and Eve looked into the lined face trying to see something of herself in the woman who was her great-grandmother. The old lady's short neat hair was completely white, so if she had been a redhead it was impossible to tell. Above all Eve could detect love in every brushstroke. Stella had loved her nana very much.

Next was *Maggie and Me*. The two young women just as they were in the photo, but surrounded by dark woodland. It changed the character of the picture completely, making it almost sinister. She saw now that the girls were holding hands and an alternative title came into her head: *Babes in the Wood*.

She must have said the words aloud and became aware of Alex behind her, his hand moving to rest on her shoulder.

'All right?'

'Just thinking.'

'You should look over here.'

He led her to one of the smallest paintings. It was of a young woman seated in a rowing boat surrounded by water that glinted with blues, greens and purples. The sky was heavy with clouds. Her red hair fell over her face as she looked down at a bundle that suggested a baby. It was called *Madonna?*

Eve was grateful for Alex still behind her because she felt as if she might fall. He pointed at the caption on the wall.

41

The woman is probably Stella's mother – apparently Stella owned a photograph of herself and Karen in a similar position. However there have been suggestions that the mother is Stella herself. Rumours persist that she had a child that she gave up for adoption a few months before her death. The question mark could support this interpretation.

Alex said very softly, 'Shall we take a moment before our meeting?'

They went down to the café. The rain had stopped and the glass-fronted room was bright. Arrows of sunshine split the clouds above the river. Not quite sure how she got there, she found herself at a table with a cup in front of her and a slice of cake on a striped plate.

She broke off a chunk of cake and swallowed without chewing or even tasting it. The coffee was only lukewarm, but it helped to bring her back to reality. She looked up at Alex. 'That baby was me. And Stella was so unhappy. You could see that too, couldn't you?'

He squeezed her hand. 'Look, I know what we want to ask, so why don't you stay here, or go back to the hotel and let me see the curator. This is too much for you.'

She pulled away. 'No, I've got to be there.' She looked at her watch. 'And we'd better go now.'

Stella

Ben opened his desk drawer and pulled out a folder, which she recognized as hers. It was the one he had picked up by mistake when they brought over her paintings. The one with her drawings in the style of George Grafton: the East End artist from the 1930s and '40s.

'I'm afraid I've been a bit naughty, but you did agree to us selling your work, didn't you?'

She wondered where this was going. 'Yes, all except the picture called *Nana*.'

'Good and we'll make sure we get the best possible price for them. I know you're not like Maggie, born with a silver spoon and all that.'

Stella shifted in her seat feeling embarrassed.

'Don't look like that, sweetie. You have everything except money. Beauty, style and above all talent, so there's nothing to be ashamed of.'

She opened the folder hoping it would make him get a move on, but it was empty and she looked up at him.

'The thing is, Stella,' he said, 'I've taken a bit of a liberty and sold those drawings already.'

'But they weren't for the show. They don't reflect my work at all.' Now she felt angry.

'Don't worry. You didn't sign them, so no one will connect them with you. But I happened to know a collector who is mad about the East End group, and George Grafton in particular, so I couldn't resist showing them to him. He was amazed at how well you'd caught George's style and he just had to have them. You've made him very happy.'

He passed her the empty portfolio. 'And if you feel like doing a few more, he'd love to buy them too.'

She didn't know what to say. 'He bought them?'

'Absolutely. And I thought you'd prefer the money in cash, so here you go.' He pulled an envelope from the open drawer and held it out to Stella.

All she could do was stare because it bulged with notes. 'How much is it?'

'Five hundred pounds and I suspect he would have paid more if I'd pushed him.'

'Five hundred pounds for a few practice drawings?'

There was that big laugh again as he leaned back in his chair and shook his head at her. 'Ah, the innocence of youth. I'm savouring it while I can. You'll soon learn how the art world works. If a collector really wants something there's no limit to what they'll pay. So take the money and go celebrate with that naughty Maggie. I'm sure she'll help you spend it.'

Eve

The curator was a tall woman around Eve's age with dark hair in a shiny bob. Her white shirt and loose black trousers looked very elegant. She shook Alex's hand. 'Good to meet you, Alex. I'm Miriam.'

Alex said, 'And this is Eve.' They had decided he wouldn't introduce her as his wife so their interest would initially seem completely professional. Eve had pulled her hair into a bun at the back of her head to minimize the mane of red that was so like Stella's.

Alex explained they were researching Stella's life, but knew little more than the information displayed outside the exhibition room.

Miriam shook her head. 'That's a shame. To be honest we were hoping you might shed some more light on her for us.'

'What about the collector or collectors who supplied the new pictures?'

Eve was glad he was getting straight to the point.

'I'm afraid I can't help you there except to say that we believe they belong to one person. We've only dealt with a firm of solicitors.'

Eve couldn't hold back. 'And these solicitors are?'

When Miriam turned to her something seemed to spark in her eyes. She had seen the likeness. 'They've asked us to keep them anonymous too.'

There was nothing to lose. Eve sat up straight and took a deep breath. 'I should tell you that I'm actually Stella's daughter and was adopted by David Ballantyne: Ben Houghton's partner.'

The curator stared. She half rose then sat down again and carried on looking at Eve for long seconds. When she spoke her voice was breathy. 'Oh my word. We actually have a note in the gallery about the rumours that she had a child — but no one seemed to know whether there was any substance to them.'

'For various reasons I didn't discover the truth myself until recently, but now I'd like to find out as much about my mother as I can. For instance, these rumours about her having a child: where did they originate?'

'As far as I know they were simply a response to the *Madonna?* picture. The mother figure looks more like Stella than her own mother, Karen, for one thing.'

'And I read somewhere that Stella was depressed just before her death. Have you heard anything about that? Or about any suspicious circumstances around her death?'

Eve felt Alex shift beside her. He obviously thought she was being too forceful, but the curator gave her a sympathetic smile and shook her head.

'Not really. Most of the reports I've come across call it a tragic accident. There are always conspiracy theorists on the Internet, but I don't take much notice of that kind of thing.'

'I read in the gallery that Stella worked in a studio separate from the house. Do you have any information about it?'

'Nothing, I'm afraid.'

Eve could sense Alex was about to speak, but she came in with: 'The main reason I've come to see you is that I'm hoping the owner of the newly discovered pictures might be able to help me. It might even be someone who knew Stella.' Eve could hear her own voice becoming breathless, but she forced herself on. 'So I'd like you to give my details to their solicitors and ask them to contact me.'

Miriam looked down at papers on her desk tapping them with a pen.

Alex spoke quickly. 'You can assure them we have no intention of making any claims on the estate. As I said we just want to find out as much about Stella as we can. Eve obviously never met her mother. And her adoptive parents know very little about her.'

When Miriam spoke her tone was careful – *guarded* – was the word that sprang into Eve's mind.

'I see, yes. Well I'm afraid I can't guarantee anything, but if you email me your details, and some evidence of your identity, I'll see what the solicitors say. And obviously, if you discover anything you'd be willing to share with us we'd be very glad to hear it.'

CHAPTER SIX

Eve

After they left the curator, Alex said, 'I think we should go for some lunch. You can come back afterwards if you want.' Neither of them spoke as they walked across the Millennium Bridge and away from the river into the busy Newcastle streets. Alex stopped outside a little Italian restaurant and looked at Eve. She nodded. Couldn't face walking any further.

When they were seated at a window table and had ordered drinks – a Peroni for Alex and sparkling water for Eve – he put down the menu he'd been holding and took her hand.

'I'm sorry. I know you hoped to find out something more concrete today.'

She said, 'Do you know the art school she went to here? Before London?'

'I've heard of it, of course.'

'You don't know anyone who was there in the Eighties when you lived here?'

'No, sorry.' It was curt, but not surprising. He always clammed up when anything reminded him of that time in his life. If he'd kept any friends from then she had never met them.

She shrugged, fighting to keep her voice steady. 'I suppose it was silly to expect anything more. It's just …' She shook her head. What she had imagined they'd find out she didn't know, but she had never felt so tired. 'I'm sorry for making you drive all this way for so little.'

'Let's try to make the most of the day anyway. I thought I'd pop into the Lit and Phil Library, and maybe check out the theatre to see if there's anything on tonight. What do you think?'

'Good idea, but I'll skip the library. I want to have another look in the Baltic.'

He didn't argue, but plunged his fork into his spaghetti and tutted as a dollop of sauce splashed on his hand.

It was raining again and Eve pulled on her beanie. She kept it on in the gallery. It felt like protection. This time she walked very slowly around the exhibition, trying to keep her emotions in check. It was difficult when she came to a painting of Stella's mother, Karen – her own grandmother. The caption said she died when Stella was nine. She was on a swing attached to the branch of a huge tree with a twisted trunk. Her hair swirling around her as she seemed to sway back and forth.

It must have been so hard growing up without a mother, and it seemed that Stella's grandmother developed dementia when she was still only a teenager.

Forcing herself to move on she came to a picture of the little town in Italy where Stella had spent her last weeks. The caption called it Sestri Levante, and Eve noted the name down. That was something she hadn't known before. The tiny beach was surrounded by tall houses and restaurants. Stella had changed the bay into a magical sea with mermaids perched on rocks.

Next to it was *Seascape with Gulls* and she was almost sure it was a view from the cliffs above Hastings, although the gulls were beautiful diaphanous creatures nothing like the screeching scavengers she knew. There were two more portraits of Maggie. Alone this time. In one she wore a red dress, her hair threaded with white flowers. Another was the strange *Mermaid* picture in which she now recognized the face as Maggie's.

Eve had seen love in every brushstroke of the *Nana* portrait and sadness in *Madonna*? The Maggie paintings were different. Some strong emotion certainly seemed to emanate from them, but Eve couldn't tell if that emotion was love or something quite different.

Back at the hotel she phoned her dad and as soon as she heard his, 'Hello sweetheart,' she felt a rush of warmth. 'I just wanted to say I'm sorry for being so horrible to you and Mum. I know you only did what you thought was right.'

'But we should have trusted you with the truth. I see that now.'

'Whatever I find out won't make any difference to us.' As she said it she tried to ignore the tiny voice asking if she was sure about that. 'But, Dad, please help me now.' She read out the names of the other artists in the show. 'Could any of these have been Stella's boyfriend: my father?'

'Now that's a tricky one. Since you started asking about her I've racked my brains and honestly I can't remember her with anyone. I assumed it was another art student. So the young men from the exhibition certainly fit the bill. I've followed their careers – those that went on to have some success – but I've never seen any connection to Stella.'

'Could you try to put me in touch with any of them?'

A pause. 'We'd have to go about it delicately.'

'I know. And I also thought I'd try to speak to Ben Houghton. He's likely to remember something about her. Might even know more about how she died. And I can't stop thinking that I was born about nine months after she met him.'

There was no pause this time. Instead David rushed on. 'Oh, no, Eve. You mustn't bother Ben. You know how things are with him.'

She knew Ben had been in a wheelchair for years, paralyzed

from the waist down. His accident was one of the reasons Houghton's had closed. Her dad was still talking.

'Granted he was a bit of a lad in his day, but he's paid the price and so have Pamela and Simon.'

'But could he be my biological father?'

'Since this started I've been thinking about possible candidates and naturally Ben came to mind, but I've remembered he was actually having one of his flings with the other girl. Stella's friend, Maggie.'

'And he couldn't have been cheating on Maggie with Stella?'

'If he did I'm sure he won't admit it at this stage. And he knows about you, my darling, so if he wanted to claim parentage don't you think he would have done so already?'

He must have heard her gasp because he said quickly, 'I'm sorry, that was clumsy. I'm just sure he's not the one and I don't want you upsetting yourself as well as Ben and his family.'

She took a deep breath. 'OK, I understand.'

Lying on the hotel bed after they'd said goodbye she held the phone to her chest and watched the early evening sun breaking through the clouds. Her father's words had only made her more convinced that she had to see Ben. Whatever his relationship with Stella it was clear he knew her friend, Maggie, intimately. So it was possible he could put Eve in touch with her, which could be crucial to finding out how Stella died. In fact, Maggie could be the key to everything.

She stared at her phone, that cold feeling creeping over her again. Much as she loved her parents she was beginning to believe they were still lying to her. And she didn't want to think about why that might be.

Stella

When Stella told Maggie about the £500 Ben had given her for the drawings, Maggie said, 'You can bet your life he got a lot more than that for them. Next time ask for double.'

50

'There won't be a next time. I don't want to get into producing copies. I need to focus on my real work.'

Still, she enjoyed treating Maggie to a meal for once even if it was only fish and chips from the corner chippie and a cheap bottle of Muscadet. They sat at the old Formica kitchen table laughing about fools who were prepared to pay out hundreds for pencil drawings that weren't even original. When they finished the wine Maggie produced a bottle of Bacardi and a few cans of Coke.

They were supposed to go to the gallery the next morning to see the exhibition before it opened the following week, but slept in and didn't get there until late afternoon. David let them in and said he needed to leave in half an hour so they didn't have long. Ben wasn't around, but Stella was glad to see the dark-haired guy, James, who had sat with her in the courtyard after the photoshoot.

He smiled and waved, but after one glance at him all Stella could see were her own paintings. Looking at them she felt breathless because, although David had promised they would be in a prominent position, she hadn't realized just how they would dominate the room.

Maggie was standing in front of her own two collages, but when she turned away from them Stella saw that her face was twisted into a scowl that was almost frightening. Then, without a word, she walked out.

James came over. 'Your stuff looks fabulous. Well done.' She managed to thank him, but when he pushed the catalogue into her hand, her heart sank. Her photograph was the only one on the front cover. The names of all the other artists were there, but it was the photo that caught the eye, of course. Inside it was even worse, because alongside the individual snaps of the four men, crammed onto one side of a two-page spread, was the one of her and Maggie together in their blue and green dresses. None of the many pictures of Maggie on her own had been used.

James must have realized she was upset because he grabbed her hand. 'Let's get a drink, shall we?'

They went to a pub nearby, and he tapped his glass against hers. 'You should be dancing in the street and instead you look as if someone died. Don't let other people put you down. Your stuff is the best in the show and if anyone is jealous then that's their lookout.'

He was very kind, but she didn't feel much better. 'It's just that Maggie has been so good to me. If it wasn't for her, I wouldn't even have been able to stay in London. And she got Ben and David to look at my work.'

'OK, so when you're successful you can try to give her a leg up. And remember, she may have helped your stuff get seen, but it's your talent they love.'

When they eventually left they bought a takeaway pizza and ate it as they walked back to the flat James shared with a couple of others. No one else was in and they collapsed on his bed fully clothed.

She woke with her mouth dry and her head thumping. Light was coming through the thin curtains, although her watch said it wasn't yet six a.m., and the room smelled of beer and sweat. She rolled off the bed, and James opened his eyes, struggling to focus on her.

'All right?' He still sounded drunk.

'Yeah, but I'd better get home.'

'OK, see you later.' He turned over and was soon asleep again.

As she got the bus back to Maggie's she told herself she was a coward for not facing her yesterday. She let herself in as quietly as she could and went to tiptoe upstairs, but Maggie shouted from the kitchen.

'No need to hide. I'm making toast so come and get some.'

Stella hovered at the door, and Maggie laughed. 'Stop looking so scared. I know it's not your fault you're so bloody talented and my stuff is shit.'

'That's not true.'

'The talent or the shit? No, don't answer that.'

Although Maggie seemed calm for the moment, Stella knew she had to be careful. Her temper was unpredictable and she had smashed most of the plates in the kitchen after her last fight with Ben and boasted that he'd only avoided a black eye by running to his car.

'Anyway where were you last night?' she asked.

'I went for a drink with James.'

'Ah, dishy James. Tell me more.'

'I stayed over at his, but before you start getting ideas, I just slept there. With all my clothes on as well.'

'Oh but next time maybe?' She laughed. 'I thought there were some sparks. We must find something great for you to wear to the opening. Me too, of course.'

It looked as if things were going to be all right, so she smiled and said, 'You looked lovely in that blue dress. And maybe I could wear the green again.' A sudden thought. 'Or what about swapping them over? And doing our hair identically? If people have seen our photo in the catalogue, they could be really confused. I'd love that.'

'Hmm, no, with gorgeous James in your sights I say we need something a bit sexier for you. And I want to be completely different. All the catalogue pictures show me in that blue dress.'

Stella felt the piece of toast she was swallowing turn into a solid lump in her throat. Maggie had rushed out of the gallery as soon as she'd seen the way her own collages and Stella's paintings were displayed.

She still didn't know about the catalogue.

CHAPTER SEVEN

Eve

Eve caught the train for London an hour or so after Alex left for work. She hadn't told him she was going to see Ben Houghton. On the drive home from Newcastle it was clear he thought all they could do was wait and hope to hear from the solicitors. Eve doubted that would ever happen, but if Alex believed she was going to leave it there it might be for the best. This was her problem, not his.

She couldn't just wait because even if the collector did get in touch he or she might know nothing about Stella. She needed to focus on the people who definitely did. Apart from her own parents that meant Ben and Maggie. If those two really did have an affair, as her dad suspected, Ben might know where to find Maggie. And Stella had been in Italy with Maggie when she died. If anyone knew the truth of what had happened it had to be her.

Ben and his wife lived in Mayfair. Eve's train came in at Charing Cross and it wasn't far on the tube after that. It was a short walk to their street, but she had begun to feel huge. It had turned bitterly cold and the wind spat rain into her face as she searched for the house. Her back ached and she rubbed her belly and made a silent apology to the baby. *I promise I'll take it easy tomorrow, my darling.*

Although Ben and David had been colleagues and had known each other since university they hadn't exactly been friends and had rarely seen each other since her dad left the business. So Eve had never met him or his wife.

The house was an elegant Regency building with stone steps leading up to a heavy front door that shone with black paint and golden brass. Eve had to stand for a moment breathing heavily before she knocked.

The woman who opened the door was not young, but in her grey woollen dress, with her blonde hair in a simple up-do she could have stepped off a catwalk. She smiled. 'Yes?'

Eve swallowed. 'Hello, Mrs Houghton, I'm Eve Ballantyne, David's daughter. I wonder if I could have a word with your husband.'

Pamela blinked. 'Well this is a surprise, but how nice to see you. The last time we met you were in your cradle.' She glanced towards the stairs and her voice dropped. 'Do come in, but can I ask you to speak quietly? Ben's having a nap.'

In the spacious hallway Pamela gestured towards a door. 'Let's go and sit down. You look tired.'

Eve felt very awkward. 'I'm fine, but I've come quite a long way, so would you mind if I used your toilet?'

'It's just there.' Pamela pointed to a door at one side of the hall. Next to it was a tiny lift with a glass door. Just large enough for a wheelchair.

The cloakroom was as big as the bathroom in Eve and Alex's house and far more luxurious. It was also beautifully warm, and Eve took her time, glad to have a chance to thaw, but also to think.

When she came out Pamela was standing at the bottom of the elegant white staircase. Eve went to speak, but Pamela placed her finger to her lips, whispering, 'I'm afraid Ben isn't up to seeing anyone. But I'm sure I can help.' She pointed to a nearby door.

In the long living room, a bow window with sweeping green curtains at one end and tall French windows at the other, Eve perched on a pale leather sofa and tried to relax. Pamela sat opposite, smiling warmly at her.

'How are Jill and David? It's too long since we've seen them.'

'They're fine, still living in Hastings, and I'm back down there now too.'

'That must be lovely for them.' Pamela looked as if she was going to say more, but Eve's movement stopped her and she made a little, *go on*, gesture.

'I'm sorry if I've disturbed you, but I just discovered that my birth mother was Stella Carr.' Pamela remained expressionless. 'As you probably know there's a new exhibition of her work at the Baltic Gallery and I wondered if Ben had contributed any works to it?'

Pamela's light blue eyes flickered towards the door. 'Actually I didn't know about the Baltic and I don't think Ben does either. We don't keep up with the art world nowadays, I'm afraid. It's a shame really, but we've never been collectors. So, no, we didn't contribute.'

Eve took a breath. She hadn't planned to say this to Pamela, but it looked as if she wasn't going to be able to talk to Ben. 'Well, I'm trying to get in touch with Stella's friend, Maggie de Santis. Do you have any idea where she is now?'

Smoothing her hair, Pamela said, 'What did you say your mother's name was?'

'Stella Carr.'

Pamela looked towards the French windows and the garden where the dark silhouette of a tree was just visible, then turned to Eve, her forehead creased. 'No, I'm afraid you've had a wasted journey. I don't remember Stella or any of her friends, and I doubt my husband does either.'

She glanced at her silver watch, and Eve took the hint and stood.

'Well, thank you anyway. Will you ask him about them for me, in case he recalls anything at all?'

Pamela led the way saying, 'Of course, but your father is more likely to know something. He organized that young artists' show. Ben just supported him. And, as David would be the first to admit, I'm afraid the whole thing turned out to be a costly mistake.'

By now they had reached the front door and as Pamela opened it a gust of cold air blew through the hall. 'I'm sorry I couldn't help you, but do give your parents my best wishes. Tell them we must catch up soon.'

On the steps again Eve stood for a moment, almost certain she could feel someone watching her. She shivered and looked left and right down the street, but there was nobody in sight.

Ben

He pushed his wheelchair over to the window. The shock of recognition when he heard that voice amazed him. It was thirty years ago. But then those few weeks were seared into his brain – and his body too.

Now he thought about it he could see there was something different. No accent. That was it. This girl sounded as if she was from round here. No hint of Stella's cute northern twang. He smiled remembering how the way she tried to hide it made her even more attractive.

It couldn't be her, but when he heard the door open and close and looked down into the street he had that sense, which happened more and more as he grew older, of absolute recognition. Of being back in time. His brain told him it wasn't Stella, but his eyes said it was.

It must be her daughter. The baby David and Jill adopted. But

57

as he watched her walk away, red hair blowing in the wind, he could still almost believe it was Stella.

He shook his head. Ridiculous. If Stella had still been alive she wouldn't look like that now. And anyway she was dead. He knew that better than anyone.

Eve

As she walked slowly along the damp pavement Eve was thinking hard. One thing was certain: Pamela had been lying.

Eve hadn't mentioned the young artists' show, yet Pamela had known Stella and Maggie were part of that. Of course, if her husband had been unfaithful to her with one or both of them she wouldn't want to be reminded.

Just ahead was a coffee shop, its lights shining onto the pavement, and Eve was suddenly overwhelmed with exhaustion. It was busy, but she found a table in a warm corner and ordered hot chocolate and a falafel wrap. Her seat was comfortable and she leaned back almost in danger of falling asleep.

'Excuse me, is this place free?' She nodded absent-mindedly as the man sat opposite. Then she did a double-take. He was almost identical to the early photographs she had seen of Ben. This had to be his son. He gave a little laugh.

'Don't worry, I'm not trying to pick you up. I'm Simon Houghton and I was at the house to see my dad just now and overheard you talking to Mum. I'm ashamed to say I stayed on the landing and listened.' Another laugh, soft and pleasant.

Like Ben he was dark and very good-looking, but this man seemed diffident, even shy, which didn't fit the image she had formed of his father.

'I was asking about my mother, Stella Carr, and her friend, Maggie de Santis.'

He regarded her silently for a moment. She knew she was flushing and was glad when the waitress arrived bringing her order. Simon asked for a coffee then turned to Eve again, shaking his head this time.

'I can't get over how much you resemble her.'

A heavy thump inside. Not from the baby, but her own heart. 'You knew my mother?'

'Hardly. I mean I was only fourteen at the time, but I saw her at the gallery because they let me come to that show. And then a few times afterwards. She was so pretty, I suppose I had a crush on her.'

Eve was glad she could fiddle with her food: pushing in a few bits of salad that poked from the end of the wrap. She knew she had gone pink. It was ridiculous. He was talking about fancying her mother not her and that was when he was a boy.

'Your mother says she can't remember Stella or Maggie.'

'That's not surprising. Maggie was one of Dad's many affairs, which didn't endear her to Mum.'

'So do you have any idea how I can find her?'

He shook his head. 'I'm sorry, I don't, and it's not likely Dad will either.'

'I was hoping she could tell me more about my mother.' She paused for a moment, but his smile told her to go on. 'Thought she might even know who my father was.'

He nodded. His eyes looked brighter blue than his mother's perhaps because of his dark lashes. 'I could tell you that knowing all about your biological parents isn't as wonderful as you might think and whatever you do find is likely to be very disappointing. But I don't suppose that would convince you?'

It was impossible not to echo his laugh. 'It wouldn't. But I'm not after anything lifechanging. My adoptive parents are wonderful, and I know my birth mother is dead. All I want is to find out what I can. I feel I owe it to my baby too.' It was very easy to talk to him.

'I can understand that and I could try and get something out of my dad if you like.' He took out a business card and wrote on the back. 'These are my work and personal contact details.' He handed her the pen and another card. 'Put yours on there and I'll get back to you if I find out anything.'

Her food was virtually untouched and she wrapped it in a paper napkin. She needed to get home in case Alex arrived early again. And it wouldn't do to meet him on the train.

Simon said he was heading for the tube station too. It had stopped raining and Eve was still so tired she couldn't walk fast, but Simon matched his pace to hers without comment. They needed to travel in different directions, so stopped by the station barriers. As they stood rather awkwardly to say goodbye Simon suddenly reached out and took both her gloved hands in his.

'Good luck. I'll be in touch if I find anything that might help you.' A lopsided smile and one raised eyebrow. 'I notice you haven't mentioned the elephant in the room.'

He let her hands drop, but carried on looking at her with that quizzical smile.

She said, 'You mean your father may have had an affair with Stella as well as Maggie?'

'Precisely, my dear Watson. And of course what follows from that. The fact that I could be your brother.'

Stella

David had asked the artists to arrive early for the show, but it wasn't easy to get Maggie moving. She changed her clothes three or four times before finally settling for a black chiffon dress, its low neckline bordered with crystals. Long earrings glittered among the shining strands of her hair. She insisted Stella try on a short red dress. Stella was doubtful until she saw herself in the dusty mirror on Maggie's wardrobe door, but the colour set off her hair. She piled her curls on top of her head and put on some red lipstick she'd bought ages ago but never worn. Maggie handed her a pair of ridiculously high black stilettos.

60

'It doesn't matter if they're uncomfortable,' Maggie said. 'We're going by taxi. Ben and David can pay.'

Stella had been close to mentioning the front cover of the catalogue more than once, but in the end she hadn't dared. Now she hoped the evening would be such fun that Maggie would be swept along in it all. And Ben would probably have the sense to make a big fuss of her.

When she saw the gallery all lit up, with big vases of white flowers everywhere and waiters holding trays of champagne, she felt a bit like Cinderella. David came up with a huge smile on his face. 'Right, now, don't be anxious; you both look gorgeous. Take a drink, and as everyone arrives it might be a good idea to stand near your pictures so people can ask you about them.'

Stella stood in the corner where her work was displayed and smiled over at James. He waved his champagne glass at her with a smile.

'Yours are my favourites.'

She was startled by a young voice coming from behind her and turned to see a lanky teenage boy with dark hair and clear blue eyes. He was so like Ben he had to be his son.

'I'm Simon Houghton,' he said offering his hand.

Shaking hands always made her feel awkward and doing it with a boy of thirteen or fourteen seemed silly. She must have shown her embarrassment because from the corner of her eye she could see James grinning at her.

When she smiled up at Simon and thanked him his ears turned pink. Poor lad. She wondered if he'd been forced to come. He looked quite used to wearing a dinner jacket and bow tie, but she was sure he would have been happier hanging out with his friends. She gulped her drink, trying to think of something to say that would put them both at ease. After all she was the adult, although she didn't feel like it at the moment. 'Is your mother around?' she asked.

It was a mistake and his colour rose again; big blotches of red marring his cheeks. 'No.'

She tried a little laugh. 'Well it's very good of you to keep your dad company like this.'

He had long black eyelashes that fluttered as he spoke. 'I came to have a look the other day and thought your work was wonderful. So I wanted to meet you.' It was so simple and so dignified that he seemed far more grown-up than his father and she felt ashamed for treating him as a kid.

Almost at once she seemed to be surrounded by people holding glasses and talking about her paintings. One man said he was planning to buy the Tyne Bridge picture and shortly afterwards David appeared, grinning broadly.

'First sale of the show,' he whispered and stuck a coloured dot on it.

James came over with another drink for her, and she realized she'd lost count of how many she'd had.

'I think I may have sold one as well,' he said and kissed her cheek before being beckoned over to his own pictures by David, who was talking to a tall man in a crumpled suit. She was grateful to have a moment to stand in silence and take it all in.

Everything glowed: a woman brushed back her copper-coloured hair, a circlet of green stones glittering on her arm. The glass tables reflected the white blooms and the flutes of pale wine; the occasional flash of colour from a dress passing by wavering and distorting. She knew she was smiling as she looked at her own paintings, their vivid hues brought to life by the perfect lighting.

Then she caught sight of Maggie.

Standing pale-faced, her arms folded, she stared across the room at Stella, the catalogue in her hand. Stella swallowed the rest of her champagne then forced herself to go over. Maggie flapped the catalogue at her.

'You could have told me about this. I've got friends coming

and they think I'm going to be on the cover or at least have a big picture inside.'

'I'm sorry.' What else could she say?

Maggie's eyes were glassy. 'I should have expected it, but it's just so humiliating.'

Stella touched her arm, but Maggie shook her off and headed for the Ladies. There was nothing for it but to follow.

Maggie sat in front of one of the mirrors rubbing at her nose and eyes with a handful of tissues. 'I knew your paintings would attract all the attention. I just thought I might get a bit of glory from the catalogue. Was that too much to ask? ' She looked up, and her face was so like a wounded little girl's that Stella, who had been choking back her own tears, crouched down and held her.

It did seem unfair. She wasn't interested in appearing in the catalogue. Hated the photo they'd put on the front.

Maggie stayed still for a moment or two, her chest heaving. Then she pushed Stella roughly away. Her eyes glittered, and her mouth was an ugly squiggle. 'You still don't realize what Ben has done with those drawings of yours, do you?'

At first Stella couldn't think what she meant. 'The ones I did in the style of George Grafton?'

Maggie's words were clipped. Hard. 'That's right. Your forgeries.'

'Copies not forgeries.' But even as she said it the look on Maggie's face sent a chill through her.

'If he gave you £500 for them, I reckon they sold for at least twice that. And you don't think anyone, no matter how obsessed they were with George Whatshisname, would pay a grand for a few copies by an art student, do you?'

'I don't know. Some people have more money than sense.' She heard her voice wavering.

'He's been doing it for years.' Maggie ran a finger under her eye to wipe away a smudge of mascara. 'Homes in on art students with a talent for copying. It's how we met.' A breath through her nose that was almost a laugh. 'Of course I wasn't talented enough, but he's had three or four doing it over the years.'

'You mean he sells them as originals?'

Her lips twisted. 'At last she gets it.'

CHAPTER EIGHT

Eve

I could be your brother. Eve couldn't stop thinking about Simon's words. Although she had guessed Ben might be her father, she hadn't really thought about the consequences, but talking to Simon, she had felt a connection. Or was she fooling herself?

The card he'd given her showed he worked for an auction house specializing in fine art. She wondered if he had ever hoped to take over Houghton's. When his dad sold up that might have been a disappointment very much like her failure to make a go of it as an artist. Although, unlike him, she had only herself to blame for that. She had been too much of a coward to face the possibility that she might not have enough talent, even though Alex and her dad had assured her she was good.

She was in the kitchen putting on some washing when her phone rang: *Dad*. A tremor went through her. It was only mid-morning. He should be busy in the shop, and after her mother's heart attack she'd begun to dread unexpected calls from him.

'Everything all right, Dad?'

'Fine, fine. I just thought I'd give you a ring. We're very quiet today and with all this rain and wind it's not likely to improve.'

She hadn't spoken to him since she came back from Newcastle and had told no one about visiting Ben's home. He talked for a bit, asking how she was feeling and how Alex was, but it was clear he had something on his mind.

She closed the washing machine door. 'Come on, Dad, spit it out.'

A gusty sigh. 'Pamela Houghton rang me last night. Said you'd been trying to see Ben. She seemed to think you imagined he might be connected with the Baltic show and was a bit cross with me for not putting you straight on that.'

'How could you? You haven't spoken to him recently, have you?'

'No, but I could have told you Ben hasn't wanted anything to do with the art world for twenty or thirty years.'

'I just asked if he might have lent some paintings to the Baltic.'

'Ben never bought art for himself. Couldn't have even if he'd wanted to. Pamela held the purse strings. And anyway, like I told you, he wasn't interested.'

'She promised to ask him if he remembered Stella. Claims she doesn't recall her or even Maggie.'

Her dad spoke slowly, as if he would rather not be having this conversation. 'Well she did talk to him and apparently he just shut off. And I can understand why he doesn't want to look back to those days. It must be very painful for him. That was when he had his accident. The same applies to Pamela. Things haven't been easy for them since then. I did warn you.'

Eve waited, listening to his breathing, knowing there was more to come.

Finally, 'Don't you think you should stop worrying over all this stuff? At least until you've had the baby?'

She bit her lip and stopped herself from snapping out a reply. *All this stuff?* A deep breath. 'Wait until I'm totally occupied you mean?'

'I'm just thinking of you. You need to keep calm.'

She said, 'Simon Houghton thinks Ben might be my father.'

'You've seen Ben's son?'

'Yes, and he seems to think it's quite likely that Ben and Stella had an affair.'

'He was just a kid at the time. What would he know?'

'He knows his dad was an adulterer.'

David's voice was low, and she could almost hear him trying to be patient with her. 'All I can say is that Stella never suggested anything like that to us.'

'I want to know what she was really like, Dad.' She could hear her voice wobbling. Felt as if she was a little girl again asking him to make everything all right.

Very gentle now. 'I know, I know. And I wish I could help more. But apart from her talent, all I knew about her was that she was a young girl in a difficult situation, just as we've always told you. She had little money, no family and no home. No one came to see her when she was here, and we were the only visitors to the hospital when she had you. So I'm afraid your biological father either didn't know she was pregnant or didn't want to know.'

'What about Maggie?'

'As I told you, we heard she went abroad not long after the show. I got the impression they'd had a falling out. So she wasn't around when Stella was pregnant. Soon after you were born Stella told us she was going to Italy to stay with Maggie and that was the last we saw of her. Then we heard about her death. I've managed to dig out that note, by the way, but it won't tell you much. There was no address, and although there was also a tiny cutting from the local paper about the fire, that said very little either.'

'Still, I'd like to see it.'

'Of course. Just don't expect too much. And since you asked I've been trying to track Maggie down, but with no luck. If she married and changed her name it would be very difficult to trace her.'

'What about the other artists?'

His breathing had become so loud he sounded asthmatic, and Eve felt bad. He coughed and when he spoke his voice was croaky. 'I've managed to trace a couple of them, but had no response yet.'

'Thank you. Please let me know as soon as you do. Whatever they say.'

'Look, Eve, it was obvious Stella was very unhappy when she was with us. It must have been so hard to give you up. But when she was gone we put her out of our minds. That's no excuse for keeping you in ignorance and what I feel most guilty for is not telling you what a great artist she was. I hope you can forgive us.'

A surge of sadness and when she could speak Eve said, 'Of course I can, but please, Dad, will you promise not to keep anything else from me?'

After she put down the phone Eve sat thinking. This was the first time either of her parents had said anything about Stella being unhappy when she was with them. It supported the idea that she was depressed just before her death. She wondered if it was a mistake on his part and they'd agreed not to mention it in case it made Eve worry about her own mental health.

She had promised herself and the baby that she would relax today, and the rain was beating off the pavements outside, so she cranked up the heating, took a book into the living room, and lay on the sofa. She had no intention of giving up her search for more information about Stella – she owed that to her own child – but it was important to avoid stress.

Hard as she tried though, she couldn't relax and the words she was reading made no sense. Eventually she picked up her phone.

And there was a reply from the journalist she'd contacted about the comment that Stella might have been depressed at the time of her death.

Telling herself it would most likely be a brush-off she sucked in a long breath, counted to five, and opened it. It was just a few lines saying how glad the woman was that someone was planning to look in depth at Stella Carr's work and that David Ballantyne's involvement was particularly exciting:

> because as far as I know he's never talked about Carr, although he's credited with discovering her.

With a plea to keep in touch she'd added a link to a 1988 article by Brock Adams, which she said might be useful. Adams was art critic for the *Observer* in the 1980s and '90s and the article was mainly about the closure of Houghton's.

> Only a couple of years ago Houghton's seemed likely to become one of the UK art world's most exciting spaces. Ben Houghton and David Ballantyne were developing as a great talent-spotting duo. In particular their last exhibition felt like the start of something big and several of the young artists featured looked set for stardom. Chief among them was twenty-year-old Stella Carr.
> Tragically that sparkling moment was followed by a series of disasters. The gallery was even then rumoured to be in financial difficulties, but Houghton insisted it would survive. These hopes were dashed when a freak accident hospitalized him for months. His recovery was only partial and he is confined to a wheelchair for life.
> Then came the terrible news that, only a year after lighting up that final show, young Stella Carr had died in another apparent accident in which a second artist from the exhibition was also badly hurt.

This was something new. So Maggie had been injured in the fire too. She wondered what *badly hurt* actually meant. And she noticed Adams used the phrase *apparent accident*, which suggested he had his doubts. She read on.

I remember spotting Stella at the start of the exhibition as a charming and vivid presence among her equally vivid paintings. However towards the end of the evening I couldn't help noticing an air of vulnerability about her. As a working class girl she must have found all the attention somewhat overwhelming. The one source who was prepared to speak to me, albeit anonymously, claimed she left England shortly before her death because of this pressure.

Houghton and Ballantyne have issued a short statement blaming the financial situation for the gallery's demise. Usually the most approachable of men, neither was willing to give an interview or add to that terse statement.

Stella

She left the Ladies without another word. Couldn't bear to look at Maggie let alone speak to her. Had she told Ben about the drawings? Maybe even taken a cut?

The gallery was still full, still noisy with chatter and clinking glasses. But the lights and jewels that had sparkled so brightly looked garish: the voices raucous, the punters overdressed and caked in lurid make-up. She felt clammy, her heart thundering in her ears and went to sit on one of the stone benches in the courtyard.

It was cool, empty and silent. There were no stars in the sky, just hazy moonlight and the drifting shadows of cloud behind the black. What a fool she'd been. If only she could unhear Maggie's words or at least believe there was any chance they might not be true. But that was impossible. They made too much sense.

Two women came into the garden followed by a group of men. One of the women smiled at her, about to say something. Stella looked away and bolted back into the gallery. If she waited she would lose her nerve.

Ben was standing with his son, talking to an older, distinguished-looking man and she didn't dare approach them. Instead she stared at Ben until she caught his eye. He smiled, said something to them, and came over.

'I need to talk to you. It's important.' She'd prepared the words as she sat in the courtyard.

His hand was on her back, shepherding her towards his office and they were inside with the door closed before she was aware of moving.

She blurted out, 'Did you sell those drawings as the genuine work of George Grafton?' hating that her voice broke.

'Ah,' was all he said with the smile she had once thought charming.

'Did you?'

'The short answer is, no.' He walked over to his desk and perched on it, his long legs stretched out in front. 'But the long answer is rather more complicated.'

Stella felt suddenly so deflated she longed to collapse on the leather sofa behind her. Instead she stayed ramrod straight glad that Maggie's painful stilettos at least made her feel a little taller. A deep breath. 'I need the long answer then.'

'OK. The truth is that I sold them to a man who probably sold them on. When he did it's likely he passed them off as the real thing.'

Stella's heart slowed to a huge and heavy thump, thump, thump, filling her chest. If she was breathing, she wasn't aware of it. But somehow she clung to her script. 'We could go to prison.' She had to stop for a second, but then forced herself on. 'At the very least any chance I have of making it as an artist will be ruined.'

When he laughed, a light unconcerned laugh, she was just able to hold back a scream.

'You have to get the drawings back. I'll return the money.' She'd spent some of it, but refused to think about that now.

Ben walked to a drinks trolley in the corner of the room. His voice was muffled, but she could hear the chuckle still in it. 'Stella, my darling, you're getting yourself worked up about nothing. No one will ever know. The idiots that bought the drawings won't have them checked, and even if they did, they wouldn't want to admit they'd been fooled.' She went to speak, but he carried on. 'And you don't think the police would waste time on something so insignificant, do you? Even major art forgery hardly ever gets exposed. Most of the big galleries in the world have fakes on their walls.' He came towards her with two glasses of whisky or brandy. 'Now let's drink to a profitable partnership and one that could do both of us a lot of good.'

She kept her hands clenched by her sides. 'We're not partners.'

He gulped some of his drink and put the other glass on a small table next to her. 'I hope this little show today hasn't deluded you into believing you're ever likely to make money from your own daubings.'

She must have flinched because he touched her arm and smiled in a kindly way.

'You're good, but not *that* good, and to make it in this business you have to be brilliant or very lucky. You might sell the odd painting every year, every few months even, but it's never likely to be enough to keep you. So why not take this opportunity? All you have to do is produce more of the same. Maybe move on to another obscure, but collectable, dead artist and I'll look after the rest. No one will ever know.'

He moved closer. The lights flickered and blurred, and she put her hand out to touch the sofa behind her, afraid she might fall. Then his arm was around her waist, his glass slammed onto the little table, and he was pressing his mouth and the length of his body against hers. He whispered against her lips. 'Come on, we can be partners in work and play. You know that's what you want.

I've seen you looking at me. Jealous of Maggie. But there's no need to be.'

She was no longer standing, but floating somewhere at a distance watching his mouth on her neck, his hand pressed into her back as the other groped at the hem of her skirt.

But then she felt the weight of him trying to push her onto the sofa. If he managed that ... For what might have been seconds or minutes that horrible sense of detachment was back and this time everything was dark. She seemed to be blinded. It was as if she was smothered in a dark cloak. But she could hear. Breathing and grunting, some of it coming from her own throat. *Oh God!* Then she forced her mind back and kicked out, her foot cracking hard against his shin, as she pushed him away with both hands. 'Leave me alone.' The words came out guttural. Nothing like her own voice.

He stumbled back and she was at the door.

When she turned to shut it behind her she saw Ben pick up his glass again and raise it in a silent toast.

Outside she stood leaning on the wall trying to catch her breath. One of the straps of her red dress had collapsed and she pulled it up, tugged at the hem, and tucked a long curl of hair back into place. Everyone in the room was chatting and drinking. Too occupied to notice her.

Except ... In the corner where her own paintings hung, their colours somehow turned dull, stood Simon. Too tall for his skinny frame; his face a sweet young version of Ben's. And he was looking straight at her, those dark lashed eyes sad and knowing.

She turned away and headed to the Ladies.

Thank God, it was empty again and she collapsed on the same stool Maggie had used. In the mirror her face was flushed, eyes fevered, and the red lipstick she'd put on so carefully all smeared and ruined.

She was wiping her mouth and trying to straighten her hair when the door opened and Maggie stood there, staring at her. 'I saw you,' she said. 'How could you?'

'I went in to ask him about the drawings, that's all.'

For a moment Maggie's eyes had the same look she'd seen in poor young Simon's. Then they took on a hard shine. 'Don't talk to me. Don't ever talk to me again.'

She turned away, the door swinging shut behind her.

CHAPTER NINE

Eve

The weather had turned wintery and Eve was forced to park yards away from the house and struggle against gusts of cold rain mixed with sleet. At her antenatal check-up the hospital had been concerned about her blood pressure. She told them she'd been rushing around, but she knew that wasn't it. Ever since meeting Simon, and reading the article about the closure of Houghton's with its comment on Stella's vulnerability, she had felt in turmoil.

As she let herself into the house her phone vibrated in her pocket. A text from Alex.

How did it go?

She rang him back as she struggled out of her wet coat and scarf. 'I'm fine. They say the baby's head is down, so it won't be long now.' There was no need to worry him about the blood pressure.

Then she called her mum and left a message. 'Had my check-up this morning and everything's good. Dad said he found that note and newspaper cutting about Stella. I'm in for the rest of the day if you want to bring them. Or Alex can pick them up on his way home.' She didn't want to give them any excuse to delay further.

As she rang off, the phone chirruped with another text: Alex, reminding her there was some lentil soup in the fridge for lunch. She heated it up and sat at the kitchen table looking through the glass doors into the garden. There were still a few withered leaves hanging from the trees, but they only made it seem colder and so bleak that even in the warm kitchen she shivered.

Her phone buzzed again. David asking if she was free to talk.

'Hello, darling,' he said when she called him back, his voice a little husky. 'I've heard from one of the other artists at Stella's show.'

Her spoon dropped into the bowl with a small splash. 'Maggie?'

'No, but you'll be interested in what he has to say.' A pause. 'Before I send it I want you to promise me that you'll talk to someone before you rush into doing anything. Discuss it with Alex if you don't want me or Mum to know.'

Her, 'OK,' was an unconvincing grunt, but she didn't care.

A moment of silence before he said, 'Right, I'll send the exchange over now.' Another pause that brought her close to screaming. 'Call me any time or come down.'

A mumbled, 'All right, bye Dad,' and she cut him off.

She forced herself to finish the soup then poured a glass of water, checking her phone every few seconds. When the emails came through she saw they were between him and James Stone, one of the names she'd written down from the Houghton programme. She scrolled down to the first email from James:

Great to hear from you, David. I still remember how kind you were to me when I was starting out. Of course I can't forget Stella. Apart from being a lovely person, she was such a talent and it was a tragedy that she died so young. I was devastated when I heard about it. I still think of her.

76

David had written back to tell him that Stella had a daughter and that he and Jill had adopted her.

Wow, David, I had no idea Stella had a child. From Eve's DOB I've worked out that she must have been born a few months after Stella and I were together. I'm guessing you were too polite to ask if I might be her dad, but all I can say is that it is just about possible, although Stella certainly didn't tell me about a pregnancy. I've since gone on to have three children myself from two relationships that in the end didn't work out. I wonder what would have happened if Stella and I had met later?

We really cared for each other, but I had the chance go to the States and the relationship hadn't go on long enough to be really serious. We were both very young and keen on our careers and I don't think either of us was thinking about kids. I imagine Stella decided on adoption for the best of motives and, although I wish she had felt able to confide in me, it sounds as if she made the right choice.

Please let Eve know that she's welcome to contact me. I'm resident in America now, but I've been hoping to get over early in the New Year to see Stella's exhibition. I'd love the chance to meet Stella's daughter then – even if she isn't mine!

Eve walked away from the table and stood staring out at the darkening garden. A single black leaf floated down from one of the trees. *Just about possible.* It was an answer of sorts. James Stone certainly fitted the image her parents had given her of a likely father, but he hadn't known Stella for long and had obviously lost contact with her months before her death. So, even though he was happy to talk, could he tell Eve anything more than her parents had already?

She went back online to search for mentions of James Stone. There was a handsome photograph that must be recent. His hair was grey now and receding a little, but he looked a good deal younger than her parents. He was wearing one earring and had a warm smile. He seemed to be mainly working in theatre design. And he had three children. What would it be like to suddenly have three siblings? Of course it would mean Simon wasn't her brother, but they could still be friends. And that might be even better.

She fired off a message to James just saying she would be delighted if he was her biological parent and would love to talk by mail or phone. She promised to put no pressure on him or to interfere in his life. She attached her own photograph and added:

> *What I really want to know is anything at all you can tell me about Stella.*

Although she knew he was unlikely to reply for ages, she kept checking her phone, pacing around the house doing mindless little jobs. She almost phoned Alex, but she didn't want to talk about this with him yet. He would only start worrying again, trying to help. But she desperately wanted someone to talk to. Someone who wouldn't tell her what to do, who would just listen.

She dug out the purse from her bag on the table inside the front door. Simon Houghton's card was still there and she added him to her contacts. She should at least thank him for his help.

> *Hi Simon,*
> *You were so kind the other day that I wanted to say thank you. It was really good to talk to someone who actually knew and liked my mother.*

She hesitated, then wrote a bit more.

I've been looking into who else might be my biological father and I've heard from James Stone. I wonder if you remember him? He says it's just possible it could be him. So it may be a relief to know that your own dad could be off the hook!

Best wishes

Eve

She wasn't planning to send the message, but it helped to imagine discussing the whole thing with Simon. Then Alex texted her from the train to say he'd be delayed and wouldn't be home for another hour and she found herself clicking open the message again and sending it as it was.

Stella

She went home with James after the show, told him she'd had an argument with Maggie over the catalogue and needed to let her cool down for a while. Maggie was nowhere to be seen.

There was no living room in the flat he shared with his two mates, so they took the beers they'd bought on the way and sat on his bed. James was drunk and happy, but Stella, although she'd had too many glasses of champagne herself, felt horribly clear-headed. But she let James talk on and on because it was a relief to sit quietly without thinking about herself.

He was so excited. Just as she'd been earlier in the night.

'David introduced me to Brock Adams, you know the critic for the *Observer*. He's planning an article about the show.'

James squeezed her knee, and she flinched, but then relaxed.

'And don't worry, I gave you a namecheck,' he carried on. 'Sent him over to talk to you, but that must have been when you were fighting with Maggie.'

'She said she never wants to talk to me again.' Unexpectedly

79

her eyes flooded with tears. James moved closer, and she turned to bury her face in his shoulder.

After a while she heard him telling her not to take it to heart. It was just a squabble.

'Both of you had been drinking and Maggie was jealous, that's all. She'll get over it.'

Of course he had no idea what she was really crying about, but she stayed leaning on him until they lay back on the bed and must have slept.

She woke to find him pressing himself against her and kissing the back of her neck.

'No!'

He let go. 'Sorry, I'm sorry. I was half asleep.'

But she was off the bed and out of the room in moments. The clock on the kitchen wall said it was four a.m.. She grabbed a jumper from the back of a chair and pulled it over her crumpled dress. It didn't smell too good, but it helped to warm her enough that she could make herself an instant black coffee and sit in misery until it was light. Then let herself out of the flat and head back to Maggie's.

Her key wouldn't open the door. Maggie must have bolted it from inside. It was still early, but she knocked and then went round to do the same at the back door. She felt ridiculous at this time of day in a baggy jumper, short silk dress and stilettos. Needed to get off the street. She had only taken a few pounds to the show, but had enough to buy some tea and toast in the scruffy little café at the end of the road. When she'd finished she stayed stirring her empty cup trying to think what to do.

The café windows were steamed up so she didn't see Maggie until she came through the door. She smiled at her, but Maggie stayed straight-faced, standing in front of her table with her arms crossed.

'I've decided to go away for a bit. Do some travelling. So I'll be selling the house.' Her eyes were cold. 'Please clear your stuff out by the end of the week. That should give you time to find something else.'

Before Stella could speak she was gone.

Eve

When Eve finally gave up trying to sleep she struggled to lever her large belly out of bed. She stood silently for a moment when she was finally on her feet as Alex turned over, disturbed by the dipping of the mattress.

All she could think of was the note and newspaper cutting about Stella's death that her mum had brought over.

Alex had begged her not to bring them up to the bedroom, but every time she closed her eyes she saw them lying on the kitchen table.

A few minutes later, huddled in her thick dressing gown, fur slippers on her feet, she sat looking at the yellowing scrap of newsprint. It was from the local paper in the little Italian town where Stella had spent her last few weeks. Eve couldn't read Italian, but it was paperclipped to a folded piece of A4 on which someone had typed a translation.

FIRE KILLS ENGLISH ARTIST

A young woman was declared dead when the garden studio where she was painting burned down. Named as Stella Carr, she was visiting fellow artist and local resident Margo de Santis. The fire caught hold very quickly and the authorities think Miss Carr was overcome before she could escape. Miss de Santis was injured and remains in a serious condition. Police are investigating.

She wasn't sure what that final line meant. Perhaps it was normal for the police to be involved after a deadly fire, but she wondered what they had discovered.

There was a blurry photograph above the report of the house before the fire – looking as if taken from an estate agent's brochure. The only thing that could be the studio was a small wooden structure that was more like a garden shed than anything else. It must have burned very fast for anyone be trapped in there.

The note from Maggie was typed, and there was no return address or date.

Dear Mr and Mrs Ballantyne

As you must know by now Stella Carr was killed in a fire at my house in Italy. I'm sorry it has taken me so long to write, but I've been in hospital for many months.

Stella had recently come into some money and as neither of us has any family we thought it was sensible to make wills naming each other as beneficiaries. However I know Stella would want me to give her money to the daughter you adopted so I enclose a cheque.

She thought back to that afternoon when her mum had given her the papers as they sat in Eve's small living room: Eve on the sofa and Jill on the armchair beside the glowing fire. She'd read very quickly while her mum used a poker to clear some ash from under the coals. When she reached the line about the cheque Eve looked up. 'You never told me about the money.'

Her mother carried on fiddling with the coals. 'It was the £10,000 we said Aunt Janie left you.' Jill kept moving the coals about in the grate avoiding Eve's eye. Eve was tempted to grab the poker and throw it on the floor. They had told her about the savings account in her name when she went to university, but said she shouldn't spend it on the fees. In the end she had used it when she and Alex bought their house.

82

A long silence until Jill put down the poker and turned to her, still not meeting her eye. 'I'm sorry, Eve. It just never seemed the right time to tell you.'

Yet another lie by omission.

Eve couldn't stay sitting. She hauled herself up and walked over to the window. Across the road was the wide expanse of grass that ran to the cliff edge and in the distance a strip of grey sea. On this gloomy day the grass was empty except for one woman in a heavy coat throwing a ball for a bounding Labrador.

What was the point of saying anything? She already knew they had kept the truth from her for years. And much as she wanted to rage at her mother it wasn't worth it.

But something didn't make sense. 'I thought you said Stella was poor.'

'That's what we thought. I mean she sold five paintings at the show and Dad managed to get her another couple of sales later on, but they didn't make anywhere near that. She obviously painted while she was in Italy, and it sounds as if her pictures survived the fire. I suppose Maggie might have found a buyer for some of them after she died. Or perhaps it was an inheritance. She says in the note that Stella had no family, but I think there was a grandmother.'

Eve said, 'Yes, the one in her painting. The old lady she called Nana. She would have been my great-grandma.'

Jill looked away, and Eve felt a twist of shame. That had been a cruel thing to say. Her mum cleared her throat. 'Yes, that was the picture she wouldn't let them sell. Her grandmother died just before Stella came to us, so maybe she inherited a house.'

'But if it wasn't an inheritance, if it was from the sale of paintings, the collector who lent them to the Baltic might have been the buyer.' She was talking more to herself than to her mother. It didn't really change anything. She had heard nothing since she had asked the curator to send on her contact details. What she needed was to find the person who had known Stella best. The person who had been with her at the time of her death. And that was Maggie.

When her mum had gone, and Alex arrived home, she showed him the note and newspaper report. He kissed and held her for a few moments, but said nothing. And after that she didn't feel like telling him about the conversation with her mum. She was almost sure he would tell her again to leave it for now. They didn't talk much while they ate, and when they finished Eve left Alex filling the dishwasher and went up to the room they'd got ready for the baby.

Sitting on the rocking chair they'd bought from a second-hand shop, and looking at the pale yellow wallpaper with its border of ducks and lambs that they'd chosen and put up together, she felt tears coming and closed the door. Even with it tightly shut she tried to stifle her sobs. Since her breakdown Alex had always been alert to her changes of mood. Too alert. But she'd been stable and happy for ages – until now.

As she rocked back and forth she told herself it was just pregnancy blues, but she knew it was because she felt so alone. She used to tell Alex everything, knowing she could trust him to be totally on her side. But she wasn't sure that was true anymore.

Now, sitting at the kitchen table in the middle of the night, she felt lonelier than she ever had. If she couldn't trust her parents and couldn't tell Alex who could she turn to?

Her phone, which had been lying on the table, chirped as its battery gave out and she got up to rake through a drawer for a charger. When she'd plugged it in she checked the display and saw a message that must have come during the day.

It was from Simon Houghton.

Thanks for getting in touch. It was good meeting you. I've been thinking about everything you said and I wondered if you'd be free to meet tomorrow. I have to be in Bexhill-on-Sea first thing to evaluate some pictures and I see it's only a couple of stops on the train from Hastings. So I could easily come over there afterwards. We could find somewhere for a late lunch before I head back to town. I'll give you a bell when I'm ready to leave Bexhill. Don't worry if you can't make it, but I'd really enjoy chatting with you again.

CHAPTER TEN

Stella

She couldn't paint. Whenever she'd been unhappy in the past it was work that had saved her, but this was different. The thought that her drawings had been sold as forgeries was allconsuming. And there was no one she could talk to.

When she got back to the house after Maggie told her she was selling up there was a note on the hall table:

Stella,
I've organized for someone to come next Monday morning
to pack the rest of my stuff and clean the place so you need
to be gone by then. I won't be back.

And that was it.

She had gone into college to check the noticeboard and found a room in a student flat right away; but three days later she still couldn't bring herself to leave. She'd only been into class once. A few newspapers had featured the Houghton exhibition and all of them made a great fuss of her. And the glances and whispers behind hands as she walked about in college were horribly

86

embarrassing. When the tutor joked that as she was obviously so photogenic she should really take the place of their model, and everyone snickered, she walked out, her face throbbing with heat. It felt just as it had when she'd first arrived as a poor girl from the north-east among all the posh kids. Until Maggie rescued her.

But Maggie was gone now.

She haunted her favourite galleries. And she was in the café at the National Portrait Gallery when Ben Houghton came through the door. It was too late to move away as he headed straight towards her.

'Just the girl I was looking for,' he said, plonking down in front of her. 'I remembered Maggie telling me you loved to hang out here.'

'Actually I'm glad to see you,' she said enjoying the way his eyelids flickered with surprise. She had been planning to go and see him, but saying what she had to say in a neutral space with other people around would be easier. 'I've got the money for the paintings David managed to sell.' She was determined not to give him any of the credit for the show. 'So I can pay you for those drawings now.'

He sat back further in his chair. 'Right,' he dragged the word out on a long drawl, 'I don't think that's going to be possible.' He raised his palm in a stop gesture as she went to speak. 'Look, I know I was out of order the other evening, and I can understand you being angry with me, but I've talked to my buyer. He's reassured me that he sold the drawings to a very reclusive chap who keeps all his art locked away for his eyes only. So there's nothing at all to worry about. In fact he's looking for some more of the same and is prepared to pay big bucks for them.'

'No.' She put her sketchpad and pencils into her bag and went to stand, but he pushed aside her empty cup and saucer and grabbed her hand, staring hard at her. Two girls in school uniform walking close to their table giggled.

'Please, Stella, just listen for a minute.'

Something different in his eyes made her sit down again, but she pulled away her hand and crossed her arms tightly over her chest.

'You see I'm in a bit of trouble, my love,' he said. 'And I need those big bucks rather urgently.'

She stifled a bitter laugh. 'You own an art gallery. And Maggie told me about your house in Mayfair.'

'Ah, well.' He rubbed his hand over his mouth. 'None of it's mine, you see. Pamela's the one with the money. And that means I can never be a free man. So I started dabbling on the stock market, hoping to raise some funds of my own. But I made a few bad investments.'

She shook her head.

He looked down at his hands and his voice sank to something so unlike his normal tooloud, too-hearty one that he sounded like a different person. 'I lost everything. And it wasn't actually mine. So if I don't do something drastic, the gallery will have to go. And this guy is willing to offer me a lifeline if I help him.'

Very aware of people walking by with trays she shifted her chair closer to him, speaking in a forceful whisper. 'I can't see how a few fake drawings could help.'

He was looking at her again and his voice had regained some of its confidence. 'I think you underestimate your skills, my darling. But in any case, they will just be a start: to show my good intentions. After that he'll organize extending my credit.'

'I won't do it.'

He leaned forward talking intensely. 'Surely you want to help save the gallery that gave you and your mates such a great start. And you like David, don't you? Do you really want to see him lose his job?'

He was pathetic but, despite herself, Stella felt a twinge of pity. But this was Ben's fault. She had nothing to do with it. She slung her bag over her shoulder. 'I'm sorry about all that, but the answer is still no. And I want my drawings back.'

'Please, Stella, you don't understand.' His voice was a harsh whisper. 'It's not just that.' The look of fear in his eyes made her pause. 'You see the guy I was telling you about, he won't actually take no for an answer. And if we don't help him out, he won't just be content with making sure *I'm* ruined.'

She needed to swallow, but her mouth was suddenly so dry she couldn't do it. As he carried on speaking the chatter and clatter from the café turned to silence. All she could hear was a horrible buzzing in her head and his words: words that would have been unbelievable if it wasn't for the emotion in his voice.

'He hurts people. People who don't do as he asks, you see. And he's threatening me – threatening us – now.'

She must have made some kind of movement because he reached a hand out to her, but she shoved her own hands into her pockets and shifted away from the table.

'It's all right,' he said. 'I haven't told him who you are, but you can see why I'm desperate. And it's always possible he might find out about you.'

Next morning she began packing up her room. What Ben had said was ludicrous, but it had shaken her and a small voice kept asking her something she couldn't ignore: had Maggie disappeared because Ben had told her something similar?

Although she'd moved in with just a couple of suitcases and her box of art materials, she had accumulated so much in the eighteen months she'd been here that it would take several trips on the tube to get it all to the new flat. When everything except her easel and the *Maggie and Me* painting she'd been trying to work on was stuffed into cases and bags, she sat on the bed for ten minutes hating herself, hating Maggie and hating Ben Houghton.

When she got off the train she carried her bags along the tree-lined street towards her new flat. It was very quiet and after what Ben had said yesterday her senses felt hyper-alert, her skin tingling as if eyes were watching her. When she heard footsteps coming fast behind her she almost broke into a run, but told herself not to be so stupid.

The footsteps stopped. She froze.

'Hi, Stella.' She turned. James Stone, smiling a nervous smile and talking very fast.

'I heard you were moving in with Laura and Jane,' he said. 'Just called round to see if you were there. Can I help you?' He didn't wait for an answer but grabbed her two suitcases. And they started walking. Without looking at her he said tentatively, 'I'm sorry about the other morning.'

'It's all right.'

When they got to the house they dumped Stella's stuff in her room, and she turned to him. 'Thanks, James.'

'I noticed a decent-looking pub just round the corner. If you want we could have a drink before you start unpacking. Help you cool down.'

'No, I can't stop. Have to collect the rest.'

He shifted from foot to foot. 'If there's much more I could come and help you.' He rubbed one hand through his dark strands of hair until it looked as if he'd just fallen out of bed. When Stella didn't speak he said, 'Or I could just piss off if you'd rather.'

She laughed. 'I'd love some help.'

At Maggie's they were able to share out the rest between them; the painting under her arm and James shouldering her easel. They didn't talk as they sat on the tube, but it was good not to feel alone.

As they walked back from the station again he said, 'So where's your mate, Maggie, disappeared to then?'

She didn't want to talk about Maggie. 'Travelling in Europe.'

'Not just for a holiday though?'

'No. She's selling the house, so I don't know if she'll come back.'

'How the other half lives, eh?' When she didn't answer he fell silent for a while. Then, 'I heard rumours there was something going on between her and that guy Ben Houghton. Is that why she's run away?'

Stella stopped and put down her suitcase. 'Look, James, I really don't want to talk about any of this.'

He turned to face her. His eyes were a warm brown and he gazed at her steadily for a moment then smiled. 'OK, I'll shut up.'

They walked on in silence, but when they reached the flat and carried everything up, he stood awkwardly in her bedroom doorway.

'I'll leave you to unpack, but I only live a few streets away so maybe we can get that drink one evening.'

And suddenly she didn't want to say goodbye. 'If you give me a hand with this, we could go after that.'

Eve

Eve arranged to meet Simon in a little wine bar near the railway station in St Leonards. It was a mile or so outside the main town of Hastings so they were less likely to be seen by anyone she knew. As she parked and locked the car she felt a qualm. She shouldn't be keeping this from Alex. But she told herself it was easier this way. He would only worry and ask questions she didn't want to answer yet.

Simon was already sitting with a glass of wine and a menu in front of him. Eve had never been to this bar before, but it looked to be a good choice: warm, woody and just busy enough to allow for a private chat without being overheard. Simon stood as she walked in and came towards her to drop a kiss on her cheek.

'Lovely to see you again, Eve. What can I get you?'

'Just a sparkling water, please.'

She picked up the menu, but her eyes followed him to the bar. He was in a dark suit, with the jacket open and his blue tie unfastened and she remembered something her dad had said about Ben: *He could always wear clothes well, of course.*

When he returned to the table he said, 'Shall we order first? Then we can talk without interruption.' His eyes never left her face, and she was glad of the excuse to look down.

They chose some tapas to share and she noticed Simon went for all vegetable options, so she did the same. The waitress took their order, ignoring Eve and fluttering beside Simon.

When she had gone, Eve asked, 'Are you vegetarian?'

'Since I was a teenager. It was mainly to annoy my parents who were big meat eaters. But I've never felt I was missing out. My wife was vegan so that wasn't a problem.' He brushed back his hair and gave a soft laugh. 'There were problems a-plenty in the marriage, but food wasn't one of them.'

'So you're …?'

'Divorced? Yes. Five years now, which is about the same time the marriage lasted in fact. No kids, thank the lord. That would have made things difficult. As it is we parted amicably, as they say.'

'I'm sorry.'

'Don't be. The single life suits me fine.'

Eve didn't imagine he would have trouble finding female company if he wanted it. And she couldn't stop a small smile as she realized she would be proud to have such a desirable man for her brother. One of his dark eyebrows rose. 'What's so funny?'

She was saved by the arrival of the food and as they ate he started talking about Stella.

'It was her work that turned me on to art, you know. I hated it before that because it was what my parents were involved with. I was an only child, so I was probably jealous that it took up so much of their time. That show was different because the artists were young. Older than me, of course – I was only just fourteen – but at that age, although you despise your parents' generation, you can't wait to be just that little bit more adult.

So I went to the gallery before the show and was bowled over by Stella's work.'

A pulse of excitement. 'Is that when you met her?'

'No, that wasn't until the opening night. Dad was pleased when I told him I'd like to come because he thought I was finally showing an interest, but all I really wanted was to speak to Stella. It wasn't just her paintings that captivated me. I'd seen her picture on the front of the catalogue and thought she was beautiful. And when I did meet her I fell in love on the spot.' He was smiling at the memory as he twisted his fork in a bowl of butter beans and olives. Then he looked up. 'Puppy love, of course, but at the time ...'

'It feels like the real thing.' She nodded. 'I know.' His eyes, clear as blue glass, clouded and he echoed her nod. 'What was she like?' she said, her breath catching in her throat.

'Very like you to look at. Pretty, tiny and kind of fragile. I was growing fast at the time, and she made me feel protective even though she was older.'

As if disturbed by the rapid thump of Eve's heart, the baby gave a sharp kick under her ribs. She sat up straighter to give it more space. Simon was talking, his eyes distant as he followed his memories.

'She came from Newcastle and had a lovely accent, but was obviously trying to disguise it, which made her even more appealing.'

'How many times did you meet her?'

He reached for a piece of bread, took a drink of his wine and turned to wave his glass at the waitress.

'Just that once properly. Although I saw her again when she came to our house a few weeks afterwards.' He took a bite of his bread. 'It was late one evening and I was hiding away in my bedroom like a typical teenager. Eavesdropping.'

'Is that where you got the idea she was romantically involved with Ben?'

'Well, I guessed that when I saw them together at the opening. They'd obviously been kissing, at the very least.' Another gentle laugh. 'God, I was so jealous.'

'I can imagine. But what about when she came to the house.'

'All I can say is that they argued. It was quite heated.'

'Could it have been about something else?'

'I can't think what. And, Eve ...' this time he took her hand, 'I listened at my door for a minute or so and I heard Stella tell Dad she was pregnant.'

CHAPTER ELEVEN

Eve

When Eve got home she found Alex in the kitchen by the open fridge. He had a frozen ready meal in his hand and had just opened a bottle of lager.

'I've been trying to call you. Been anywhere exciting?'

They never kept things from each other, but she hesitated. She hadn't told him about the visit to Pamela and Ben yet, so he didn't even know she'd met Simon. Instead of answering right away she pulled out her mobile. 'Sorry.' Two missed calls and a text from him. The music and chatter in the wine bar must have prevented her hearing. She was still in her coat, still with her bag over her shoulder, and she turned back to the hall to take them off. Calling out as she did so, 'I went to meet Ben Houghton's son, Simon. I've been trying to talk to Ben. He won't see me, but Simon happened to be down here today, so we met up.'

When she came back into the kitchen she knew from the way Alex was standing, with his arms crossed, that he was upset. 'So when were you going to tell me about this?'

She felt a surge of something that might have been annoyance or maybe guilt. It wasn't the fact that he wanted to know, but the way he'd spoken that made her answer come out so spikily. 'When I found out something worth telling you.'

Alex shook his head and turned away. His voice was very quiet. 'And have you?'

'Yes, I have. Simon is pretty sure Ben is my father, which would mean that Simon and I are brother and sister.'

He twisted back, looking down at her and speaking in his normal voice. 'I thought Ben had a relationship with her friend?'

'It sounds as if he had multiple affairs. Simon saw him kissing Stella at the gallery opening and later on she came to their house to announce she was pregnant.'

Alex rubbed his chin. 'That sounds convincing, but how old was Simon at the time?'

'Fourteen.'

Alex took a fork from the drawer, pierced the plastic cover on the frozen pasta and put it into the microwave. 'It's strange that your dad, David I mean, didn't know about this.'

Eve switched on the kettle, dropping a herbal tea bag into a mug. 'I think he and Mum just want the whole thing to go away. Like they said, they started thinking of me as their real child and wanted to forget all about Stella. So they ignored any suspicions they might have had and distanced themselves from Ben. Dad told me he hadn't seen much of him since he left the gallery.'

The microwave pinged and Alex opened it and stirred the pasta. 'Do you want any of this?'

She shook her head. 'We had lunch so I'm not hungry, but I'm cold. I think I'll have a bath.'

She lay in the hot scented water sipping her tea and trying not to be annoyed with him. She couldn't shake the feeling that he thought she was incapable of doing this on her own.

Closing her eyes she found herself thinking about Simon. Although Ben didn't sound like the kind of man she would like for a father she'd be very happy if it turned out that Simon was her brother. She felt a definite connection with him and the way he talked about Stella was oddly comforting.

The water had cooled, but she stayed lying there until Alex knocked on the door.

'Are you all right?'

When she came out wrapped in her dressing gown he put his arms around her. 'I'm sorry if you think I'm prying. I just want to help.'

Eve rested her head in the curve of his shoulder and when he stroked her damp hair she rose on tiptoes to kiss his warm lips. 'I'm sorry too. I don't mean to shut you out.'

'There's some pasta left if you want it.'

She shook her head. 'I'm tired so think I'll go straight to bed. Maybe read for a while.'

He spoke into her hair. 'What about some food? I could toast a piece of that nice bread.'

She realized she *was* hungry. 'Yes, please. With some of the hummus I made if there's any left.'

They walked back to the bedroom arms entwined and when she climbed under the covers he tucked them around her.

'Back in a minute.'

She must have dozed because he was back with a plate and mug. Still in his clothes he lay on the bed beside her.

She said, 'I've also heard from one of the other artists at the Houghton: James Stone. He was Stella's boyfriend for a short time and says it's possible he's the one.'

'Well that sounds more likely to me. Are you going to try to meet him too?'

'He lives in America, so that will be difficult, but he's hoping to get over here in the New Year.'

He sat up. 'That's good. Sounds like you've got it down to two candidates. Why don't you wait until the baby's born then ask James and this Simon Houghton to do a DNA test? That could put your mind at rest completely.' He swung his legs onto the

97

floor. 'Anyway, I've got some work to do. Call me if you need anything.' Then he gave her a long sweet kiss. 'Just in case you're asleep when I come to bed.'

After he'd gone she lay for a few minutes. He still didn't understand that she couldn't wait. Nor that it wasn't the identity of her father she was bothered about but what had happened to her mother.

Alex had brought her phone up with him and after she'd eaten her toast she saw there was a message from James Stone:

Thank you so much for the photo. I'll treasure it. You look just as Stella did when I knew her.

I was so pleased to hear about her exhibition at the Baltic and the fact that she produced more paintings before she died. But you're an adult now and I can understand why you need to know as much about your mother as possible so I'm going to be completely honest with you.

You see when we were together she couldn't work. The huge success she had at Houghton's didn't make her happy. In fact it was obvious to me that something went wrong around the time of that show. She wouldn't talk about it, but she seemed almost afraid at times. I had an inkling that something had happened between her and Ben Houghton. It was clear she was angry with him, although she never admitted they'd had an affair and I didn't ask.

She'd also had a really unpleasant bust-up with her best friend, Maggie (sorry I can't remember her surname). I have to say that from what I saw and heard of her I didn't like Maggie and I suspect that the estrangement was mainly because she was jealous of Stella's talent.

But Stella was very fond of her and I was glad to hear they reconciled and Stella began to work again before she died.

I just wish she had been happier when she was with me. Or that I could have helped with whatever was bothering her.

If he was telling the truth, and she had no reason to doubt him, he'd certainly confirmed that Stella was troubled during that last year. And he knew Ben was part of the problem – so he was still in the frame as a potential father. James hadn't used the word *depressed*. Instead he thought she was unhappy and angry. But the phrase that jumped out at Eve was: *she seemed almost afraid.*

Stella

Stella had been lying awake since the early hours. James was beside her in bed and she tried to keep still so as not to wake him. He had been more or less living with her for the past few weeks. She wasn't in love with him, but she liked him a lot and when they made love she could almost forget the pain of being unable to paint and having lost Maggie. It quietened that nagging anxiety about Ben Houghton's warnings too.

Around six thirty James rolled over in bed and said, 'You didn't sleep again, did you? No wonder you can't work.'

She sat up and groped around on the floor for her glass of water. She'd only put it there last night, but it already tasted dusty.

James rubbed her arm. 'Why don't you tell me what's bothering you?'

'I still feel so bad about Maggie.' She half-hoped he would say he didn't believe that was all. Maybe then she could force herself to tell him the whole truth. But when he simply carried on stroking her arm, she lay down again staring at a series of cracks across the ceiling that reminded her of the spokes of a broken umbrella.

He kissed her, and she let herself forget again as she pulled off her baggy T-shirt and helped him do the same.

Afterwards, she lay with her head on his chest and reached up to play with his earring. He laughed and squeezed her hand.

'You should get *your* ears pierced. You'd look lovely with big gold hoops showing through your curls. I'd like to paint you like that.'

'I don't think there'll be time.'

He kissed her hard on the top of the head. 'Get them done and I'll work fast. I'll even buy the earrings.'

She pulled away and sat on the edge of the bed. She didn't want to think about this. Him leaving for Philadelphia in two weeks. He had a scholarship for a course in set design and would be gone for at least a year. They both knew it would mean the end of their relationship. It wasn't love, but she had begun to wish it was because maybe then she could tell him the truth. Or the part that concerned him, at least.

In the bathroom she opened the window. Outside it was the loveliest summer morning. Down in the garden belonging to the flats there was only a scrubby lawn, but the grass shone with dew and the bushes around the fence were covered in a green haze of leaves.

In the shower, her face raised to the jets of warm water, she tried not to think, but that was impossible. She was pregnant. She'd done a test yesterday to confirm it. There was no point in telling James because he would be gone in a fortnight and the thought that he might feel obliged to stick with her made her cringe. It couldn't work.

For the first time in years she kept thinking about her mother. The mother who had regretted having her and told her so almost every day until she was nine years old. 'You ruined my life,' she said. 'I should have got rid of you.' And then she was dead.

Stella came home from school one day and found her slumped with her drug paraphernalia all around her. That wasn't unusual, so Stella took a packet of crisps and a glass of lemon squash to her room and climbed into bed to keep warm. In the morning her mam was still curled up on the sofa. The way she was breathing made her sound like the old dog that belonged to Mrs Ahmed

100

next door. There was no breakfast and as she left the flat Stella was only thinking about how long it would be until her free school dinner.

When she got back that afternoon Mrs Ahmed rushed out to her and took her into her own flat. She made Stella sit on her sofa. It was covered in white dog hairs. Mrs Ahmed's usually smiley face was so serious Stella knew something was wrong. Her mam had died, and after Mrs Ahmed told her she said, 'Didn't you see she was poorly, pet?' Stella shook her head.

That was when she went to live with her nana. And Nana told her, 'Your mam wasn't right in the head. I tried my best with her, but nothing worked. Thank the lord you're more like me.' Stella wanted so much for that to be true.

But now her nana's mind was gone and she didn't even recognize Stella. Maggie was gone too, and James soon would be. She rubbed the towel slowly over her stomach. She seemed to lose everyone who meant anything to her. And maybe that was her own fault.

Eve

They usually had Sunday dinner with her parents once a month, although Eve had put them off for the past two weekends. But today, eating her dad's roast beef in the warm kitchen above the shop made everything feel normal again. Alex told her parents they planned to name the baby Ivy, and her dad poured himself more red wine and raised it in a toast. 'Here's to Ivy and let's hope she's never poisonous.' Jill slapped his arm and told him not to be horrible, but everyone laughed and clicked their glasses.

After dinner they usually went for a walk along the seafront, but when David stood and began to pull on his coat her mum stayed where she was. 'I think I'll give it a miss this time. Have another cup of coffee and get on with the washing up.'

Alex hadn't moved either and he avoided Eve's eye when he

said, 'No, I'll do the washing up. You can relax, and Eve and David can have some father and daughter time.'

Eve guessed it had been planned, but it was still nice to bundle up and hold her dad's arm as they braved the windy promenade. 'We'll just walk as far as the pier, shall we?' David said.

Despite the cold wind there were plenty of other walkers out today. A crowd of noisy teenagers, shouting and laughing in French, nearly collided with them and her dad quickly moved in front to protect her, saying, 'Careful, careful now.'

She squeezed his arm. She loved him so much. But although she knew he had something to say to her, she wasn't going to help him out. The way he and her mum had deceived her still hurt.

A seagull flew so close its wings stirred her hair before swooping down on a woman just in front of them to snatch a chip from the paper bag she was carrying. When the man with her gave a loud guffaw she began pelting him with chips. More screeching gulls dive-bombed the scraps of potato.

David steered Eve around them, but they were both chuckling. When they reached the pier the wind had died down, so they headed along to lean on the railings at the end where it was quiet and empty.

Close to the pier the sea churned and foamed with white but further out the grey clouds had turned it into swirls of molten steel. David coughed and touched Eve's gloved hand on the railing.

'Are you still in touch with Simon Houghton?'

She put her hand in her pocket. 'Of course. He could be my brother and, even if he isn't, he's one of the few people who's happy to talk about Stella.'

'Does Pamela know he's seeing you?'

'I have no idea.' She turned away from him to look back at the town and the cliffs rearing behind it. 'And, before you say he was only a kid at the time, he was fourteen and he remembers Stella coming to their house to tell Ben she was pregnant.'

A long silence. Then he took her arm again and they began walking back towards the promenade. 'Well, if Simon really did hear that it seems pretty convincing. All I can say is that we never heard anything like that from Stella.'

They had reached the pier café and he said, 'Let's get a coffee, shall we? Warm up a bit.'

At a table facing the sea they sat stirring their drinks and Eve said, 'Pamela may be able to stop me seeing Ben, but she can't prevent me from keeping in touch with Simon.'

'That's true, but ...' He was leaning both elbows on the table and it trembled as he took a noisy breath. 'The thing is, if you're going to keep seeing him there's something I should tell you. Something you'll probably find out anyway if you go on like this.'

A heavy thump from her heart and an answering kick from her baby girl. She rubbed her bump. 'Go on.'

'You say Simon told you about Stella coming to their house?'

'Yes, that's when he heard her say she was pregnant.'

'And that's all he said?'

'Yes.'

He picked up his mug, took a long drink of coffee and wiped his mouth with a paper napkin. 'He didn't tell you when this happened?'

The baby was kicking hard. 'No.'

'Apparently it was at the same time as Ben's accident.'

A cold band tightened on her throat. 'And?'

Her dad gripped her hand very hard, looking into her eyes as he spoke. 'According to Pamela the accident happened on the same evening that Stella came to the house.'

Silence.

'Dad?' She shifted her bulk towards him. 'What is it? What are you trying to say?'

'Pamela says it happened during an argument. With Stella.'

Eve stared out at the swirling sea, suddenly so dark it was

almost purple. She couldn't look at him anymore: couldn't breathe. But she couldn't stop herself hearing.

'She says she arrived home to find Ben injured on the hall floor. And ...' He rubbed his hand over his jaw as if checking whether he needed a shave.

'Dad?'

'Ben was still just conscious enough to tell her Stella had pushed him down the stairs.'

Eve must have made some kind of noise because he pulled her towards him and held her tight as he spoke. His breath was warm on her ear. 'His back was broken, Eve. He was paralyzed for life. And, according to Pamela, Stella was responsible.'

CHAPTER TWELVE

Eve

As they walked back from the pier Eve's mind screamed at her that it wasn't true. Pamela just wanted to discourage her husband's illegitimate daughter from trying to make contact again.

It was beginning to grow gloomy as the winter night drew in. The promenade had emptied out, the coloured lights edging it were beginning to flicker on, and the sea was disappearing into darkness. Soon there would only be the shush, shush sound of the waves. They walked in silence, matching their paces, arms linked.

Finally, Eve burst out, 'If that's what really happened. Why didn't they tell the police?'

'Apparently Ben begged Pamela not to say anything. He told everyone else he had no memory of the accident and insisted on her backing up his story that he must simply have tripped.'

'What about Simon? Does he know?'

'I've no idea. And she only reminded me so you would know why you can't see Ben. It would be cruel to force him to think about Stella. And you looking so like her would make it painful for him to meet you.'

They had been walking steadily, but Eve stopped and turned to face him. Over his shoulder she could just make out the stark outline of the pier dotted with a few lights.

'You said she reminded you of this. So you already knew?'

'Yes, Pamela told Mum years ago, but we were never sure if it was true.'

'Do you believe her now? I mean if Stella and Ben had an affair, and I'm the result, I can't imagine his wife being keen on me.'

He leaned forward to kiss her cheek with very cold lips. His nose was red, there were purple blotches on his cheeks, and she registered for the first time that he was getting old. When they moved on he put his arm around her, their bulky coats making it difficult to get close. 'That did cross my mind of course, but ...'

'What?'

He shook his head. 'Nothing.

In the car on the way home Alex didn't ask her what she and her dad had talked about. Instead he chuckled. 'I don't think my washing up met Jill's standards, and I wouldn't be surprised if she started doing it all again the moment we left.'

Eve forced herself to smile, grateful that he was giving her a breathing space, and he rubbed her knee.

When they got in he went straight up to his office. 'I'll come down about nine and we can have a snack and watch that TV programme if you like.'

She lit the living room fire and checked her phone. There was a message from James Stone.

I've been worrying about what I told you in my last message.
Didn't want to imply that your mother was always miserable.
She certainly wasn't and we had some wonderful times
together. She was only twenty, twenty-one, and at that age

we all go through periods of unhappiness and insecurity, don't we?

I just wanted you to know as much truth as I could tell you. If I am your father I wish she had told me, but I can imagine that giving you up for adoption was a wise decision if she was feeling troubled.

On that note I've attached a portrait I painted of her not long before we separated, which I thought you might like to see. She looks great, and not at all sad, doesn't she?

The picture showed Stella sitting at a table with a vase of flowers next to her. Her red hair hung loose and bright in the sunlight from the window behind her and gold hoop earrings glinted among her curls. She was smiling down at a book on her lap. She didn't look pregnant, but must have been in the early stages. Eve touched the screen. How strange to think she was hidden in the painting too.

She hesitated for a moment and then posted the picture on Instagram without a comment. It was a long shot, but it was possible someone who had known her mother might see it.

Then she reread James's message. She remembered what he'd said about Stella and Ben: *it was clear she was angry with him.* Angry enough to want to hurt him?

But, no, Eve told herself, it could only have been an accident. Perhaps Ben had been trying to make her leave and she had pushed him away.

Still thinking about it she heated up a pizza and called upstairs to Alex. They sat on the sofa with plates on their knees and he went to turn on the TV.

'Before you do that have a look at this from James Stone,' she said, holding out her phone.

He put down his plate, but instead of reaching for it he took both her hands in his, looking into her eyes. 'You don't have to show me if you don't want to.'

Eve found herself comparing his eyes with the vivid blue of Simon Houghton's. Even though Alex was fair his eyes were brown with a ring of gold in the centre. She hoped Ivy would have that too. She smiled at him and when he put his warm palm against her cheek she rested her head there for a moment. 'I want you to read it. And look at the painting too.'

He checked the picture first and turned to smile at her. 'Ah, that's lovely.' When he'd read the email she told him what her dad had said about Ben's accident. A frown creased his forehead as he listened then he drew her to him, holding her firm and tight.

'We may never know the truth. But just remember that Stella Carr is not you. She might look like you, might have given you life and half your DNA, but she isn't you.'

Stella

James finished her portrait before he left, and she had worn the gold earrings every day since. She had also started wearing loose shirts over her jeans because she couldn't fasten the top button.

One day she found a note in her college pigeonhole.

Dear Stella, I'm wondering if you've had time to reconsider whether you might be able to do that work for me. It really is very important and I'll make sure it's worth your time.
I'll pop by your flat this evening and we can discuss it.
BH

He must have found out where she lived. The idea that she couldn't get away from him would have been upsetting anyway, but if he really was mixed up with some dangerous people … Her already queasy stomach churned.

She screwed up the note then pressed it flat again and tore it into the tiniest possible pieces.

When she got home there was another envelope waiting for

her on the hall table. Maggie's handwriting was on the front and there was no address or stamp on the envelope, so it had been hand delivered. Inside was a folded note and another envelope addressed to her at the old house.

The note was from Maggie herself, and she read it as she walked upstairs to her room.

I came back to check the house before it was sold and found this letter for you. I'm still travelling and don't have a permanent address so if anyone asks you, please tell them they can get in touch via this PO box.

That was all – no invitation to meet or words of friendship.

The letter was from David Ballantyne asking her to call in at the gallery.

To pick up the painting you didn't want to sell (although I could have done so several times!) Congratulations again on your success and do keep in touch.

Stella lay on her bed thinking about Maggie. She must be in London, but didn't say where she was staying. Stella had passed the old house a couple of times, but it was all shut up. If only they could see each other so Stella could tell her about the baby. Hot tears filled her eyes. It was just wishful thinking; Maggie didn't want to know her. She wiped the tears away with the corner of the sheet.

The pillowcase on his side of the bed still smelled of James and she held it to her chest wishing he was with her. Maybe she should have trusted him, not just with the truth about her pregnancy, but with the Ben Houghton business.

She must have dozed because the light had changed when she opened her eyes to hear a tap on her bedroom door. Shaking her head to clear it she went to the door. Her flatmate, Laura, stood, pink-faced, in the corridor.

'Ben Houghton's here wanting to see you,' she said. '*The* Ben Houghton from the gallery.' Her face asked a dozen questions.

A deep breath. 'Please tell him to go away.'

A look of panic passed over Laura's face. But it was no good, he was already bounding up the stairs.

'It's all right, I won't keep you a minute.' A brilliant smile for Laura. 'Thanks so much.'

Laura avoided Stella's eye as she headed down.

Ben looked as handsome as ever standing in the doorway in jeans and a dark jacket, and she could understand why Laura had been so flustered. She let him go past her and sit on her bed, but stood with her hand on the door holding it open and hoping he realized Laura was probably lurking at the bottom of the stairs.

'What do you want?'

He glanced past her at the landing. Yes, he knew he could be heard. Good.

'As I said in my note, I was hoping you might have had second thoughts about doing a few more of your wonderful drawings for my contact and his collector.' He spoke formally and with a smile, but his foot tapped a fast rhythm on the floor and he touched his knee as if to calm it.

'And, as I keep telling you the answer is no. I'd also like my original pictures back. So if that's all, you can leave.'

He sighed and stood, but when she stepped aside to let him pass he reached around her and tried to pull the door closed. Her heart gave one huge beat that seemed to make it jump into her throat, but her foot worked automatically to hold the door open. Her stomach lurched so much she swayed and had to lean on the wall.

But he stood back, holding up his hands in a gesture of surrender. 'All right, it's all right. I've learned my lesson.' He smirked. 'This time I only want to talk.'

Shaking her head she held the door wide. 'There's no point. Now please will you go?'

Instead of leaving he went back to sit on the bed, one foot drumming fast again. Although he was no less handsome, his face looked gaunt and there were dark shadows under his eyes. He coughed and began to speak, his voice sounding hoarse. 'Please, Stella, I'm begging you.' The look of despair in his eyes was shocking. 'Just one more set of pictures. Six or seven, at most, and we'll be fine.'

Her stomach twisted with a different kind of fear. He tried the old charming smile, but his mouth quivered until he rubbed it with the back of his hand. A deep breath in which, horrifically, she thought she might have heard a sob. He patted the bed beside him. She stayed where she was, but closed the door.

'You see.' He seemed to choke on the words and had to start again. 'You see, what I didn't know when I met my contact was that he is part of a – well a syndicate I suppose you'd call it – quite a powerful group actually. And it was they who lent me the money I lost. Now he tells me the only way out is for you to produce another set of drawings – to show good faith.'

Her knees felt so weak it was difficult to stay standing. He was still talking, his voice a flat monotone. 'They know who you are, I'm afraid, and they are threatening us both now.'

Her voice finally worked, although it sounded so clogged she hardly recognized it as her own. 'Threatening us with what?'

He stood up. 'Nothing, it's nothing, I'm sure. They'll expose us as forgers, I suppose.' He was beside her now, gripping her arm, and she hadn't the strength to push him away. His eyes were dark pools in which she saw tiny distorted reflections of her face. 'All you need to do is to give me half a dozen more and it will all be over. And I'll pay you well, of course. Please, Stella.'

She couldn't believe this. There was a spear of pain in her chest as she tried to breath in enough air to get the words out. 'Are you telling me I'm in real danger?'

111

His face crumpled into so many tiny lines he suddenly looked like an old man. 'I'm so sorry, Stella. I didn't know the kind of people I was getting us mixed up with.' He dropped a light kiss on her forehead, and she was amazed at herself for registering how good he smelled – how expensive – before she flinched away. 'I promise you, everything will be fine, if you just do this one little thing.'

'I don't know. I can't think.' The words, breathy and quavering, came out without her knowing she meant to speak.

'OK. I'll go now. But they want an answer soon. Please don't let me down.'

CHAPTER THIRTEEN

Eve

Eve had arranged to meet Simon in London. She needed to know if he was aware of what Pamela had said about Ben's accident. Alex was teaching that morning, so they went up on the train together. He couldn't understand why she didn't just email. 'And what's the urgency, anyway? It's thirty years ago, so waiting a few weeks or even a few months won't change anything. Why on earth did your dad tell you at a time like this?'

Eve had no answer except that she needed to know now. After days of feeling tired and washed out she was suddenly so full of energy she couldn't face sitting at home torturing herself with the thought that her mother might have ruined a man's life. And she needed to see Simon's face when she talked to him.

He was busy at work and could only spare her a few minutes, so they'd agreed to meet near his offices. When they got off the train it was too early for her to go to the café. It was just round the corner from Foyles bookshop, so she decided to spend an hour browsing there while she waited. Alex said he'd come to Foyles when he finished his tutorials. Then they could go to lunch.

Dipping into books while she waited helped to relax her, and when she arrived at the café Simon was already at a table. She was surprised to feel a pulse of pleasure when he looked up from his paper, smiled and waved at her. He was on his feet, pulling out a chair for her before she reached him, and their kiss seemed so natural she felt as if she had always known him.

'I'm sorry I don't have long today, but it's lovely to see you again. Next time let's make it dinner,' he said.

'I'd like that. Although we'll need to put it off until the baby arrives.'

He glanced at her bump. 'Do you know what it is?'

'A girl. We're going to call her Ivy.'

A huge grin that made him look very young. 'Well whatever you discover about your parentage I shall still consider myself her uncle.' His smile was infectious and when he clapped his hands and said, 'Right, coffees all round, is it?' she wished this was just a friendly get-together.

Yet again she found herself studying him as he stood at the counter. He was about Alex's height, but looked bigger because he had broad shoulders. When he came back he caught her eye and raised one eyebrow in a silent query. And a flush of heat rose in her cheeks. To cover her embarrassment she laughed.

'I'm sorry I keep staring at you. It's just that I never imagined having a brother.'

He pushed a cup towards her and glanced at his watch.

She squeezed her hands together. 'I know you don't have time for chit-chat, so I'll just blurt out what I came to ask you. It's about what your mother says happened the night when Stella came to your house.'

Simon stirred a sachet of sugar into his coffee. 'But she wasn't there. I imagine Dad told Stella to come when the coast was clear. They weren't bothered about the teenager, of course.' He tapped his own chest. '*He* wasn't expected to notice anything.' He tossed the crumpled sugar sachet onto the table.

Eve sipped her coffee, but could hardly taste it. She leaned forward keeping her voice low. 'Your mother says when she arrived back home she found your father lying at the bottom of the stairs and he was able to tell her that Stella had pushed him down then run away.'

He didn't speak, just sat hands clasped in front of him. A deep breath. 'I'm sorry, I'm trying to take this in,' he said.

'So this is the first you've heard of it?'

A slow nod, still thinking hard, his eyes clouded with memories. 'Do you know I didn't even realize the two things happened at the same time. I remember the argument. My mum certainly wasn't home when Stella arrived, and I have no idea when she got back because I stopped listening when I heard Stella say she was pregnant. I was really upset and – like a typical teenager – I threw myself on my bed in a sulk, put on my headphones and turned my music up to top volume. Then I fell asleep.'

'When did you find out about the accident?'

He scratched his head. 'Not until late next morning. I suppose that's why I haven't connected the two things before. I used to sleep till lunchtime at least when I didn't have school. So it must have been nearly twelve when Mum woke me and said she'd just come back from the hospital. I've always thought Dad fell downstairs when he got up in the morning. I'm almost sure that's what he told me must have happened.'

'According to your mother it was the night before. When Stella was there.'

Simon steepled his hands and pressed his fingertips against his lips. 'I must have slept through it all.' He was squinting, trying to see back into the past. 'I'm not certain, but I may have a vague memory of some kind of commotion. A couple of voices I didn't recognize – the ambulance people I suppose – but I always thought that was in the morning.'

'And neither of your parents ever told you it might not have been an accident? Never mentioned Stella in connection with it?'

A slow headshake.

When his clasped hands dropped to the table, Eve reached out to hold them between her own. 'I'm sorry, Simon, I didn't mean to upset you.'

He shook his head then gave her a weak smile. 'Don't be sorry. It's certainly not your fault. But I can't help thinking that, if this is true and I'd carried on listening, instead of getting into a strop, I might have stopped it happening.' He rubbed his hand over his face, and Eve could see the young boy he must have been back then.

'It's been horrible all these years,' he said. 'You know what it's like with teenage lads and their fathers. Well Dad and I were just starting to be friends again – but his accident changed him. He became bitter and angry. Thought he wasn't a proper man anymore. Mum gave up her whole life to look after him, but he resents her for it. They lost the gallery and would have lost the house if her parents hadn't helped out.'

Eve didn't know what to say. She sat staring into her cup, and it wasn't until he moved his other hand that she realized she was still holding it. He looked at his watch.

'I need to go and I'm sorry for reacting like this. You're the one who's had the greater shock. But remember, I didn't actually see anything. And my father has always said he has no memory of it. So for all we know it might not be true. I love my mother, but it wouldn't be completely out of character for her to make this up to stop you trying to see Dad.'

'You don't really believe that, do you?'

He shook his head. 'I honestly don't know.'

Outside the café they stood looking at each other, and he said, 'However this turns out, I hope it doesn't stop us from being friends.'

She reached for him and they held each other close for a long moment, and although she knew there were people milling around them, it felt as if they were completely alone. And standing in the cold street with his arms around her, the only thing she knew for sure was that she didn't want to lose him.

Stella

Stella found another note from Ben in her pigeonhole. It pleaded with her to get some drawings to him very soon.

If you don't we are both in serious trouble. Please, Stella, I am begging you.

A swell of fierce anger went through her. She had done nothing wrong and if it came to it she would go to the police and tell them everything. But first she decided to see his wife. Maggie had pointed out his house to her one day when they passed it on a bus. It seemed obvious that Pamela didn't know what Ben was doing, and according to Maggie she was wealthy, so surely she would deal with her husband's debts. Then it would all be over. If it ruined their marriage, that wasn't Stella's problem.

On the doorstep of the big house in Mayfair that evening she nearly lost her nerve. Although she'd rehearsed what she was going to say to Mrs Houghton, she'd forgotten most of it now.

Almost without meaning to she found she had rung the big brass bell. A minute passed and she began to turn away, more relieved than disappointed. But then she heard fast footsteps pounding the stairs and the door flew open. It was the boy; the son. She couldn't remember his name, but he seemed to recognize her. His face and neck blotched with pink and he put his hand into his tangled dark hair.

When she'd thought about this moment Stella had imagined being met by some kind of servant, and this was so unexpected she couldn't speak. The boy seemed stunned too. *For goodness' sake pull yourself together. He's just a lad.* Although he was much taller than her, she stood as straight as she could and tried to talk like a grown-up. 'Could I see Mrs Houghton, please?' If only she didn't have her bloody accent.

The boy hadn't moved and was still staring at her as if he couldn't understand what she was saying, but then Ben's voice came from somewhere upstairs. 'Don't just stand there, Simon. Let her in for fuck sake.'

Simon flinched. He glanced back to the stairs and stepped aside without a word. The tiled hall was bigger than the whole ground floor in her nana's house. Ben was leaning over the banisters at the top of the stairs, and he called down, 'Stella, darling, I'm in my office, come up.'

Simon had closed the door, but was moving from foot to foot in front of it, hands shoved into the pockets of his jeans. The hems were frayed and he was wearing no shoes. He noticed her looking at his odd socks and rested one foot on top of the other, as if that would somehow make them invisible. Ignoring Ben she turned to smile at him.

'I came to see your mother.'

His Adam's apple moved as he gulped and his voice came out hoarse with a slight squeak at the end. 'She's out. Should be back soon.'

Ben's shout echoed down again. 'Bring her up, you clown, she can wait here.' Then the hectoring tone disappeared to be replaced by his usual friendly bellow. 'Pamela will be a few minutes at most. You can wait here. Have a drink.'

Shoulders slouched, the boy headed upstairs. Stella hesitated. Ben had probably guessed what she was planning, so she wouldn't be able to try this again. It was now or never. She climbed the curved staircase. Mainly white, but with shining wooden treads made of dark wood instead of carpet and twisted ironwork balusters, it was intimidating. The metal handrail was smooth and surprisingly warm and she was glad of its support.

Ben was on the landing by an open door. Behind him she saw crowded bookshelves, a big antique-looking desk and an office chair. Simon went into the room next door. At least they weren't alone in the house.

Ben gestured for her to come into the office, but she shook her head. 'I'd rather wait for Mrs Houghton downstairs.'

'Don't be silly.' He gave one of his loud chuckles. It made her think of the men in those old-fashioned comedy films her nana used to watch. 'You'll be quite safe.'

She crossed her arms tight over her chest. 'Does your wife know what you did with my drawings?'

'Of course not. I needed the money to be free from her.' His laugh was a loud crack that made her jump, and she looked at Simon's door. A spike of sadness for him. She hoped he hadn't heard.

'But now it's turned nasty, you have to ask her to bail you out,' she said.

'You seem to forget it's her money I've lost. Even if she wanted to help, which is unlikely, she wouldn't be able to.'

Stella backed away from him until she was pressed against the banisters. 'You have to do something. At least get me out of it. I'm going to have a baby.' She hadn't meant to tell him, and for a moment she felt dizzy, because it was the first time she'd said it aloud to anyone except her doctor. A hard lump lodged itself in her throat and she fought back a sob.

After a quick flash of surprise Ben pasted on a concerned smile. 'Oh my dear. I'm not sure whether to congratulate or commiserate with you. I can't stand kids myself, but whether you're planning to keep the little tyke or not you'll want some money, won't you?' He took her hand, holding so tightly she couldn't pull it free. 'Just think of it. If you come in properly with me, this could be the start of a great future for you.'

A rush of something dark and bitter powered up from deep inside to fill her chest. She felt like an angry child again. Wanted to smash her fist into his smug face. Instead she jerked her hand away and spoke as calmly as she could. 'I don't ever want to see you again. I'm going to the police. They'll protect me. And you can be sure of one thing: I'll try to make sure they prosecute you and the people you're working with.' Her voice sounded so harsh and unfamiliar it frightened her.

As she turned and tried to go down the stairs, he grabbed her arm. 'Stella, my love, think what you're doing. You drew the pictures after all. And I'm a respected businessman. You're – well, I don't know what you are – but I gather from Maggie that your family isn't anything to be proud of. Wasn't your mother unstable? Killed herself, didn't she?'

A flash of her mam gurgling on the sofa in that filthy room. And Mrs Ahmed saying, *Didn't you see she was poorly?*

She pushed him hard away. 'Shut up, just shut up, and leave me alone.'

She ran downstairs, her eyes blurred with tears. When she reached the hallway her foot slipped on the tiled floor and she almost fell, grabbing the post at the end of the stairs with one hand and clutching her stomach with the other. The front door seemed miles away, her breath coming hard and fast. When she reached it she fumbled at the brass latch, her fingers clumsy. Finally it began to move. The door was heavy, so heavy. She thought she could hear him coming after her.

But at last she was out and staggering down the stone steps. At the bottom she collided with someone on the pavement. 'Sorry, I'm sorry.'

She didn't stop running through the pouring rain until she passed her bus stop and the next two. It wasn't until she reached the third and saw a bus coming that she put out her hand. She found a seat and looked back the way she had come, almost sure someone had been chasing her. But there was nobody. It was only then that she registered how wet she was. Her coat soaked through, her hair hanging in wet hanks around her face.

She'd made a mess of everything. If Ben was telling the truth, his wife couldn't afford to pay off his debts. Even if he was lying he knew what Stella had planned and would make sure she couldn't try again. Whether they were really in any danger from these people he claimed were threatening them or he was just desperate to recoup his money, she knew she was in trouble.

She spent much of the next day in bed, trying not to think about anything. Her only option now was to carry out her threat and go to the police, but she was scared.

When she finally made herself get up and have some cornflakes it was almost evening. Laura and Jane were both out and it was so quiet she put the radio on in the kitchen.

It was an old house and she was used to its creaks, but even with the radio on she found her ears straining for other sounds. She switched it off, but the silence was too much. She'd feel better in her room again with the door tightly closed.

Cereal bowl still in her hand she headed up the stairs. A loud rap at the front door broke the silence, making her jump and spill some milk down the leg of her jeans. She couldn't see who was there, but the window at the side meant whoever it was might be able to see her. Another rap.

It was probably one of her housemates' friends. She crept down, put her bowl on the telephone table and, as quietly as she could, slipped on the security chain. A deep breath then she eased open the door.

Pamela Houghton, looking pale and so haggard she must be ill. Stella took off the chain and let her in. The woman didn't speak just stood looking at her, one hand on the telephone table as if in danger of falling.

A surge of hope. Ben must have told her everything and maybe she still had enough money to bail them out. But then Pamela's mouth hardened. When she spoke there was ice in her voice. 'You might prefer it if we talk in your own room.' She looked down at the cereal bowl and shook her head. Then followed Stella up.

Unlike Ben she stayed standing, narrowing her eyes at the clutter and the rumpled bed. Stella waited, trying to keep her expression steady and her fists from clenching.

121

It was clear Pamela was struggling too. Her breath was uneven and her hands twisted together at her waist. When she finally did speak, Stella couldn't take in her meaning.

'The hospital tells me Ben will never walk again.'

It was so surprising, so different from what she had been expecting, that Stella could only stare at her. And her next words made even less sense.

'At the moment he's letting everyone think it was his own carelessness and neither of us has mentioned that you were even there. I don't like it, but he insists that's what he wants.'

A shudder inside. 'Ben has had an accident?'

Pamela laughed a mirthless laugh. 'You're asking *me* that? You know very well what happened. You were there trying to get money out of us, but it didn't work because there is no more money.'

'You don't understand.'

'I understand perfectly well, but that's not important. What is important is that I came home to find him at the bottom of the stairs. Where you left him.'

The room shifted and she grabbed the bookcase next to her to keep steady. 'What?' It was more a gasp than a word.

Pamela's voice softened. 'Oh I realize you may not have meant to hurt him, at least not as much as this, but that doesn't excuse you running away instead of helping him. He'll never walk again, and if I hadn't come back when I did, he could have died.'

Stella tried to say something, but Pamela just shook her head slowly. 'Luckily for you Ben doesn't want any fuss, so neither of us has said anything to the police.'

Finally Stella found her voice. 'Mrs Houghton. I didn't do anything. I just came to talk to Ben. And when I left he was fine. It must have been that gang, the forgers. They've been threatening us.'

Painted eyebrows raised, Pamela stared at her. 'What on earth are you talking about?'

'I drew some pictures and Ben sold them as forgeries.'

Pamela snorted and tucked her black patent leather bag under her arm. 'This is ridiculous and I can't imagine how you think it will help you. But it doesn't matter anyway because, as I said, Ben can't face talking to the police. He just wanted you to know the full extent of the damage you've done.' When Stella tried to speak she held up her hand. 'That's all I have to say.' She turned away.

Stella followed her downstairs. 'You have to listen to me, Mrs Houghton. They threatened to hurt him and they must have done it. We need to tell the police.'

At the door Pamela wheeled round so fast Stella almost collided with her. 'You're living in a fantasy world, you silly girl. A *dangerous* fantasy world. And if my husband ever does decide to speak to the police, it won't be about your imaginary gang – it will be about you.'

CHAPTER FOURTEEN

Eve

Alex was hardly talking to her. As they'd agreed, he'd been waiting outside Foyles when she got there after saying goodbye to Simon. It was very cold and Alex was so pale and silent that at first she thought he was freezing. 'I didn't think you'd be here this soon. You should have waited inside the shop,' she said as they walked to the little restaurant they liked. He didn't reply and she left it until they were sitting at their table and had ordered. Then she reached over and touched his hand. 'What's wrong?'

'My last meeting was cancelled, so I came to the café. Timed it so I would catch you as you left. Thought it would be a chance for you to introduce me to Simon Houghton.' He pulled his hand back and began tracing patterns on the table with the end of his knife, his eyes focused on what he was doing. 'You never told me what he looked like.'

'What's that got to do with it?'

'I saw you outside the café. The way the two of you were clutching each other.'

This was ridiculous. 'For God's sake, Alex, I'm hugely pregnant and he's probably my brother.'

'Well, you didn't look like brother and sister to me.'

Their food arrived, and she bit the inside of her mouth until it hurt to avoid making a scene. When the waiter was gone she was able to clamp down on her anger and talk normally. 'You don't really think I could have feelings like that for him, do you?'

He started to eat. She tried to talk to him, but he carried on methodically cutting, chewing and swallowing, and when he'd finished, he glanced at her nearly full plate.

'Are you going to eat that?'

She shook her head, and he called for the bill.

As their train pulled out of Charing Cross, Eve's phone rang – *Simon* –she rejected the call. Alex glanced over, but said nothing. A message:

Good to see you again and we really must get together for longer soon, hopefully to talk about more pleasant things. Let me know if you'd like me to ask my mother about what you told me today. Good luck with the baby and keep in touch. Simon X

Alex was pointedly staring out of the window. She replied:

Nice to see you too. Please don't say anything to your mother. There's no need to upset her. If she hasn't told you before then she obviously doesn't want to talk about it. Look forward to seeing you again fairly soon. Eve X

Alex had taken out his laptop and was tapping on the keyboard. Although she wanted either to cry or to shout at him that he was being childish, she made herself put on her earphones and listen to some music.

When they got home he lit the fire in the living room then went straight up to their office. Eve had hardly eaten anything at the restaurant, so she made herself some soup, but didn't call Alex. Let him sulk.

It was becoming bitterly cold and she huddled close to the fire. Outside a few flakes of snow floated past the window.

She had switched on the TV to distract herself when a fierce surge of pain went through her. So strong she couldn't breathe. It must be the baby, although she wasn't due for two weeks. When the contraction stopped she waited, breathing steadily and trying to stay calm. Everyone said first babies took their time and it could be a false alarm.

When Alex came down two hours later she was in the middle of another contraction and his face turned almost as pale as hers must be. Sitting next to her, he very carefully took her hand. Squeezing his helped her ride out the pain, but when it was over and she looked at him he rubbed his hand roughly over his face.

'I'm so sorry,' he said. 'It's just, oh I don't know, but you never mentioned how goodlooking he is.'

Eve smiled and kissed his cheek. 'Is he? I didn't notice.'

'I'm a pathetic, jealous bastard and I don't deserve you.' She rested her head on his shoulder, and he stroked her hair. 'How frequent are they?'

'Not regular yet. So let's just sit here for a while, shall we?'

He kissed her hand and rubbed her bump and they stayed like that into the early hours when she said, 'I think we'd better go now.'

Stella

The nursing home in Newcastle called Stella to say her nana was seriously ill. Pneumonia and problems with her heart on top of the dementia. 'I'll be there tomorrow,' she said, hardly able to get the words out. Then she went back to her room and lay on the bed dry-eyed. They wouldn't have rung unless it was serious.

At her last visit her grandmother had only briefly been aware of who Stella was and when she did recognize her she had begun to cry and plead to go home. It had been a relief when she lapsed back into confused apathy.

It was still sometimes possible to think of her as her old self, pottering about in the tiny, spotlessly clean house where Stella had grown up. But if – when – she died that would all be over. And Maggie was gone too. James had filled the aching gap for a while, but soon there would be no one. Stella would be utterly alone.

Except, of course, she wasn't alone. She rested her fingers on her stomach. There was a little life fluttering inside her.

Staring up at the cracks in the ceiling she remembered how James had laughed when she told him they looked like the spokes of a broken umbrella. The room had seemed cosy and comfortable when he was with her, but now she could only see the scuffed paint on the door, the flaking wood on the window frame. The sun shone outside, and she knew the garden next door was full of flowering plants. But when she swung her legs over the side of the bed she felt a swell of nausea and could only see the sun showing up a mass of grimy smears on the window pane.

Her easel was standing in the corner with a canvas propped on it but every time she tried to work she felt queasy. Any strong smell was likely to send a surge of sickness through her, but underneath the physical nausea was a constant sense of unease. Ben Houghton had warned her they might both be in danger. Had those people made good their threats?

Accusing her of causing his accident could be his way of stopping her from going to the police. And it had worked. She couldn't risk it.

Pamela had ridiculed her when she mentioned the forgers, and Stella knew he could have invented the gang to frighten her into doing what he wanted. But she had no way of sifting the truth from his lies. It was clear he had been drinking that night, so falling downstairs could have been a simple accident.

She scrubbed at her hair until her scalp hurt. It was no good going over and over this. The only thing that mattered right now was seeing her nana. It might even give her the strength to find the best way out.

On the bus north she tried to remember her happy childhood and teenage years with Nana. But her mind kept straying back earlier – to her mother. And those were times she never wanted to revisit.

The sun shone hot and bright through the coach windows, forcing her to close her eyes, and she drifted in and out of sleep. Whenever she jerked awake it was with garbled snatches of dreams lingering in her mind. They were daylight nightmares. In each one she was running away, terrified that the horror she'd left behind would catch up with her. She couldn't always see the horror. But when she could – oh when she could – she was with her mother in that filthy room again, watching her mam's eyes bulge with fear, as she gurgled and reached out for her. Sometimes it was Ben, all crumpled and bleeding at the bottom of his grand staircase, begging her to help him.

At last they reached Newcastle and in the bus station toilets she splashed her face and neck with cold water. It helped to clear her head, and at the nursing home she was able to paste on a smile. 'I've come to see Mrs Carr, Thelma Carr.'

The gentle tone of the nurse's, 'Your grandmother's quite poorly, you know,' told her everything.

Stella nodded and followed her. Always before her nana had been sitting or wandering about in the day room or in the garden outside. Today she was bedbound, so pale and thin Stella's heart stumbled for a moment, thinking she was already dead.

The nurse patted her arm. 'If you talk to her she usually comes round for a while,' she said.

Sitting beside the bed Stella took her nana's hand. The blue-veined skin was so thin it felt like damp tissue paper. 'Hello, Nana, it's Stella.'

Her nana's eyes opened. For a moment Stella saw them as they used to be: sharp green buttons. Then they darkened and took on the muddy puzzlement she'd grown used to in the past few years. Still holding her hand Stella talked about things she hoped might trigger memories. Jumping back and forth over the years just as Nana's mind seemed to do nowadays.

'Remember when I told you I was painting your picture? Well I've finished it and I've put a garden full of lovely flowers all around you.' No response. She cast her mind back further. 'Remember when we used to go to Whitley Bay? The Spanish City fairground and that ice cream shop where you always let me have a banana split?'

Nana's eyes sprang open. 'That was years ago,' she croaked. Then something sparked, bringing the green back to her eyes. Her hand tightened on Stella's. 'You're a good girl.'

Stella bent to kiss her dry cheek. 'Hello, Nana. How are you?'

But her grandmother's hand had gone loose again, her eyes had closed and her face was a blank once more.

Stella sat with her for an hour, until the nurse came with a bowl of something beige and mushy. She hoisted Nana up in the bed and pushed a pile of pillows behind her. Passing the spoon and bowl to Stella she said, 'Why don't you have a go?'

Although Nana took a couple of spoonfuls, eyes mostly closed and jaw working awkwardly, there was as much of the mush on her lips and chin as in her mouth and she soon turned her head away. 'Don't like it.'

'Please, Nana, try for me.'

As she said it her nana's eyes shot open, staring at Stella's swelling stomach. Then, with something close to hatred. 'It's no good coming crying to me now, Karen. You got yourself in trouble, so you have to get yourself out of it. I wash my hands of you.'

The nurse who had just come in put a warm hand on Stella's shoulder. 'Pay no attention, pet. She doesn't know what she's saying. She's not talking to you.'

Stella stood looking down at the bed. She forced herself to nod and give the woman a pinched smile. 'I know.' She thought, but didn't add, *She was talking to my mother.*

Stella had lived with Nana in her rented house from the age of nine to eighteen, but they never owned it and when Nana went into the home she had to give it up. So she spent the night at a B&B nearby. The room was poky and the bathroom along the corridor didn't look too clean. The sheets on the bed were scratchy. But even if it had been palatial Stella wouldn't have been able to sleep.

Sitting up in bed she turned on the light and grabbed the book she was trying to read, but her mind wouldn't stay still. She hadn't known her grandmother well until her mam's death. They had visited her occasionally, but Stella had only vague memories of lovely food, days marred by arguments and her mam drinking even more than usual. Then when she was eight she had spent the whole of the summer holidays with her. It had been the best time in her life, and when her mam came to pick her up, in an old banger owned by an occasional boyfriend, Stella had cried.

'You could leave her with me, if you like. She's no bother,' her nana had said. But her mam just shook her head and pushed Stella into the back seat. And Nana stood watching as they drove away.

When they got home her mam told her, 'That old bitch won't be happy till she's taken everything from me. We won't be going there again.'

Her nana had given her a scrap of paper with her phone number on and Stella kept it, although she never dared call her. But when her mother died she gave the details to the social worker, and Nana came for her.

She sent Stella to school on the day of her mother's funeral.

'That's all over with. Best forget her.' Another time she said, 'She ran away when she was fifteen and had you a few months later. Only good thing she ever did. And you're much better off with me. I always told her that. She wasn't capable of looking after herself, let alone a child.'

Stella hated it when Nana talked like that, but she did try to forget. And most of all to forget the day her mam died.

In the grubby B&B, with the open book on her knee, the words making no sense, she couldn't stop herself remembering the next morning when her grandmother came for her and was so cross with Mrs Ahmed who kept saying the same thing over and over: *I'll never understand why Stella didn't run next door to me. Must have realized her mam needed a doctor.*

CHAPTER FIFTEEN

Eve

Eve had never been so tired. Even though they had waited to go to hospital until the contractions were coming every ten minutes or so, Ivy hadn't made her appearance for many sleepless hours. The first night home it felt as if she woke, screaming, every half hour. She was in her carrycot on Eve's side of the bed, but Alex got up several times to hand her over. 'Maybe we should buy some formula milk so I can do a few of the feeds,' he said the third time he'd struggled round.

Eve, fighting to keep her eyes open, shook her head. 'I'll try to express some milk tomorrow. Put a few bottles in the fridge.'

At 4 a.m. Alex was sleeping heavily and Eve, wide awake, took the baby downstairs. At least one of them should get some rest. With just the little lamp on the table beside the sofa she tried to read. She had no idea how Alex was feeling. In the moments after the birth they had clung together, and when he looked at Ivy, Eve could see he was as overwhelmed with love as she was.

But now he felt far, far away from her. Everyone did. Eve's parents had come to the house while she and Alex were at the hospital and decorated it for Christmas. There was a beautiful tree in the corner of the room and cards and flowers everywhere. When she and Alex arrived home her dad waved a bottle of champagne at them, popping the cork as her mum carried in a pretty pink and white cake inscribed *Welcome Ivy*. Everyone was smiling, but Eve just wanted them to go away, to let her crawl into bed and hide her head under the covers.

Instead she smiled and sipped the small glass of wine her dad poured for her. 'One drop to wet the baby's head won't harm you.' The kiss he dropped on her hair felt too heavy. Outside it was icy cold, but the crackling fire, which usually made her feel cosy, seemed to turn the room hot and airless. She pulled at her jumper, which had suddenly become so scratchy she wanted to tear at the skin of her neck and chest.

Downstairs, at 5 a.m., she was woken by Ivy grizzling in her carrycot. Her nappy was dry, so Eve tried to feed her, but the baby turned her head away and continued to whimper. It grew louder and louder and Eve carried her over to close the door tightly. Rocking her and holding her upright she whispered, 'Please, be quiet, my darling.'

Back on the sofa Ivy finally latched on and sucked away. Eve put her head back and closed her eyes. *Just for a minute.* A cry brought her back to herself. *Oh God.* Her hands had loosened and the baby had slipped down onto her lap. She clutched Ivy to her and the cries turned to screams. Pacing up and down, desperately rocking and pleading, 'Please, please, don't cry,' didn't work. Finally she realized it was a wet nappy this time.

They had changing stuff ready in the living room, so she could do it right away, but she felt clumsy, her hands shaking and slipping as Ivy squirmed. And when the baby was back in the carrycot asleep at last, Eve was completely awake.

She hobbled to the kitchen to make some tea and switched on her phone. Sent Suzanne from school a photo of the baby, then messaged Simon:

133

Our daughter Ivy has arrived. She is beautiful and we are both very well.

In the sitting room Ivy was sleeping soundly and Eve curled up on the sofa. Her mobile chirruped: *Simon.*

Insomnia can be useful! Congratulations and welcome to Ivy. Love and best wishes to you and Alex. XX

Knowing he was awake Eve was tempted to phone him, but her voice might wake Ivy and she knew what Alex would think. She turned the mobile to silent and tucked it under the cushion beneath her head.

When she woke it was light and Ivy's carrycot was empty. She was on her feet, her head spinning before she heard the little gurgling sound she'd begun to recognize as a happy Ivy and Alex rattling dishes in the kitchen.

She collapsed on the sofa again. As Alex brought her in, Ivy began to cry and he handed her over. 'I think she's hungry. I know I am.' Eve smiled at him and nodded as he said, 'Milk for Ivy and bagels with scrambled egg for Mum and Dad, what do you say?'

They ate with Ivy cooing on the sofa between them. Then Eve took a shower.

When she was dressed in loose trousers and a fleecy top, clean hair combed and dried, she felt a bit better. Alex loved her, Ivy was well and her old self would return in time. Standing at the top of the stairs she heard a rap on the front door and stepped quickly back into the bedroom. She couldn't face seeing anyone.

Alex's voice, 'Thank you,' and the door closed again. Looking down into the hall she saw him place a huge and beautiful bunch of flowers on the hall table.

She called, 'They're so lovely, but you already gave me some.'

He jumped and looked up, his face unreadable. 'They're not from me.' Then he walked into the kitchen.

The card on the flowers read.

Congratulations and welcome to Ivy. With much love Simon X

Stella

Her nana died in the night, and Stella had to spend the next day organizing everything. It was clear that however cheaply she tried to do it the funeral would eat up most of her money. Money she had hoped to use for a deposit on somewhere to live with the baby.

As she moved around Newcastle in a trance, unable to believe that Nana was gone, she had never missed Maggie so much. The people at the home were kind, but she needed someone to confide in. And practical help.

Perhaps she would talk to David Ballantyne at the gallery when she got back to London. He was kind. He really seemed to like her work. And it had sold. Surely she would be able to paint again soon and he might agree to take something. If she admitted she was hard up he might even pay her in advance. It was the only hopeful thought she'd managed to dredge up, and she tried to ignore the voice in her head that kept reminding her that Ben had said the gallery had no future. She knew he was a liar and she had to believe he was lying about that too.

With the funeral organized for the following week, she headed back to London. The B&B was costing money she couldn't spare and there was nothing else she could do in Newcastle. As soon as she got back she went to the gallery. It was closed, but she rang the bell by the side door and David, in dusty looking jeans and a T-shirt, answered.

He stood back to let her in. 'You've come for your beautiful picture, have you?' he said.

Ben hadn't been lying. Apart from a few pictures all packaged up, the gallery was empty. It had seemed such a large airy space before, but with the sofas gone it felt cavernous. There were marks on the floor where the sofas had stood and patches of dust.

David made a little gesture with his hand: a kind of sad and quizzical answer to the question she didn't ask. 'Better come into my office. I still have chairs. And coffee too.' His voice with that soft Scottish lilt was instantly comforting, although she knew there was no way he could help now.

A coffee maker was already bubbling away, and his office still looked lived in. They settled on either side of his desk with their mugs, and he cleaned his glasses with a tissue. Without them on he looked younger, his face naked and vulnerable. Replacing them he pushed back his fair hair.

'You know my partner, Ben, has had an accident?'

She sipped her coffee and nodded. He clearly knew nothing about her involvement.

'It was very serious. He's still in hospital and they don't expect him to walk again, poor guy.' His chin wobbled; then a breath. 'It means the gallery has to close, at least for a while, I'm afraid. Otherwise I'd love to offer you an individual exhibition.'

Swallowing down her misery she asked, 'What will you do?'

'Oh, my wife and I have a house down on the south coast: Hastings. There's a little shop we plan to buy. Our own gallery.' He shook his head, looking at her with those kind grey eyes. 'It will be much lower key than Houghton's, of course. Mostly local artists. So although I'd love to give your work a spot, it wouldn't be worth your while. But I'll put a word in for you with some friends in other London galleries. Just let me know when you have a few new things to show.' He passed a card across the table.

She tried to thank him but, to her horror, a flood of tears filled her eyes. He pushed back his chair and came to sit beside her, handing her a tissue. She wiped her eyes. 'I'm sorry. It's just that my nana, my grandmother, died a few days ago.'

He patted her hand. 'Oh, dear. I'm so sorry.' They stayed sitting together, and she was glad he didn't try to say more. After a while he refilled her cup and she took a sip. He gave a tiny laugh. 'I would offer you something stronger, but I see that might not be appropriate.'

And that did it. She found herself spilling everything out to him. Not the situation with Ben, but her pregnancy and the fact that her nana's funeral had swallowed up all her earnings.

'First of all don't even think of carrying that painting home. I'll have it delivered. Then please come to me if you need money for the deposit on somewhere to live. I'm not rich and I'm having to use every penny I have to buy the new gallery, but I know you'll be able to pay me back as soon as you have some work to sell.'

She thanked him. Couldn't say that she hadn't been able to paint for months. 'Thank you for everything and good luck in Hastings.'

He shook her hand. 'And the very best of luck to you. Please don't forget my suggestions. I really would like to help.' At his office door he turned to smile at her and paused. 'A possibility has just occurred to me. If you wanted a quiet place to work and to be free from money worries for a few months before the baby comes, I'm sure my wife would be very happy for you to have our spare room. It's lovely and light. Plenty of space too. And later on there will be a flat available above our new gallery.'

Her face felt hot and red. This was so unexpected she couldn't answer.

He went on. 'No need to answer now. It may not suit you at all. Just think about it. We, my wife and I, love children. Haven't been able to have our own, but Jill wouldn't forgive me if I didn't offer to help you out.' His face flushed pink, and he took off his glasses again. A laugh. 'And selfishly, I'd be able to boast I helped you on your way when you make it big, which I know you will.'

She could only blurt out her thanks. 'That's so kind.' There was no way she could accept, but it made her feel just a little more hopeful.

He had already turned away, putting his glasses back on and his hands into the pockets of his jeans. 'You can let yourself out. Just make sure the door closes properly. I'll have the painting delivered tomorrow and that offer is there if you ever need to take it up.'

Alone in the empty gallery she looked around her, thinking back to the evening of the exhibition.

Then the main door came open and Pamela Houghton stood there dressed as elegantly as ever, but her eyes puffy and her mouth a thin line. Stella stretched as tall as she could, folding her arms as if that might distract from the obvious bulge under her shirt.

Surprisingly, Pamela's smile was almost gentle and she spoke softly. 'After our meeting I talked to Ben and he admitted there was some truth in your story about the forged pictures. But he claims you passed the drawings off to him as the real thing that you found in a secondhand shop and recognized as genuine. So he sold them on innocently.' A toss of the blonde hair. 'To be honest I'm more inclined to believe you, but my opinion will count for nothing if the police get involved.'

She glanced down at Stella. 'And it looks as if you could do with a quiet life for a while.'

'I'm not going to say anything. I just want to put this whole thing behind me.'

'Good. I'm glad we've been able to clear the air.' Another glance down and a lowered voice. 'But remember, if you have any ideas about claiming from Ben for that child, there really is no money.'

Before Stella could speak – and she was so surprised it took a moment to understand Pamela's words – David's office door opened and he called out, 'Pamela. How are you? Come in, come in.'

And she stood there staring as the door closed behind them.

CHAPTER SIXTEEN

Eve

It was strange seeing Simon for the first time in a plain white T-shirt instead of a suit and tie, but he still managed to look stylish, even Skyping from home at 9 p.m. She had emailed him to thank him for the flowers and perhaps said too much, because he had suggested using Skype:

Get yourself a drink and we can pretend we're in a café. Being at home with a brand-new baby must make you stir-crazy.

Tonight had been really difficult. Ivy had screamed for hours and nothing Eve could do would comfort her. So Alex said he would take her out for a walk. 'The movement of the pram seems to soothe her and if that doesn't work I'll pop her into the car and drive round for a bit.'

So she decided to take Simon up on his offer and by the time they had talked for a few minutes she was already feeling more like her old self. It was good to chat to an adult who was more interested in her than the baby. She burst out, 'I don't know why you're wasting your time listening to me moan.'

He smiled, leaning closer to the camera, and she wondered how he could look so handsome even on Skype. Didn't dare think about her own image.

'I like you, Eve, it's as simple as that. And my dad's affairs caused me and mum endless unhappiness even before his accident. Now they've brought you along – a good thing to stack up against all the bad.'

She turned away to hide her expression. If he'd been in the room she would have been tempted to kiss him.

'And even if I never get any further with finding out what happened to my birth mother I'm glad I started. Or we would never have met.'

'I'd say you've done pretty well anyway. Finding two possible fathers is a lot more than some adopted folk manage. And if it helps I'm very willing to give a DNA sample.'

'Thank you. I might take you up on that.'

He ran his hand through his hair. 'I shall be disappointed if it turns out we're not related. I've kind of got used to the idea.'

'We can still be friends though, can't we?'

'Absolutely. And will you be all right if this is as far as you can go?'

She shook her head. 'I don't know. Since Ivy has come along I haven't had time to think about it. But I don't think I can give up yet.'

The front door opened. Alex coming in very quietly. Ivy must finally be asleep. Eve was in the office with the door closed, but she spoke softly and a little hurriedly. 'That's Alex and Ivy. I should go. Thank you so much for listening.'

'Not at all. Go back to your family. But call me anytime.'

When she ran down to Alex he put his finger to his lips and pointed to the pram. 'Let's leave her there. Come and sit with me. I feel as if we never speak to each other nowadays.' He put his arm around her, and she stood on tiptoe and kissed his cold cheek.

He had bought a bottle of wine and persuaded her to let him pour her half a glass. They sat close together on the sofa and it felt just as it used to. She held her glass up to watch the firelight glinting in the deep red.

'This is lovely. And you're right: I need to talk.' When he kissed the top of her head she took in a breath. 'It's a lot harder than I expected.'

'I know.' His breath stirred her hair.

Then Ivy began to cry from the hallway, and they both sighed. 'She needs feeding,' she said. 'You stay there and finish your drink.' As she stood Alex took her hand and squeezed it.

Upstairs she sat in the rocking chair, and Ivy was soon feeding greedily. To keep awake she picked up her phone. She had some likes and comments on Instagram. Lots of the likes were for a picture of Ivy she'd posted, and there were several comments about how beautiful she was.

There was a single comment under the painting of Stella that James had sent her.

Ivy had finished feeding and was lying contentedly in her arms. With utmost care, because she didn't feel quite steady, she stood and put the baby in her cradle.

The comment was by someone called *intheshadows,* and when she looked the account up she saw it had only a few followers and most of the posts were rather bland pictures of landscapes. If this was a troll it was a strange kind. But it was one who clearly knew how her mother had died. So, although she was tempted, she didn't block it. Even though the comment made her feel sick.

It said:

Burn, baby, burn!

Stella

After her nana's funeral, Stella headed straight back to London. A few of their old neighbours had turned up at the church and were obviously put out that there was no food or drink on offer, but she couldn't afford it and hated the idea of standing around in some pub or hotel while other people behaved as if they were at a party. She had lost the last person who mattered to her; the last one who cared whether she lived or died.

At the flat Laura was sympathetic. 'Come out for a drink with me and Gary tomorrow night, why don't you.'

Stella nodded. 'Thanks,' knowing and hoping they would have forgotten about it by then. Upstairs she emptied her bag and put out the few things she'd kept from Nana's room at the home. There was a photo album with lots of pictures of herself and a few of her mother as a child. None of Nana's wedding. But her grandfather was there. He had died in his forties and looked a bit of a roughneck. Stella couldn't remember her nan saying anything nice about him. She had told Stella that Karen, Stella's mother, took after him, adding as always, 'But you're more like me.'

At the time Stella had just been glad her nana loved her, but for a mother to talk about her own daughter the way Nana talked about Karen was surely wrong. And Karen had been indifferent to Stella. Nothing mattered to her but her next fix. So, what if Stella couldn't love her own child?

There was just one happy family photograph in the album. Nana and her brother with their parents. It was old and faded, but there seemed to be real affection in their smiles. Stella suddenly felt lonelier than ever.

And for some reason David Ballantyne's face, smiling so kindly at her, came into her mind. What had he said? *My wife and I love children. Haven't been able to have our own, but Jill wouldn't forgive me if I didn't offer to help you out.*

If Jill was as lovely as her husband, it might be good to be with them while she went through the pregnancy. And there was the possibility of a flat later on. Above all it would be a relief to be out of London. She still didn't feel safe. Didn't know what to believe of the things Ben and his wife had said. Of the threats they'd made. But if they knew she was no longer around she could at least hope they would forget about her.

She took one of her nana's notelets. Best to write and address it to both of them so Jill could refuse if she wasn't keen. She asked to come stay with them soon after Christmas. The baby was due in February and that would give her time to settle in and arrange things with the hospital. She promised not to over-stay her welcome and would understand if David had changed his mind.

Eve

It was a couple of days before she mentioned the Instagram comment to Alex. He said, 'And this was under a picture of your mother?'

'Yes.'

'Must be some nasty troll who's read about her and thinks that kind of thing is fun. You should block them.'

'I don't know. It seems personal.'

He shook his head. 'It's just one of those monsters that lurk on the Internet.'

She wished he hadn't phrased it like that, but for now she decided to do nothing. An online remark couldn't hurt her.

Alex said, 'Let's get a takeaway tonight. We're both exhausted and I don't fancy any of those casseroles your mum put in the freezer. I'll go and collect it.'

They settled on Chinese food, but when Eve had made her choice a wave of weariness came over her and she said, 'I think I'll lie down while I wait.' Ivy was in her carrycot fast asleep by their feet, and Alex took her upstairs as Eve dragged herself after him.

These days sleep came like a shutter descending. One minute she was listening to Alex in the hall putting on his coat, the next she was struggling up from the depths to Ivy crying beside the bed.

A noise – Alex coming in again – made her jump and Ivy snuffle and let out a little grizzle, but looking at the time Eve stifled the urge to call out. It was too early for Alex. She raised her head from the pillows to hear better. Nothing. Must be the wind. But, no, there it was again coming from the kitchen or the back door. Ivy was working herself up to cry, so she scooped her from the carry-cot and rocked her for a few minutes until she slept again.

But she couldn't relax. Slipped her phone into the pocket of her joggers and, with Ivy dozing on her shoulder, lowered her legs over the side of the bed and tiptoed onto the landing. All was silent, so she switched on the hall light.

Another creak. Her heart thumped. It was the back door. Was there a shadow behind the glass? Alex wouldn't come in via the kitchen. He didn't keep a key for that door with him.

She stood totally still. Listening.

The same noise again. A rattling or scratching coming from somewhere – maybe the garden. Probably just a cat or a fox. She should go back into the bedroom, close the door and try not to hear it. Alex wouldn't be long.

But she couldn't move. Imagined someone creeping around downstairs. The tiniest movement from Ivy made her breath catch in her throat. She mustn't wake and start to cry.

She felt horribly exposed; something icy crawling up her spine. Wished she hadn't turned on the hall light so she was visible through the landing window. Holding Ivy tight she pulled out her phone. Hand shaking she clicked on Alex's number. The recorded voice asked if she wanted to leave a message. She fought not to scream at him to come home.

It was nothing, just a few noises, and she didn't want him thinking she couldn't be left alone for five minutes. She began to edge back towards the bedroom.

Another rattle. The front door this time. Her heart juddered.

'Eve, are you all right?' Alex coming in with the food. 'Why did you ring?' She breathed again as she headed down to him.

On the stairs, Ivy still in her arms, her foot caught. She was falling. The wooden floor rising towards her. The solid wood floor. *Ivy. Oh God, Ivy.*

Somehow she grabbed the banister with one hand, clutching Ivy with the other and, instead of falling, she stumbled on to one knee, the trapped foot twisting in agony. Then she was on her feet staggering in a half run to the bottom of the stairs.

Ivy began to scream, and Alex and dropped the bags of food with a cry. A bottle smashed and red wine poured across the floor. Then he was there clutching her and trying to take Ivy from her, but she clung on, holding Ivy to her face, kissing and stroking. 'Oh, God, oh God.' Her knee was a fiery agony, but she managed to say, 'It's all right. We're all right.'

When she let Alex take the baby he carried her into the sitting room, and Eve staggered over to close the front door. Alex had put Ivy on the sofa and Eve picked her up gingerly and held her saying, 'It's all right, it's all right now,' through gasping breaths.

He knelt in front of her, his hands on her knees. 'What happened?'

She moved the hand that was resting on her sore leg and rubbed the place. 'Caught my foot in the stair carpet.'

He sat back, forehead creased. She clung to Ivy's warm softness.

'I thought I heard a noise. Thought someone was trying to get in. That we'd left the kitchen door unlocked.' She put Ivy down on the sofa again and reached for him. He held her without speaking, his hands loose on her back. Then he stood up and went away.

Eve sat, unable to do anything but wait and listen to him clearing up the mess in the hall. When he came in he had the carrycot, put Ivy into it and placed it on the floor. Then he went back for the food, spreading everything on the coffee table.

'Alex?' Her voice was hardly there. 'It was the carpet. There must be a loose bit or something. And I thought I heard someone trying to break in.'

He was piling his plate with food and took a long swallow of water. 'Yes, you said. It's all right, I checked the back door and it was locked, but I couldn't find anything wrong with the carpet. You must have tripped over your own feet.'

Her knee and ankle were throbbing and there was a hard lump in her throat. 'It was an accident, Alex.'

He kissed her cheek. 'It's all right. No harm done. But I was worried. You called me, but didn't answer when I rang back.'

Eve looked at her phone, and he was right. There was a missed call from him. A flush of heat as she realized she had switched it to silent to avoid waking Ivy. She just shook her head.

When she got to the bedroom she turned up the sound on her phone, feeling her mouth twist in a bitter smile as she realized she was doing it so Alex wouldn't know how stupid she had been.

Then she saw there was another Instagram comment under the portrait of Stella.

Starry girl, starry girl, just had to die. No good will come of wondering why.

Stella

David drove Stella and her belongings down to Hastings then wouldn't hear of taking any money for the room. 'It's just going to waste at the moment.' The college had agreed to her taking some time off. Her tutor must have guessed why she needed it and why she had fallen so far behind with her work.

146

David had phoned when he got her letter and told her she could come right away if she wanted to, but she said she was fine in the flat and had paid the rent until the middle of January. That much was true, but she lied and said she had college work to finish and was spending Christmas with friends in Newcastle. She told her flatmates the same story. In reality, her Christmas consisted of hiding out in her room. But she was happier like that than in someone else's family home.

David's house was actually what she would have called a cottage. It was on the outskirts of the town with a garden that looked pretty even on a winter's day. There were window boxes filled with snowdrops and lavender bushes edging the brick path. David would only allow her to carry her shoulder bag.

The woman who opened the front door had to be his wife, Jill. 'Come in, come in, Stella, we're so pleased to have you.'

Stella hesitated in the little hallway. It smelled of polish and the old wooden floor shone nut-brown in the weak sunlight.

'David can take your things up. You go through to the kitchen.'

Mrs Ballantyne had a round and rosy face surrounded by a halo of brown curls. Stella guessed she must be a similar age to David. She had made a chocolate cake, and Stella had to sit at the big pine kitchen table and take a huge piece and the mug of tea that Mrs Ballantyne, *it's Jill please, Stella, you make me feel like an old woman*, held out to her. It was a lovely room with worn tiles on the floor. Some kind of green plant tapped at the window and she guessed the garden would be beautiful. A good place to paint.

David came in, took some cake and settled himself in an easy chair beside the Aga that was giving out a gentle heat. Apparently his gallery, which he was still setting up, was right in the centre of the Old Town as he called it. 'It's where the fishermen have always lived. They draw the boats up on the shingle beach there. That area of town is very picturesque.'

Eventually Jill showed Stella to her room at the back of the house overlooking the garden. Even this early in the year it was filled with light. Another perfect place to paint.

The floorboards, like those in the hallway, looked old, but shone with polish. David had set up her easel in one corner by the window and placed on it the carefully wrapped painting of herself and Maggie she had been trying, and failing, to complete.

Stella said, 'It's lovely, thank you.'

Jill touched her arm. 'We're very glad to have you and you must stay as long as you like. There's plenty of space.'

They stood awkwardly for what seemed ages, Jill looking at her with a smile. When she finally said, 'Well, I'll leave you to it,' Stella closed the door and lay on the bed staring out of the window at the ice blue sky and listening to the shriek of gulls that reminded her of home and childhood visits to Whitley Bay.

This wouldn't just be the perfect place to paint. But the perfect place for a child to grow up.

CHAPTER SEVENTEEN

Eve

When Alex came up Eve was lying awake. He put Ivy's carrycot beside the bed and kissed Eve's hand. His brown and gold eyes glimmered. 'I don't know what I'd do if anything happened to you and Ivy. It's not easy for you, I know, and I'm getting a lot of things wrong. I've been trying so hard to do it better than with my first children. I was hopeless with them.'

She sat up and went into his arms, but the movement made her knee and ankle throb so she couldn't hold back a little yelp of pain.

'Let me see,' he said. A big bruise was forming on her knee and her ankle looked puffy. Alex went into the bathroom for two flannels soaked with cold water.

She watched as he undressed and found herself feeling more remote from him than she could ever remember. The second Instagram comment had chilled her and her first instinct had been to show it to him. But she hadn't done it – worried he would pass it off as nothing to worry about.

He climbed in beside her, stroking her hair before turning away and falling quickly asleep. Eve lay awake trying not to think. Trying not to let dark thoughts overwhelm her.

When Ivy began to whimper she crawled out of bed, wincing from the pain in her leg and limping into the room they had so much enjoyed getting ready for their baby. Sitting in the rocking chair she told herself to get a grip. This should be the happiest time in her life. And she was spoiling it. Alex was obviously struggling too, however much he tried to hide it. He had told her he would never forgive himself for being so wrapped up in work that he had left the care of his first two children to his ex-wife. 'That was why I lost their love,' he told Eve soon after they met. 'And it was only what I deserved.'

He was trying so hard this time.

But tonight Eve had felt he thought Ivy might not be safe with her. And he could be right. Why hadn't she just left her in the bedroom in her carrycot? And how had she managed to trip like that? She had been so sure there was something wrong with the carpet, but it had been her own carelessness. Her stupid panic that someone was trying to break in just because she heard a noise. It must have been a cat or an urban fox getting at the dustbin by the back door. She would never have been frightened by something like that in the past. So maybe Alex was right to be worried. Maybe she should be too. Instead of getting into a state about some random stranger lurking in the garden or a couple of peculiar Instagram comments.

Her thoughts twisted in tortuous circles, and Ivy took ages over her feed, twisting and mewing. By the time she had fallen asleep, Eve was so tired she could have slept there and then in the rocking chair. But that wouldn't do. What if she let Ivy fall?

She carried her – oh so carefully – back to the master bedroom, knelt on her sore knee to place her in the carrycot and crawled into bed again. But she couldn't sleep and lay staring at the grey windows, imagining the wide stretch of empty grass out there, the cliffs, and beyond them, the dark sea.

In the morning she woke to see Ivy sleeping soundly beside

her. She had only stirred once more in the night and Eve had stayed in bed to feed her. After that she fell into a restless dream-filled sleep. In one she was in a small boat on a wild sea clutching Ivy to her until a wave tossed the boat into the air and she lost hold of her. She watched helplessly as Ivy disappeared down, down into the depths and was gone forever. Eve screamed so hard it hurt her throat, but the sound was lost in the wind unheard even by herself.

Alex leaned over and kissed her. She opened her eyes, glad to have woken, and shivered.

'It's trying to snow again out there,' he said pulling the duvet up. He nodded towards the carrycot, keeping his voice low. 'She slept well.'

She sat up gathering the covers around her shoulders. 'Yeah, she only woke twice.'

'What about you? You seemed to be crying in your sleep at one stage. Bad dreams?'

'I don't remember.' As she said it a wave of sorrow came over her. Only a short time ago she would have told him the whole thing right away knowing he would kiss her and make her feel better.

He climbed out of bed. 'I know I'm still on leave, but one of my students is having a serious wobble, so I should to go in and talk to her. Will you be all right for a few hours? There's plenty of food in the fridge. I'll light the living room fire before I leave, but keep the heating on too.'

Eve kissed him. 'We'll be fine.' When she heard the door close behind him half an hour later she told herself the relief she felt was only because she would be glad of a quiet few hours on her own with Ivy.

After she'd had breakfast she sat in front of the fire and for the first time was able to simply enjoy the warm weight of her baby in her arms.

The back door opened and she tensed, but the, 'Only me,' from her mum made her lean back with a sigh. Jill bustled in. 'I used my key so as not to disturb you if you were having a nap. Alex called to say he had to go into work, so I thought I'd pop round and ask if you needed anything.'

'I wish you'd knocked or called before you came. I had a panic yesterday when I thought someone was trying to break in.' She tried to clamp down on her annoyance.

Her mum sat beside her touching Ivy's little pink mouth where she must have spotted a strand of hair or cotton. 'Yes, Alex said. And you hurt your leg too. What a nuisance.' She reached for Ivy. 'Shall I take her for you?'

Eve stood, pain shooting through her leg. 'I'm fine. I'm going to put her in her big cot for a while. Start her getting used to it during the day.'

Jill stood. 'I'll make us a cuppa.'

'Have one yourself, but I'm all right.' She didn't dare look at her mum because she knew she was being unkind. But as she carried Ivy upstairs she was very aware of Jill standing at the bottom. Poised to catch them if they fell. She wanted to scream. Instead she put the baby in her cot and sat on the rocking chair, rocking back and forth very fast, until Ivy began to whimper with hunger.

She slept as soon as she was fed and changed, and Eve left her and went down to find her mum mixing eggs for omelettes. Cheese omelettes were one of Eve's favourites. Jill turned to her, her face crumpled and pink. She had been crying. 'I'm sorry, love, I was only trying to help. We all are.'

Eve put her arms around her. 'I know and thank you.' She cut some bread and added a few tomatoes to the little salad Jill had put ready on the kitchen table.

While they were eating her mum started talking about the book club she belonged to. 'You should come when Ivy can do without you for a bit longer.'

'I'll be back at work by then I expect. Won't have much time.'

She shouldn't have said it because she knew her mother thought she should take at least a year off.

After they'd finished Jill said she would wash up, and Eve went back into the living room picking up her phone to see if she'd had any messages from Alex.

There was an email from Ben Houghton.

Ben

He regretted it almost as soon as he'd pressed *send*. Pamela was right, he should have kept out of it. But then perhaps the email would do what nothing else could and draw a line under the whole sorry business. Pushing his wheelchair over to the window he watched the snow coming down. He'd always hated the British winter. Used to dream of living in Italy. And this weather made getting out of the house even more difficult.

Thank the lord for Mark. He could always rely on him for running errands as well as the more basic stuff. Been with him for years. His *carer* Mark called himself when they first hired him. Ben wouldn't have that, was tempted to call him *my valet* but could see that wouldn't wash. So they'd settled on assistant.

Wasn't much of a job for a man in Ben's opinion. Although there was the heavy lifting and Ben had to admit he wasn't getting any lighter. Mark was a decent chap – not too bright, but that was an asset as far as Ben was concerned. He'd been really useful these last few weeks, of course. Unlike Simon he did what he was told and asked no questions. Had been keeping an eye on the situation, making his presence felt.

Ben had done what he could too, within his limitations. And in a way had quite enjoyed it. But nothing seemed to have had much effect. They'd have to step it up.

And he needed to talk to Simon, at least try to persuade him to stop seeing this girl. But that needed serious thinking about too. They'd never discussed it, so he had no idea what Simon remembered of that night. It had always seemed best not to ask. And of course Simon didn't know how much Ben recalled either.

He forced himself to go back to the laptop on his big antique desk – the desk he loved and that Pamela never stopped trying to get him to sell – and called up the message to Eve Ballantyne. She was still using David's name, he noticed, even though she was married. Bloody David. A lot of this mess was due to his interference.

Dear Eve.

He shook his head. Had dithered over that for ages.

My dear Eve.

Too familiar and she might even think it condescending – or worse – fatherly!

Dear Eve Ballantyne

Too formal. At that stage he almost gave up. If he couldn't get that right, what was the point?

Dear Eve,
I hope you don't mind me contacting you, but I gather you are anxious to find out all you can about your poor mother, Stella, although I doubt anything I say will be particularly helpful.
As you know I am wheelchair bound and have been for many years.

God how he hated writing that. Still if it made it harder for her to suspect him of anything untoward, and encouraged her to leave the helpless invalid alone, it was worth it. *Your poor mother* was a good touch, he thought. Before going in for the kill as it were!

> *Unfortunately (for you although not for me!) I have a blank in my memory from a few hours before the accident until I woke up in hospital a day later. However my wife tells me I was able to talk to her before lapsing into unconsciousness and to tell her that Stella caused my accident. She actually saw Stella not far from the house and my son confirms that she visited that evening.*

(He had originally put *and I have no reason to doubt them* but deleted that. Best to be definite and allow no room for alternative interpretations.)

> *Pamela was in a state of shock immediately afterwards, as you can imagine, and very much focused on looking after me. So she said nothing about it until I regained consciousness. When she told me I begged her to keep silent. I could see no benefit in ruining Stella's life as well as my own.*

(He was pleased with that bit.)

> *Although, I will admit that I was not the most faithful husband in my youth,*

(David, bloody, Ballantyne would have told her that already no doubt.)

> *and I can understand why I might be a suspect, I have to tell you that I am categorically not your father.*

He originally started the next sentence: *As you probably know I was friendly with Stella's friend, Maggie.* But he deleted that. If the waters needed muddying a bit more in future he could always mention Maggie, but best to keep to the point at this stage. Instead he wrote:

> *My relationship with Stella was totally professional. My memory of that whole period is hazy so have no idea why she came to my home, but I assume it was to persuade me to feature more of her work at the gallery. She was possibly upset by my refusal.*

Pamela would be furious if she found out what he'd done. She didn't believe in committing things like this to writing. Face to face was always the best way according to her. It was more powerful and you could deny everything if need be. That could be Pamela's motto.

Deny everything.

Stella

Living in David and Jill's house reminded Stella of when she used to peer into other people's windows in Newcastle. Her nana's terraced cottage was clean and quiet and, unlike the flat she had lived in with her mam, there was nothing to frighten her. No strange men or haggard women came calling. But when she was older she saw how poor her grandmother was, how worn and tired the furniture and carpets were, and she used to dream of moving into one of the spacious villas in Jesmond: the better part of town.

The Ballantynes' house wasn't grand and intimidating like Ben's place, but was so pretty and comfortable that it was difficult to imagine anyone being unhappy there. Although, of course, she was unhappy.

It wasn't their fault. They couldn't have been kinder. They had a car, but they both liked walking, and if David went up to London

Jill drove him to the station. Mostly the car sat in the garage, but Jill took some time off work to drive Stella to her first antenatal appointment at the hospital.

'Do you have a licence?' she asked as Stella sat dumb beside her. She nodded. Nana had a little old rust bucket and had taught her to drive. She passed her test first time at seventeen. 'Well I'll get you put on the insurance and you can come on your own in future. Take the car if you want to go into town anytime too.'

Jill worked at the local library and brought back books she thought might interest Stella. David was busy either in London winding up the gallery or setting up his new place in Hastings, so Stella often had the house and garden to herself. When she said she should give them some rent or at least pay for her food they wouldn't hear of it. David told her, 'You can pay us back with a picture if it will make you feel better.'

But she still couldn't paint and wandering around the house during the day all she could think of was what a wonderful place this would be for a child to grow up in. What perfect parents David and Jill would make.

And more and more, as her bump grew, she couldn't help noticing a hungry expression coming into Jill's eyes when she looked at her.

After a hospital visit one day she took the car into town and walked about for a while. Sat on a bench overlooking the sea. It was too cold to stay long, so she drove back slowly, thinking hard. Although Jill had never put it into words it was obvious she wished Stella would let them adopt her baby. And the more she thought about it, the more it began to make sense. There was nothing she could give her child that could compare with what they offered. They were the kind of parents she had dreamed of having herself.

When she arrived back she parked the car carefully in the garage. There was a door from it that opened into the kitchen and she heard voices. It must be later than she'd thought and Jill was already home from work. But it wasn't David in there with her.

She froze. The voice coming from the kitchen belonged to Pamela Houghton.

CHAPTER EIGHTEEN

Eve

Ben Houghton's email was no help: even if he was her father she guessed he would never admit to it and, if he didn't remember the night of the accident, she was no closer to the truth about that. She took her phone into the kitchen and showed her mum the message. She still had a feeling Jill wasn't being honest with her and, if nothing else, Ben's words might help to get her talking.

'What do you think? I mean you and Dad seem convinced that Ben couldn't be my father, but Simon actually heard Stella tell him she was pregnant. Why would she do that if he wasn't?'

Jill tapped the screen with one finger. 'All I can say is that Stella gave us to understand that the father was a boyfriend who was no longer around. So that would fit this chap James you've discovered and he admits they had a relationship at the right time.'

'She could also have been talking about Ben, if he rejected her.'

'No, no, she said it wasn't him.' Her mum's voice wavered, as if she realized she'd made a mistake. Eve's breath caught. This was something new. Jumping up, Jill took her half-full mug over to the sink, turning on the tap so that water gushed out very loud.

159

Eve waited a moment then spoke quietly, trying to sound matter-of-fact. 'You never told me she actually talked to you about Ben.'

Her mother picked up a tea towel and looked at it. 'This needs a wash.'

Eve slapped the table. 'Mum, tell me. Did you actually ask Stella if Ben was my father?'

Jill, still beside the sink, was rubbing the cloth over and over the mug. 'Yes, I did and she was very definite that he wasn't.' When Eve said nothing her mum came over to the table and leaned with both hands on the back of a chair. 'I'm sure she was telling me the truth.'

Eve's jaw was clenched so tightly it began to hurt. She took an enormous breath. 'Why on earth didn't you tell me this right at the start?'

Jill pulled out the chair and sat, arms pressed across her chest, not looking at her. 'I'm sorry. I just didn't want you getting into all that. And there was no reason you should suspect him.'

She couldn't hold back a snort of anger. 'But *you* obviously did at some point. Why was that?'

She felt like a little girl again. Begging her mum to take away the thing that was hurting her. But, head down, her mouth a twisted thread of pale pink, it was Jill who looked like a child, a guilty child. When she spoke it was so soft and fast Eve had to lean closer.

'Pamela came to see me and it was obvious she suspected that Ben and Stella had been having an affair. So I asked Stella.'

'And you believed her when she denied it?'

Jill nodded. 'Absolutely.'

'I wonder what Pamela thought when she heard you'd adopted me?' Jill shook her head. Eve swallowed. She needed so much to know this. 'Why did Stella agree to let you adopt me?'

Jill sipped her coffee and said, 'I've told you already. She thought you would be better off with us.'

'And she had no qualms about leaving me?'

'Of course she did. And if she'd changed her mind—' She stopped short. Her hand went to her mouth.

'How could she change her mind if you'd adopted me?'

It came too quickly. 'Well we had to foster you first. It doesn't happen overnight, you know. You have to be thoroughly checked out.'

'But surely once she'd signed the adoption papers?'

Her mother pulled at the sleeve of her cardigan.

Eve's words were almost a gasp. 'She never signed the papers, did she?'

Jill swayed and held on to the edge of the table.

'Mum?' Her voice sounded harsh, and she saw her mother wince, but she couldn't stop now. 'Tell me, Mum.'

'She let us foster you and went to Italy. She couldn't come back to complete the adoption formalities, because she died.' When her mother touched her hand Eve pulled it away. 'You had no one else and we'd looked after you since you were born. The case worker agreed we were ideal parents. So they let it go through anyway.'

A loud cry from Ivy upstairs that made them both jump. Eve stopped at the door when her mother said, 'Please, Eve, darling. Tell me you're all right. We're all right, aren't we?'

She could only manage to shake her head. 'I don't know.' Then she ran upstairs. If she'd stayed she would have said the words that were pounding through her head: *It was very convenient for you and Dad, wasn't it? The fact that Stella never had the chance to change her mind.*

Stella

One afternoon Stella was sitting by the window in her room trying to sketch. It wasn't much good. Footsteps on the stair and a tap at her door and Jill came in holding out an envelope. 'A letter was forwarded from your old flat.'

Stella took it. An Italian stamp and Maggie's flamboyant hand-writing. She wanted to rip it open, but made herself drop it onto her lap. Jill sat on the bed.

'It was with a pile of our stuff. Bills mostly, of course.' She didn't look as if she was going anywhere.

'It must be from my friend, Maggie. She's the only person I know in Europe.'

Jill nodded and when Stella said nothing more she hovered by the door for a moment, then said, 'Well, I'll leave you in peace.'

Once she'd gone Stella held the letter to her lips almost afraid to read it.

Darling Stella,

I'm really sorry for the way I treated you. I'm a total bitch and I would understand if you never wanted to speak to me again. Last time I was in London I should have come to see you, but I was still in one of my stupid rages. You know I was really pleased and proud about your success at Houghton's, but that bastard Ben had built up my hopes about the catalogue. It was childish and spiteful of me to take it out on you.

Anyway apology over. I heard about you and the baby and the mutterings that it might be Ben's, but I know that isn't true. Whatever happened between you I have the feeling you are more sensible than me and I'm guessing it's the dishy dark guy you palled up with.

I tried to see Ben when he was in hospital, but that bitch Pamela was standing guard over him.

What I'm really writing for is to tell you I'm staying in Milan and hoping to buy a little place on the Italian Riviera. The one I have my eye on looks gorgeous in the photos and there's a tiny studio in the garden. So when I move do come and stay – the longer the better – I'm dying to see you again.

Please, please, please forgive me, darling Stella! And please come.

Love and kisses. Maggie XXXXX

After that she couldn't go back to drawing. Maggie could be temperamental and she would have to make sure she got painting quickly so that she had something to sell if she suddenly needed money, but it might just work.

Jill called up asking if she wanted some tea and, despite her bulk, which always surprised her when she tried to move or bend, she ran down the stairs. As usual Jill was opening a cake tin.

'Haven't had time to bake this week, but these ginger biscuits should still be all right.'

She started getting things out to make dinner then came and sat at the table, breaking a biscuit in half, but not eating it. The silence turned awkward and Stella guessed she was wondering about the letter.

'My friend is buying a place on the Italian Riviera. She's invited me out there.'

Jill said, 'How lovely.' Then she coughed and sipped some tea. 'Stella, it's none of my business, but Pamela Houghton came by the other day. I don't know if you saw her.'

Stella picked up a spoon and stirred her tea, although she didn't take sugar so there was no need. 'Yes, I did.'

A deep sigh and Jill pulled at one of her silver earrings. 'This is difficult, but she said …' A little cough, 'well she said your baby might be Ben's.' As if expecting Stella to speak she raised one hand. 'Please don't be upset. I'm not trying to interfere, just to help if I can. I mean if you were thinking of making any claim on Ben …'

Stella was so surprised she almost laughed. She had been worried about Pamela's visit, thinking she might have told Jill something about the accident, but not this. 'I don't have any claim at all on him and you can tell Mrs Houghton that I hardly know him.'

Jill moved her chair closer. It made a screeching noise on the tiles. 'The only thing I'm concerned about is that you aren't bothered about anything at a time like this.'

Sitting back in her chair again Stella tried to smile. 'I'm sorry. You've been so kind to me.' She took a deep breath. Why did she feel like such a child around Jill and David? 'Pamela told you other things, I suppose?'

Jill nodded. 'I know life hasn't been easy for you.'

Maggie was the only person she had told about her mother and the rest of it. But Maggie, especially when she'd had a drink, could never keep her mouth under control. She shook her head. 'I've been luckier than lots of people.'

Jill was so close now Stella could smell a warm scent, like vanilla, coming off her. She touched Stella's shoulder very lightly. Her voice became husky. 'If it's too much for you. The baby, I mean.' She gave a gentle smile. 'David and I would be very happy to look after it. For as long as you like.'

Stella swallowed. *So here it was.* 'Adopt it you mean?'

Jill stood quickly and walked over to the chopping board. 'Or just take care of it for you until you're settled.' When she turned back her cheekbones were glowing red. 'I know the original plan was for you to leave when the baby was born, but there's really no need. You can stay here as long as you like. Or that flat above the gallery will be ready soon if you want independence with babysitters to hand.'

They didn't speak again for a while. Jill sliced some onions, and Stella washed up, dried the mugs and plates and put them away.

Jill rinsed her hands, wiped her eyes and sniffed. 'Those onions are very strong,' she said. Then she took the tea towel from Stella and grasped her hands. 'We know you want the best for your baby, and so do we. So just think about it. We'll go along with whatever you decide.'

Stella nodded. There was nothing she could say.

Eve

Eve knew she had upset her mother when she left without saying a proper goodbye. But she was so stunned by what Jill had said she could do nothing but sit in the rocking chair trying to take it in. Of course the fact that her real mother had never got so far as actually signing the adoption papers meant nothing. She had left and gone to live in another country, so she clearly didn't want her. But why hadn't her parents told her all this?

Ivy was sleeping well in her cot, so eventually, Eve turned the baby monitor right up and forced herself to move. Although it was only mid-afternoon it was already getting dark outside and she began to feel very alone in the house. It helped to keep busy and she had some Christmas presents to wrap, so she brought them to the kitchen table.

But she was too on edge to make much of a job of it and when Ivy began to cry she was glad to stop. The feeding and changing routine was becoming easy now and it helped her relax. She sat in the warmth afterwards with the baby lying contentedly in her arms and a deep sense of peace flooded through her. Finally she was coping. Without Alex, without her mum, she was doing fine.

It was fully dark outside when the house phone rang from downstairs. Shortly afterwards her mobile vibrated from the kitchen. It would be Alex. Probably ringing from the train. Reluctantly, she put Ivy in her cot. Better check if he'd left a message.

As she stood she heard what she was sure were footsteps in the garden. She crept to the window, her hand resting on the cot as if that would keep Ivy safe.

Heart racing she stared down into the darkness outside. And froze. There was a shadow. Moving across the grass. Then still. Too tall to be an animal.

She wasn't breathing. Didn't dare move.

The shadow wavered. Still she held her breath. Eyes straining. Trying to make out details.

And then the shadow merged into the dark. And was gone.

She stood for so long that her eyes blurred, her legs began to ache and she was shivering with cold rather than fear.

A sound. Close to the front of the house. A glance at her watch. It could be Alex now.

Leaving the landing in darkness, and Ivy's door closed so that the light from her little lamp didn't show, she ran downstairs. No sign of Alex. She checked all the doors. They were locked and secure. Still in the dark she stared from the kitchen window. Nothing but the grey outline of the leafless tree.

Slowly she went back up. One more check from Ivy's window. Nothing.

Ivy was stirring, probably sensing something and she took her back to the rocking chair longing for the return of that wonderful sense of peace.

But it was no good and she knew she must tell Alex and show him the second Instagram comment. This affected him and Ivy too.

When the front door opened he shouted, 'Hello,' and ran upstairs to her. Something must have shown in her face because he said, 'What's wrong?' Going down on his knees and looking not at her, but at Ivy, 'Is she all right?'

It was as if her body was flooded with heat, and she clenched her hands so tightly her nails bit into her palms. *Don't overreact.* 'Of course she is. We both are.' She knew she shouldn't but found the words bursting out anyway. 'Didn't you think she'd be safe with me?'

He reached out to touch her hair, but she jerked her head away.

'I'll put her down then get on with the dinner.'

'I can do that.'

She noticed for the first time that his hair was thinning slightly at the back. 'Don't worry, I won't drop her.'

A sigh as he stood. 'I know you won't. I meant I'd start the dinner.'

She didn't look at him just put Ivy into her cot and stood fiddling with the mobile of brightly coloured birds above her head. She wanted to tell him about her fears, but what if he didn't believe her?

When she turned back he had gone and she plonked down in the rocking chair again. *Why was she being like this?* In the old days she would have told him everything as soon as he got home. They would have talked it through and he would have helped. He was always so calm and reasonable and that was one of the things she loved about him. *And she did love him.*

Her mobile was ringing downstairs again. Then the home phone shrilled.

Alex's voice, sounding strange. 'Eve, come down, please,' and she knew something was very wrong.

CHAPTER NINETEEN

Eve

Her mother was in hospital. Another heart attack and a serious one this time. She left Ivy with Alex and drove there fast. Her dad was all alone, looking almost green under a flickering strip of fluorescent light.

When he saw her his face crumpled as he tried to hold back his tears. He reached for her and they held each other but, instead of making her feel safe, it made her want to cry. Not just for her mum but for how shrunken he seemed and how sharp his shoulder blades felt through his clothes. When they parted she recognized his jumper as an old one Jill was always threatening to throw out. There was a stain just where he had the beginning of a small paunch. All she could think was: *Mum will be so embarrassed when she realizes he's been out in that grubby old sweater.* But it didn't matter because her mum might never see it. Might never see anything again.

'It's bad,' he said. 'They're doing a bypass right now.'

She took his hand. There was nothing to say.

She seemed to drift away for a while and wasn't sure how long he'd been talking.

'Can't think what she was doing. Even in good weather she should never have thought of walking all that way. But in that terrible cold wind and rain.'

'Dad?'

His eyes were misty grey. 'When did she leave you?' he said.

'Just after lunch. About half one I think. Why?'

'She didn't come home, so I thought she must still be with you. Tried ringing her a couple of times. Tried you, too, but when neither of you answered I thought you were busy chatting or had gone out with the baby.'

If only she'd answered her phone. 'Where was she?'

'It looks like she walked for hours along the beach. In that awful weather. Why would she do that?'

Because I upset her, that's why. 'So what happened?'

'A man found her collapsed on a bench on the seafront and rang 999. He was just in time, but it was touch and go at first. Still is, I think.'

She squeezed his arm. 'Oh, Dad, I'm sorry.'

He kissed her hand. 'It wasn't your fault.' A wavering croak: an old man's voice.

But it was my fault.

'She was conscious for a few minutes, when I got here. Kept saying she loved us and made me promise to tell you that.'

Fire in her throat. Acid tears in her eyes. All she could do was shake her head and grip him tighter.

'And I had to tell you she was sorry. I don't know what she meant, but she kept saying it.' He gulped and pressed his fist to his mouth. 'They told her she needed to lie still, but she was trying to sit up, grabbing my hand.' Another huge gulp. 'She kept saying the same thing over and over. 'I'm sorry. Tell Eve I'm sorry.'

Stella

The birth was nothing like she'd prepared for. In the weeks leading up to it she had read all the books she could get her hands on. Jill had brought her several from the library.

In the end it happened a week early. She had been in agony all day, pacing up and down in her room, and wanted to wait a bit longer, but when Jill realized what was happening she insisted on driving her to the hospital. It was just as well because everything went wrong from then on. Apparently they had been worried at her antenatal visits that she was too small, or the baby too big, although she couldn't remember anyone telling her.

She ended up having a caesarean. As they got her ready and wheeled her into the theatre she watched the strip lights passing by over her head and heard her nana's voice. 'I had a terrible time with your mother. They had to cut me open because I was so tiny. Couldn't get out of bed for ages. Was never the same after that.'

They allowed Jill to come in and sit beside her head, while the rest of her body was hidden behind a screen. And Jill's smiles and soft words helped to keep her from thinking about what was happening.

It didn't take long, but she lay waiting and listening for endless minutes before she heard a tiny cry. When they told her it was a girl she managed to mutter to Jill, 'I want her to be called Eve.'

They gave her a quick look at the baby before they sewed her up. Red blotchy face, crumpled little nose, purple-tinged eyelids closed fast against the light. Or maybe against the sight of her mother.

What had her mam said? 'I was just a kid when you were born and the way you looked at me, after all I went through, well I could see you didn't like me. Should never have had you.'

Strands of ginger hair on the baby's head. She had hoped it would be dark, like James. Tears spilling down. The nurse moved the baby away and all she could do was follow the little bundle with her blurred eyes. The books all said early bonding was vital. But they whisked her out of the room.

Next day sitting up in bed and feeling as if she'd been cut in two, she tried to breastfeed like all the other women in the ward seemed to be doing so easily. But the baby jerked and wailed in her arms, and the nurse told her she might not have enough milk, and she gave up and let them bring a bottle. They said she could try again later, but it had hurt so much and she'd been so embarrassed that she didn't want to. Anyway, Jill said at least this way she would know that Eve was getting enough nourishment. And formula these days was very good.

Jill and David visited, bringing flowers and chocolates, and the other mothers assumed they were her very young-looking parents. She didn't contradict them. It was nice to feel like everyone else with their families around them.

When she was released both David and Jill turned up in the car for her. They had fitted a baby seat in the back, and she was able to sit there with Eve. Climbing from the car she winced and held onto the door as Jill bustled round to help her while David carried Eve indoors.

'You go up and lie down in your room and I'll bring you some lunch. We'll watch the baby for you.'

As a surprise for Stella's homecoming they had bought a beautiful Moses basket. David moved the wooden blanket chest from the end of the bed in her room to the side so that she could easily reach the baby during the night. But Jill said, 'We'll have her in with us for the first night. It'll give you the chance to get some proper sleep.'

The kitchen was always warm and cosy, so Eve spent most of her time in her basket near the Aga and more often than not it was Jill who fed her; Jill who prepared her bottles. Stella knew she should be grateful, but sometimes she wanted to grab her baby and run away with her.

When the plump and laughing health visitor, who introduced herself as Vicky, came to see her, Jill was there too. Vicky was not much older than Stella and after she'd looked at Eve and cooed over her a bit she sat and ate a piece of carrot cake. Licking her fingers, she looked from Stella to Jill. 'I gather you aren't related?'

Jill answered, 'Just good friends.'

Vicky smiled.

Leaning back in her chair Jill said, 'Stella is an artist. A hugely talented one.' When Stella made a noise she laughed. 'Unfortunately she's too modest for her own good. She has no family, but when my husband featured her paintings in his gallery we kind of adopted her. We love having her here.'

Vicky asked if she could wash her hands, turning to Stella as she dried them. 'Well it all seems fine. I'm glad to see you so settled and baby is looking wonderful.'

Stella followed her to the door and then to her car. 'You know I haven't been able to feed Eve myself?'

Vicky touched her arm. 'Don't you worry about that, love. We encourage breastfeeding, of course, but bottle-fed babies do perfectly well too.'

'What about letting other people feed her. Is that all right?'

'Of course. And if it gives you a chance to relax and rest that's all to the good. A relaxed mum is always best for baby.'

She climbed into her car and rolled down the window. 'I'll be back next week, but call me if you have any concerns at all. You're staying here permanently, are you?'

'Oh, no. Just for a while.'

'Ah.' She had put the keys in, but took them out and rested them on her lap. 'Well do be sure to let me know your plans and I wouldn't rush away too fast if I were you. It can be difficult when you don't have the support of a partner, especially without close family nearby.'

'I don't have *any* family.'

Vicky looked at her watch and started the engine. 'Well then

172

you're very lucky to have found Jill. She's obviously a really caring person and this is such a lovely house. You couldn't be better off. Nor could baby.'

She was painting in a kind of frenzy. Painting every day for as long as she could. Ignoring the pain from her stitches and her aching back. If she could get three pictures finished, she could give one to David and Jill to pay them back for everything they'd done for her.

She'd written to Maggie to tell her about Eve's birth and that she hoped to visit. Maggie replied that she was just about to move into the new house. She didn't mention the baby.

The weather's beginning to warm up here. If you come soon we can have a wonderful summer together.

The painting was going well. The *Maggie and Me* picture was complete and she'd started two more. One was a view looking out to sea from the cliffs above Hastings. The seagulls were transformed into fantasy birds with white feathers so they looked almost like angels. The other was of the Ballantyne's cottage with David and Jill standing in the doorway. She had put a coronet of flowers on Jill's curls to turn her into a May queen, or a bride.

She kept both pictures covered and worked on them at the same time, something she'd never done before. Didn't go out much because she still felt sore from the operation and she didn't want to leave Eve. Jill had said she could carry on using the car, but, 'I've taken an extended leave from work, so I'm always available to babysit.' She offered to buy a pram, but Stella refused. 'You've spent enough on us already.'

Jill was at home most of the time now. Occasionally she went shopping or for coffee with a friend and then Stella would sit singing and rocking Eve, feeling as if she was doing something wrong. Watching this tiny bundle with bubbles around her pink mouth yawning and trying to focus her eyes, she still couldn't think of her as her daughter. And when Jill returned – always too soon – she would put the baby back into her basket and go upstairs to her frantic painting again.

When she finally completed the pictures she waited until both David and Jill were home. It was evening, but the spring sunlight was perfect. They stood just inside the door where they could get a good view of the easel beside her bedroom window. When Stella took off the cloth to show them the painting of themselves, neither of them spoke for a few minutes while Stella stood, heart pounding.

Finally David said, 'It's wonderful, Stella. I can see real development.'

Jill spoke very softly. 'It's beautiful, thank you.'

'Are you sure you don't want me to try to sell it for you?' David asked her. 'I can offer it to one of my old friends in London. They could get you a very good price.'

'No, no, it's yours.'

The others were leaning against the wall and they hoisted them up one by one. Each time David stood back again shaking his head and smiling.

'Do you think you could sell these?' she said.

'Of course. I'd love to have them in my gallery down here, but couldn't get you as much as they deserve. I'll take them up to London when I go next week. You could come with me if you want.'

Stella said she didn't feel up to it yet and realized she was almost afraid to leave Eve with Jill. She had come into the kitchen yesterday to find her sitting by the Aga feeding the baby and the look on her face transformed her from a plump woman on the verge of middle age into a cherubic beauty. Her skin was flushed and her eyes gazing down at Eve were filled with something more like adoration than love. *Madonna and Child.* That was the thought that came into Stella's mind and she wanted to snatch the baby – her baby – up and run, run out into the street and as far as she could go.

She had never felt so tired. The baby had been with her all night and neither of them had slept much. Jill knocked on her door first thing to ask if she should take Eve down and she hadn't argued. Was desperate for sleep. When she woke she lay looking out at the sunlit garden forcing herself to think. The facts were plain enough. Jill did everything better: calming the baby, feeding her, getting her to sleep. It all took longer and was more difficult when Stella tried to do it. Jill was a born mother, David would make a wonderful father, and they had a home and enough money to give Eve a comfortable life.

When she came down Jill was preparing bottles of milk. Eve was asleep in her usual place by the Aga. As if she'd heard Stella's thoughts Jill turned to her, shaking a bottle of formula, and said, 'Have you given anymore thought to the future?'

Stella went to sit by the Moses basket, looking at Eve sleeping. She seemed to grow plumper and prettier every day. 'I can't impose on you much longer.'

Jill lined up the bottles in the fridge and wiped her hands, coming to sit on the nearest chair and turning it to face her. 'Don't be silly. We've loved having you. And David was just saying we won't know what to do with ourselves if you go.' Her hands twisted together in her lap. 'And what about Eve? You know how happy we'd be to look after her. Maybe foster her officially while you decide what to do.' Her voice dropped as if she was talking to herself more than to Stella. 'Or adopt her if you think that's best'

She was suddenly so frightened her breath seemed to have stopped, and Jill must have seen it.

She came to kneel beside Stella's chair. 'Oh, no, don't be upset. I shouldn't have brought it up now after your bad night.'

When Stella made a sudden move, feeling like running away again, Jill stood and walked round the table, her hands twisting and twisting. 'I know you want what's best for Eve. If you did let us look after her, you could see her anytime. But it would mean you could get on with your work knowing she was safe and happy.'

Stella looked away. Staring at the wall. David had put her painting up there. It showed a perfect home and a perfect couple. But she turned her eyes to the blank plaster above it. Couldn't bear to look at it. And couldn't face the real Jill standing in her lovely kitchen – the Jill who would make a wonderful mother.

It might be best for Eve if Stella gave her up, but oh ... There was a pain in her throat and in the place where her heart must be.

Far away, Jill was still talking, her voice bright, 'You said your friend has invited you to Italy, so why not go for a few weeks? Give yourself time to think. Have a proper holiday. And leave Eve with us.'

176

CHAPTER TWENTY

Eve

There was nothing to do but wait under the flickering strip light, jumping every time a door opened. The waiting room was empty and it would be hours yet, but if something went wrong it could happen any minute. Eve and her father didn't talk for a while. She rang Alex to tell him she wouldn't be back until they knew how the operation had gone. Then she went to the foyer and brought back a couple of bottles of water. Her dad dropped his on the chair next to him as if he was too weak to hold it.

'I upset Mum,' she said. 'Asking about Stella.'

He nodded. 'I thought it must be something like that.'

'I didn't know you had only fostered me when she went to Italy. Why didn't you tell me that?'

He ran his hands through his thin grey hair. 'What? Well, it was so long ago. And we did adopt you shortly afterwards, which is what we told you.'

'But you didn't do that until Stella was dead.'

'No, but as soon as we could.'

'So why is Mum saying she's sorry. What has she got to apologize for?'

He didn't answer for a while and then it was only, 'You won't say anything when she comes round, will you? She'll need us. Need to know we love her.'

They sat in silence again. Eve drank some of her water, walked up and down. When she sat beside her dad again he took her hand. His was cool, the skin papery.

'Promise me you won't say anything to Mum until she's better.'

'Of course, I won't.'

She thought that was all, but he took a shuddering breath.

'I think she feels guilty because of the way we persuaded your mother to leave you with us.'

A jolt inside almost like one of Ivy's kicks, her hand going instinctively to her stomach. It was still surprising to find it flat and empty. 'What do you mean?'

He squeezed her fingers just a bit too hard, but she stayed still. 'Stella loved you, Eve, but although we didn't want to believe she had attacked Ben, we did think she was unstable. For one thing we knew her background was very troubled. Her own mother was a drug addict, apparently.'

'Did you hear all this from Pamela?'

'Some of it. But Ben mentioned something early on. During the exhibition at Houghton's. I imagine he got it from her friend.'

'Maggie, you mean?'

'Yes, and Ben also said she came to his office once accusing him of stealing some drawings she'd done.'

His grip on her hand was too tight and she moved her fingers to make him release it. He stretched out one leg and then the other, and she saw a twist of pain skid across his face.

When he sat back she said, 'I don't understand what you mean about persuading Stella to leave me.'

He sighed. 'Your birth was quite difficult and she was very young, so Mum did an awful lot for you right from the start. Stella hadn't painted at all while she was pregnant, but she suddenly started going at it full pelt. So Mum began to help out more and more.'

He got to his feet and walked stiffly around the waiting room, his hand pressing at the small of his back. 'Shouldn't keep still for so long.' When he did sit again he rubbed his knee where she knew he often had arthritis.

She waited. 'We hoped Stella would stay nearby, in Hastings, where we could keep an eye on you both. But she started talking about visiting Maggie in Italy, which we didn't think was a good idea. I mean from what I remembered Maggie wasn't very reliable. And she had turned against Stella once before.'

'But she did go, and without me. Why was that?'

'She was clearly under a lot of stress and frankly we were worried about both of you, so we suggested she go on her own. Have a holiday and think things through.'

'And she just let herself be persuaded?' Who was she feeling so angry with? Stella was dead. There was no point in feeling bitter towards her. And when she heard a huge sigh from her dad she felt even worse. This wasn't the right time to be cross-questioning him. 'I'm sorry, Dad. You're feeling awful and I'm not helping.'

'I just want to be sure everything will be all right between you when Mum comes round.'

She couldn't answer. Was still too confused.

She could hear him breathing hard and fast. His flimsy plastic chair gave a loud creak as he twisted towards her. 'Eve, my darling, I'm very tired and I don't know even now if I should tell you this.' A little cough that turned into a longer wheeze. He pulled out a tissue and wiped his mouth. 'As I said, Stella seemed to be suffering from stress. She was painting as if she was possessed and the rest of the time she was either tramping the streets or sleeping so deeply that she didn't wake when you cried.'

The look on his face told her there was more. 'Dad, please. It's too late to hold anything back now.'

'We couldn't stop her from leaving, but we needed to make sure you were safe.'

A silence such as she had never known before. 'Safe from my own mother? What do you mean?' *Please don't say it.* But she had pushed him too far and, even if he didn't tell now, she knew the truth. Better to say it herself. 'Did my mother try to hurt me?'

He took both her hands in his. 'I'm so sorry, Eve. But she did and we thought – and the health visitor agreed – that she could be a danger to you.'

Stella

The London gallery had sold the paintings David had taken there. So she'd have some money soon. And Maggie had written again to say the purchase of the Italian house was moving forward. If she wanted to take Eve, she would have to get her a passport. But Jill kept suggesting she go alone. 'I've no need to go back to work, so it won't be a problem.' She mentioned it to the health visitor, Vicky, when she called round. 'Stella's friend has asked her over to Italy for a holiday.'

And Vicky, 'Ooh you lucky girl. Wish I had friends like that. And it won't do Eve any harm at all to leave her with Jill for a couple of weeks. They're very adaptable at this age. In fact it's better to go now rather than later when she's really attached.' She added that she could see Stella was finding things difficult *like so many young single mothers do,* and Stella ran her fingers through her hair wishing she'd combed it this morning. When Vicky suggested she ask the doctor for something to help her relax, Jill nodded and said that was a good idea, but Stella could feel herself flinch.

Vicky's voice, telling her it would only be for a short time of course, then Jill's saying she'd taken Valium herself when she went through a bad patch, became a nasty background hum. It failed to drown out the loud whine in her head, which was her own

180

mother's voice: *It was those sleeping tablets and the tranquillizers they doled out to me when you were tiny that got me onto the rest of it. Ruined my life.*

The health visitor must have spoken to the doctor because he came by later on and spent five minutes asking Stella how she was before eating a piece of cake and writing out a prescription. Stella just smiled, like the little girl they were treating her as. She wasn't going to take the pills, but didn't say that. All she needed to focus on now was getting to Italy *with* Eve.

The cheque from the gallery arrived on a Wednesday morning when Jill always went for coffee with a friend who lived on the other side of the park. She walked there, so Stella planned to take the car, go to the bank to pay in the cheque and get the forms for Eve's passport. There was no need for Jill and David to know about it until the last minute.

Eve was deeply asleep in her Moses basket, and a door off the kitchen led into the back of the garage, so it was easy to carry her through and load her into the car seat.

The main garage door at the front was an up-and-over design that was very heavy to move and sometimes stuck. When she bent down to it she pushed carefully knowing it was likely to creak as it opened.

After that everything moved so fast she could never recall exactly what happened.

The door squealed as it started to move. Eve began to grizzle.

A crash behind her. And Eve screaming now. *Oh God.* She turned back.

Jill stood by the open kitchen door. It had slammed against the brick wall of the garage as she flung it open. Her handbag was on the concrete floor by her feet where she must have dropped it. Her eyes were wide, mouth open. She seemed to be saying something, but Stella could only hear Eve shrieking.

Then Jill was pulling Eve from her seat and out of the car.

181

And she was gone. Back into the kitchen with Eve in her arms.

When Stella got there, Jill was still holding Eve, pacing up and down by the window. Eve was screaming louder.

Stella stood frozen by the door her mind whirling, heart thumping. Something was wrong. But what? She tried to ask, but her voice wouldn't work. All she could do was watch as Jill rocked Eve and whispered to her. When the baby's cries turned to soft hiccupy sobs Jill came to sit with her beside the Aga.

She looked up at Stella standing by the door to the garage and said, 'Please shut that. It's chilly. Then why don't you make us some coffee.' Stella closed the door, but otherwise she couldn't move. It had taken all her effort to get this far. Jill's voice was little more than a whisper. 'I only came back early because I forgot the biscuits. Thank God I did.'

Stella managed to say, 'What do you mean? What happened?'

Eve had stopped crying and Jill stood, still rocking her. 'Let's not talk about that just now. I have to make a phone call.' She took the baby with her.

So dazed she didn't know what else to do, Stella found herself putting on the coffee maker, fiddling with cups and milk. After a few moment's Jill came back. 'She seems fine now,' she said. 'Why don't you take her?'

Sitting in the easy chair Stella tried to slow her heart. Eve gazed calmly up at her, and Jill bustled about looking in cupboards, turning on taps, rattling in drawers, still not explaining. Stella's voice was a croak. 'I don't understand. What was wrong with Eve?'

The front door opened. 'Hello, folks.' David home early. He kissed Jill's cheek, walked over to the coffee maker and touched the glass with his palm. 'Great,' and poured himself a mug. A huge sigh. 'How's it going?'

Jill said, 'We've had a bit of a shock, but it's all fine now.'

David gave Stella one of his gentle smiles, rubbing his hand over his jaw. 'I gather you had a bad night with Eve?'

She could only shake her head. 'Sorry.'

'There's nothing to apologize for. That's what babies do.' He gave a little chuckle that didn't sound genuine. 'Or that's what they tell me anyway.'

Why was he here? Why was any of this happening? She looked at Jill. 'I don't understand.' If she said it often enough …

Jill gave another of her sweet, sad smiles and a slow headshake. 'You have to be more careful. I'm sure it was just because you were so tired, but I can't understand why you had the engine on with the doors closed.'

She stared from Jill to David in shock. They looked back with sad, concerned eyes until she managed to croak, 'I didn't.' And then because they obviously didn't understand. 'I was going to the bank.'

The cheque, yes, the cheque would prove that at least. But, of course, she had left her handbag on the car seat and the doors unlocked. Her purse and the cheque from the gallery were in there, and the up-and-over door wasn't too secure. She lowered Eve gently into her basket very aware of Jill and David watching her, then took the car keys from the table where she'd dropped them.

It was cold in the garage: the main door was half up and the back door of the car was still open. Stella's bag was on the front seat.

Except it wasn't.

She looked in the back, under the seats, in the boot, then bent down to peer under the car. Her bag was gone, along with the cheque.

David was by the door to the kitchen just where Jill had stood earlier on. 'Anything wrong?'

Wanting to scream, but knowing she mustn't, she said, 'I can't find my bag. It had the cheque in it.'

David closed the boot, took the keys from her limp hand and locked the car. 'Maybe it's in the kitchen.' He put his arm around her and she longed to rest her head on his shoulder. But she pulled away. She needed to find the bag.

Back in the kitchen Jill was heating a bottle for Eve, who was rubbing her face with tiny pink fists and beginning to make little squeaks of irritation. Jill turned to Stella and gave her the same kind smile as always. 'Do you want to feed her?'

Shaking her head, hardly able to breathe, Stella said, 'Did you bring my bag in from the car?'

Jill frowned, glanced at David and said, 'No, I didn't even see it. I don't think you had it with you.'

Of course she did. She was going to the bank. And she hadn't turned on the engine. She clung to those thoughts.

Jill was asking if she had looked in her room. And although it couldn't be there Stella ran up.

It was sitting in the middle of her bed. Everything still inside.

How had this happened? Surely she hadn't been up here since taking Eve to the car? She stood, breathing hard. Her windows were open and a chill breeze blew the curtains, making her shiver. She dragged at her hair. Felt as if she was going mad.

CHAPTER TWENTY-ONE

Eve

My mother tried to hurt me. Eve didn't ask her dad anything more. Didn't want to know the details yet. Wasn't sure she would ever want to know them. She walked fast away from him, down the long corridors and out through the main doors of the hospital all the time trying not to hear her own thoughts. *My own mother was a danger to me.* She had left her coat hanging on the back of her chair in the waiting room and she was shivering even before she got out into the night.

It was too late to call Alex and she wasn't sure she could tell him anyway. Instead she paced up and down. Followed the lights to walk all the way round the main carpark and then towards the back of the hospital.

It explained everything, of course. Why they'd tried to keep Stella's identity from her. And all the little evasions once she did find out.

And just like that the memory that had been teasing at the edge of her consciousness all these weeks came back to her. Long ago there had been a painting in the same style as Stella Carr's in the kitchen of their old home. It was of her mum and dad and the house. It had to be one Stella had done while she lived there. And that could explain why Eve started drawing all those shooting stars. And why the signature looked so familiar. She had been very young, but seemed to recall her mum telling her not to keep drawing the same thing over and over; to try something else. And instinctively she'd known her mother didn't like the stars.

When she had grown into a teenager, were some of the problems she had with Jill because Jill could see her likeness to Stella and it worried her?

If that was true she knew why now and wished she'd left it alone. *Stupid, stupid.*

A huge shiver shuddered through her. *What was she doing?* Mum was back there, her real mum, fighting for her life.

When she got to the waiting room a woman in doctor's scrubs was sitting by her dad, her seat turned so close to his that their knees were touching. She stopped by the door, wanting to run back outside. *Please no.*

Then her dad looked up and the tiniest of smiles allowed her to breathe again. 'Doctor, this is my daughter, Eve.'

The woman stood and shook her cold hand. Hers was warm and soft. Comforting. She was smiling and her brown eyes gleamed in the harsh light. 'I've just been telling your father that it all went as well as we could have hoped. She's not out of the woods yet and she'll be in the high dependency unit for a bit, but it's looking good.' She turned back to David. 'A nurse will be out in a minute to take you in to see her.'

The nurse would only let her dad go in and when he had stumbled away after her, Eve texted Alex. It was 3 a.m. and she would probably be home again before he read it. Then she tried to clear her mind of everything except the sense of relief.

Even on the uncomfortable chair she kept slipping in and out of a dreamlike trance so that she had no sense of time and it seemed only seconds had passed when her dad was touching her arm. She jolted upright. 'How is she?'

He crumpled into the chair next to her. 'Hasn't come round yet. They say I should go home, but what if something happens?'

'They'll call you. And you can't do any good while she's out of it.'

When they parted at his car she reached up, kissed his cheek and smoothed down a few wisps of hair blown by the wind. Watching him drive away she put her hand to her diaphragm where a pain had been lodged for hours. Her mum already felt like an absence.

In her own car she shivered again. Once the engine was running she turned the heating to full, but knew it wouldn't get properly warm before she was home. She switched on the radio and tuned it to a music station. Didn't care what they were playing so long as it was noisy and cheerful enough to stop her from thinking. About what might happen to her mum. About how her dad was going to cope.

And about her other mother.

Ben

Even dead, dead for thirty years, that girl was a menace. Ben rolled his chair into the glass lift and pressed to take himself down to the hall. Pamela was out and he'd heard the post arrive. Wanted to get to it first in case it was something he didn't want her to find.

Why had he ever got involved with Stella bloody Carr? Because she was so fucking talented. That was why. He had desperately needed money. Tried everything to fend off the loan sharks and those drawings had been a last, desperate, throw of the dice. If only Stella had been sensible it could have worked out amazingly for him and she would have been fine too. But, no, she had to be awkward. And because of her stubbornness she was dead and he was in this bloody wheelchair.

And now there was the new exhibition. Bringing calls from

people who thought he might have supplied the pictures. The folks he still owed money had long memories and, although Pamela had persuaded them that they'd squeezed all they could get out of him – out of her really – they would be coming back for more at the first sniff of a windfall. And if they thought he'd had a treasure trove of artwork concealed all these years ... Well, it didn't do even to think about that.

He'd thought at first that David might be behind the sudden appearance of all this stuff, but that always seemed unlikely. And apparently he and the silly woman he was married to had never told the girl about her mother. Sensible decision in his opinion. But they would have known a new Stella Carr show would cause questions.

He opened the little cage behind the letter box. Just bills, as per usual, which, for once, he was glad of. No, it had to be that other bitch, Maggie. Another one he wished he'd never met. Stella was with her when she died, so it made sense that Maggie would have got her hands on the paintings she left behind. She didn't mention them in that pathetic letter she sent him after the fire, but, of course, she wouldn't want him to know.

The only surprising thing was that she'd waited so long to make use of them. Probably scared of what might happen if she made waves. Must have run out of cash now and got desperate. Thought it was all so long ago that she was safe.

He had tried to tell Simon to keep away from the girl, the daughter, but he never listened to his dad anymore. Couldn't seem to understand that it was crucial to close this down – and fast. Because the loan sharks weren't the only thing they had to worry about.

Eve

Her mum was out of intensive care the day after the operation. They said she was making progress and, although she didn't look well, she was sitting up and talking.

188

When Eve visited she gripped her hand and whispered, 'I'm sorry,' just as her dad said she had after her attack.

'It's all right, Mum.'

Her dad rubbed Jill's knee through the bedclothes. 'They say you'll be out for Christmas.'

'We'll make the dinner this year,' Eve said. 'You've already done the cake and the puddings. Alex and I will handle the rest and you can relax and enjoy your granddaughter.'

But when David went out to stretch his legs, Jill slid closer to her, wincing and putting a hand to her chest. 'Eve, I have to talk to you.'

'If it's about Stella, don't worry. Dad told me enough for now. Like I said, let's all have a lovely Christmas together with Ivy.'

Jill shook her head on her pillow. She must have missed a hair appointment because there were lots of silver strands in her parting and framing her face. It made her look much older. 'I blame myself for what happened, you see. I took over caring for you. Was too pushy. I don't think I helped her confidence. But I always worried about her.'

'Did you believe she hurt Ben?'

'At first I thought Pamela was just jealous because she imagined there had been an affair. But then she told me about Stella's background and that she tried to blame Ben's accident on some kind of criminal gang, which was ridiculous.'

'What happened?'

'I think she felt she would never be a good enough mother. I took to it, you see. Loved it and you were such an easy baby with me, but she always struggled.' Her mother seemed to be talking to herself now. Her lips looked chalky and Eve held up the cup of tea they'd brought round a couple of minutes earlier, but Jill shook her head. 'It was only luck that I came back that day. She knew I'd be out for an hour or more. Must have planned to have just enough time.'

Oh God.

Jill reached out for the tea and Eve handed it to her. She drank the whole cup in a few gulps as if suddenly very thirsty. Then wiped her hand across her mouth. It was a clumsy gesture; one that Eve had never seen from her before. When she spoke it was slowly and her eyes became distant.

'I found her with you in the garage. The door was closed. You were strapped into the car and she had turned the engine on.'

'Oh, Mum.'

Her mother looked at her as if surprised she was there and began talking faster. 'Yes, the door was closed tight, the engine was on and she'd left everything behind. Her bag, all her painting stuff, Eve's clothes and toys.' It was obvious Jill had said all this before. To David if to no one else.

A gasp that was almost painful caught in her throat. 'So she might have killed us both?' When she could speak properly she said, 'Did you try to get her psychiatric help?'

Jill pulled at her curls. 'We wanted to, but she wouldn't have it. So we alerted the health visitor to the fact that she wasn't coping. Didn't tell her the details and she was just a young girl, so she accepted what we said. That Stella was feeling inadequate, not eating or sleeping well. That she wasn't able to care for you properly.'

'So why did she go. To Italy, I mean?'

A slow headshake. 'I think, having made up her mind it was best to part with you, she needed to get right away.' She reached for Eve's hand and held it tight. 'And I encouraged her. Thought it was a good idea. I can't help feeling guilty about that.'

'You've no need.'

'But if she hadn't gone away she wouldn't have died.'

'That wasn't your fault.'

'It's just,' Her mum shifted as if she was in pain, but when Eve asked if she was OK she said, 'I'm fine, I just can't get it out of my head that she was so unhappy during those last days with us.'

Eve pressed her other hand over her mother's. 'It's years ago now, Mum. Don't think about it.'

'I know the fire was ruled an accident by the Italian authorities, but it took a while, so there's always been a nagging worry in the back of my mind.' Again it was as if she was talking to herself.

Eve said nothing because she knew what her mum meant and it made sense. If Stella had tried it once she might have tried it again – and succeeded.

Stella

After *the little accident in the garage,* as Jill kept calling it, Stella walked down to the bank on her own. Then she carried on walking. Not thinking, not feeling, just putting one foot in front of the other until she found herself back in the house. Straight up to her room to take off her shoes. One of her toes was sore and her sock was sticking to a blister that had burst, but she just tore off her clothes and dragged herself under the covers. Everything ached and she was so cold she thought she might be ill.

Had it happened as she remembered or as Jill said? She couldn't be sure of anything.

Jill insisted on taking Eve in with her and David overnight. 'To allow you to have a proper rest. You're obviously exhausted.' And she slept. Without dreams. Without movement. As if dead.

The health visitor turned up first thing. It wasn't her normal day and Stella was still in bed when Jill called her. She didn't dare delay and threw on the clothes she'd dropped on the floor the night before. She knew she must look terrible. Her shirt was crumpled and there were stains on her jeans. Even with the shirt hanging out it was obvious her trousers were gaping open. Her stomach was still flabby and her scar hurt when she tried to do the zip up.

Vicky was in the kitchen standing with her back against the sink, sun streaming through the window behind her and turning her face into a fuzzy halo. Impossible to see her expression.

Jill was at the Aga pouring coffee. The room smelled rich with it, but when Stella pulled out a chair with its little patchwork cushion and sat at the table she caught a hint of another, more delicate, fragrance. There was a pottery vase of fresh yellow and white freesias in the middle. It was all so beautiful and comfortable she wanted to let her head fall back, to close her eyes and sleep again.

Vicky patted her hand and she jumped because she hadn't noticed her moving to sit beside her. She must be saying something, but Stella could only hear muffled words. Fragments of sentences floated around her as if drifting through water. Warm and fragrant water. *Difficult … young mother … on your own.*

She forced herself to listen.

'I hear things aren't getting any easier? Are you taking the tablets the doctor gave you?'

She knew she should say something, but couldn't find the words. Any words. So she nodded, not sure what she was agreeing to.

Jill's voice. 'We've been talking about fostering Eve officially so that Stella can go on her Italian break without worrying.'

Vicky gave her broadest smile, deep dimples forming in her cheeks. 'That sounds like a grand idea. We're all quite worried about you, you know, Stella love. No one wants to take baby away from you, of course, but you shouldn't be alone with her until you're feeling better.'

They sat there with their coffees in front of them and smiled at her, while Eve cooed in her basket and Stella fought not scream and pick up the plate of beautiful homemade biscuits that Vicky was eyeing so longingly and fling them down on the shiny tiles.

CHAPTER TWENTY-TWO

Eve

Although they said her mother was on the mend she was very subdued and didn't take as much interest in Ivy as Eve had expected. On Christmas Day she sat in a chair by the fire and held her, smiling down at her now and then, but handing her to David after a few minutes. He hovered around her all day, helping her out of her seat, bringing her drinks and asking if she was warm enough. In fact, after days of ice and sleety rain the weather had become muggy, the cloudy sky turning everything grey outside. The lights in the tree in next door's garden were hardly visible and the flickering electric sparkles in windows along the street did nothing to lighten the gloom.

But Eve should have been happy. Almost as happy as Alex obviously was. Ivy was feeding well, sleeping for longer at night and sharing the feeds with Alex meant Eve felt much more rested. Christmas dinner went well and Jill brightened up enough to laugh at the cracker jokes and put on her paper hat as they all crowded round the kitchen table.

'This is lovely,' she said and joined in with the clapping when

Eve brought over the pudding that, for once, she'd managed to get flaming successfully.

Everyone made a fuss over it, and Jill chuckled, saying, 'It's the same old recipe. No need to go overboard because I nearly popped my clogs.'

It didn't last. When Alex suggested they put Eve in her pram and go for an afternoon walk, and David reminded her that the doctors said walking was good for her, she pulled off her paper hat and shook her head. 'You go. I'm a bit tired.'

All her movements nowadays were careful and her hand seemed to be permanently pressed to her breastbone. As Eve watched her she knew her dad was doing the same and tried not to catch his eye.

Of course he decided to stay too, but Alex and Eve wouldn't leave Ivy behind. And once they'd got out with the baby bundled up against the misty rain she felt able to breathe a bit more easily.

When they got down to the town there was a chill wind coming off the sea, so they cut back along a little cobbled lane with walls on either side and into the narrow High Street. All the shops were closed, for once, and the old-fashioned lamppost lights struggled against the mist. Alex tucked Ivy's covers closer to her chin and said, 'Don't worry about your mum. She'll soon come through this and be able to enjoy being a grandmother.'

Eve said nothing. There were so many things she should talk to him about, but she didn't want to spoil his happiness. And when they got back to the house, Jill was pottering about getting a few things ready for tea with her beautifully decorated Christmas cake in the middle of the table. Alex caught Eve's eye to signal, *I told you so*, and she smiled at him, glad she'd kept quiet.

But when she took Ivy upstairs to feed and change her she heard Jill go into the bathroom next door. The usual sounds: toilet flushing, water running. But then, instead of the door unlocking, she heard something else.

Quietly, but not quietly enough, Jill was crying.

Lying in bed on Christmas night, Eve almost told Alex about what she'd heard, but stopped herself. Jill would hate anyone else to know. Instead she said, 'I can't help worrying, because Mum seems so depressed. Last time she was ill she was really positive.'

'Don't forget she was close to death at one point.'

'How can I forget? It was my fault.'

He turned to her so forcefully the mattress dipped. 'Stop that. None of this is down to you. I haven't liked to say too much, but your parents were very wrong to keep all this stuff about your birth mother from you. I wish …' He lay back heavily on his pillow.

'What?'

'Oh nothing. I just wish I'd been more honest with my kids. Told them how much I loved them for one thing.'

'I'm sorry,' she said.

'At least they'll soon be old enough to make sense of it themselves. To see their mother's told them a pack of lies. But when I think what she may have said to them it makes me feel sick. She was just so vindictive.'

Her beside light was on very low and she twisted so she could look at him. This was probably the most he'd ever said about it. 'I'm sure they'll find you as soon as they're able.'

He gave her a long kiss and then they made gentle love, Alex asking over and over if it was all right. Did she feel all right?

Afterwards she told him what she'd learned about Stella.

He said, 'Well that explains why your parents didn't tell you.' When she shifted beside him he reached for her hand and kissed it. 'I'm not saying it excuses the lies, but it does make them more understandable. One day you should think about meeting James Stone. Get a DNA test if it will set your mind at rest. But not just yet.'

She took a breath, ready to tell him about the new Instagram comment and those frightening noises she kept hearing. But his breathing had changed and she realized he was asleep.

She woke to Ivy's first cries and was able to take her into the other bedroom without disturbing him. Sitting in the rocking chair she smiled down at her baby. All was quiet and when Ivy was asleep again she put her in the big cot and checked the garden. It was still and silent. Maybe it had been her imagination after all.

After a while she picked up her tablet intending to read for a bit, but spotted two messages. One was from Simon:

Wishing you and Alex a great first Christmas as parents

and she smiled to think he might be also be awake in these dark hours. It was comforting.

The other was from James Stone:

Have a good Christmas and New Year. I'll be in the UK in early January. Very happy to meet up then if you'd like to.

That made her smile too. The search for her birth mother hadn't turned out well, but it had brought these two men into her life.

She looked through some of the photos she'd taken today wondering if she should send any to James. There were so many of Ivy it was difficult to choose.

Then she couldn't stop herself from looking on Instagram.

A lurch inside. Under a picture of newborn Ivy was something else from *intheshadows*.

Clutching the fleece around her she turned off the light and went to the window, pulling the blind back just enough to let her stare down into the dark garden as the words echoed in her head: *Listening at the window, Standing on the stair. Watch your step my darling. Unless you know who's there.*

To anyone else it would seem just a silly rhyme, but Eve shivered, her eyes straining into the grey night, remembering how she'd stood on the landing listening to those noises from the garden. If someone had been out there they could have seen her through the window. Seen her trip on the stairs.

Now every night-time creak and rattle she'd made herself ignore since then came back to her. Perhaps they had been nothing, as she'd told herself, but she was sure now that someone had been in the garden the night she fell, and the second time when she stood frozen on the landing, too.

Someone who knew about her connection to Stella. Someone who wanted her to know they were watching her.

Stella

Walking, walking, walking. It seemed to be all she did in the days following *the little accident*. Each morning, after she had given Eve her first bottle and swallowed a piece of toast, she would head down towards the sea. It was a cold spring, but she didn't care about that. Even preferred it on the days of spitting rain when the sea boiled grey and waves whipped right over the pavement as if determined to soak her.

Vicky had come back with another health visitor, obviously someone senior. They spoke very kindly, but made it clear that she couldn't go to live on her own with Eve. 'We just feel you should have a little more support until you're back on an even keel. The doctor agrees. There's no need for any formalities as you have Jill and David on hand, but we must think about baby's safety above all.'

All she could do was sit and let their words float through the fog that permanently surrounded her these days.

Later, in the warm kitchen, David mentioned that the flat above the gallery was nearly ready. 'If you want to get away from us, you could move in there in a few days. Rent-free in exchange for keeping an eye on the gallery on the odd occasion when I can't do it.'

A spark of hope before Jill came in with, 'And, of course, you can come over to see Eve whenever you want.'

David smiled at her, taking off his glasses to polish them.

'Eventually, when you're feeling better, you could have her there with you. Stay permanently if it suits.'

Jill, stirring something on the stove said, 'Yes, as soon as Vicky thinks you're well enough.'

And the spark that had flared again faded and died.

So she walked, and if she wasn't walking she slept. In the pretty bedroom overlooking the garden, she'd sleep as if dead before dragging herself out for another walk. In the afternoons it was usually up on one of the hills overlooking the sea, the wet grass squelching under her feet as she tramped through it.

By the time she got back to the house she was so tired she often fumbled with her key, and Jill would come and let her in. After a couple of evening meals where she sat silent as Jill and David chatted away, trying too hard to include her in the conversation, they gave up and Jill said, 'If you're too tired to sit with us, why don't you take your plate up to your room to eat.'

Her sleep these days was dreamless, and for someone who used to be plagued by nightmares that was a wonderful blessing. But when she woke she never felt rested, but weighed down. It was as if she had aged ten or twenty years.

One afternoon she came back so exhausted her legs felt as if they had turned to concrete.

Jill sat cradling Eve who was sucking on her bottle eyes closed in bliss. 'You missed a phone call.'

'Who was it?'

'Your friend, Maggie, ringing from Italy. She said she's still in Milan, but will be going to her new place next week.' Jill lifted Eve onto her shoulder and began rubbing her back, her hand circling and circling while Stella stared at the flash of the diamond engagement ring on her finger. 'She says you can visit any time after next Monday.' Both hands busy, Jill nodded towards a scrap of paper on the table. 'That's her phone number from then onwards.'

Jill stood, Eve still in her arms, and handed her to Stella. She continued talking as she opened the fridge, took packets from the cupboards, a knife from the rack and placed a chopping board on the work surface. All with her usual quick efficiency. 'Maggie's obviously dying to see you. I told her you might come on your own.'

On your own. A sick lurch inside. Stella's jaw clenched so tight it hurt, but Jill's voice chirped on.

'She thinks that's a good idea too. So you can have a proper rest and get on with some painting. Apparently this new house has a studio in the garden.' She turned, the knife in her hand dripping liquid onto the floor. 'Sounds like heaven to me.'

Stella waited until she had gone back to her chopping and stirring. Then she kissed Eve, who was sleeping, laid her in the Moses basket. And went upstairs.

She needed to get away. To be able to think properly. To decide what was best. Being with Maggie would help. Maggie, who had rescued her when she was feeling so lonely in London surrounded by people who smiled at her accent and made her feel she was dressed all wrong. People who made her think her scholarship must have been a mistake or awarded to her out of pity. But Maggie was different. She looked like them, talked like them, but she despised most of them. And what was most wonderful of all she laughed at them.

Stella could talk to her as she had never been able to talk to anyone. Being away from Eve would be agony, but maybe that was what she needed if she was to work out what to do.

CHAPTER TWENTY-THREE

Eve

Although she kept scanning the garden every night, listening for unusual noises, as well as constantly checking Instagram, Eve waited several days again before she told Alex about her fears that she was being watched. Somehow the fact that he didn't know made it all seem less real. And deep down she couldn't help worrying that he wouldn't take her seriously.

But when she finally came out with it as they were eating breakfast at the kitchen table he looked at her with horror. 'Oh my god, why didn't you tell me right away?'

A spurt of anger. 'I did, on the night I fell down the stairs with Ivy.'

He shook his head. 'Did you? All I remember is you saying you caught your foot in the carpet.'

'But before that I heard someone in the garden. And it happened again when you went into work the other day.'

'So always when you've been alone?'

She could feel her jaw tightening. 'What does that mean?'

He took her hand. 'Only that it's more worrying if someone is targeting you when you're on your own. You and Ivy.' When she didn't speak he said, 'I think I should extend my leave until you feel safer and we should get a burglar alarm fitted.'

Why did she feel as if he was humouring her?

'There's something else,' she said, taking out her phone and calling up her Instagram page.

But when she looked for the comments from *intheshadows* they were gone – deleted.

Alex was trying to look at the screen, but she turned away from him. 'I had some more weird comments on Instagram, including a little rhyme under a picture of Ivy that really scared me.'

Before she could recite the rhyme he said, 'You haven't been broadcasting pictures of Ivy to the whole world, have you?'

'It was just one photo. Just on Instagram.' She felt sick. Looked at him and could see what he was thinking. That she might have put Ivy in danger.

'What about this rhyme?'

It was so curt she felt a swell of tears in her throat. She recited it to him, her voice weak.

'And this was under a photo of Ivy?' he said.

'I'm sorry, I didn't think.' She was talking more to herself than to him.

He came behind her chair and put his arms round her, squeezing her and resting his head on her shoulder, his voice very gentle. 'I'm sorry too. I didn't mean to sound so harsh. I was just frightened.'

She stood and he held her for a long time. Then they sat again and he said, 'I suppose we could tell the police, but without any evidence I doubt they'd do anything. So we'll just have to make sure the house is secure, and until you feel completely safe I'll be here all the time.'

Eve nodded and he went on, 'It's Stella Carr, isn't it? Your search for her has obviously disturbed somebody.'

She thought about James Stone saying that Stella seemed afraid of something and then her mum's words came back to her. Stella had blamed Ben's injury on *some kind of criminal gang*. But Alex went on, 'I always worried that this collector might think you were trying to claim the paintings for yourself. So this could be an attempt to intimidate you.'

It made more sense than what she'd been thinking. 'Yes I can see that.'

'I suppose the best thing to do is to contact the Baltic and tell them you've had no luck with tracing the owner yourself and if there's been no response from the solicitors then you're giving up.'

'Yes, and I'll take the painting of Stella off Instagram and the photo of Ivy. That should send a message too.' It felt good to have a positive plan.

Alex arranged to have a burglar alarm fitted, but of course it couldn't be done until after New Year. He made Eve promise to wake him if she heard anything suspicious at night and to show him any worrying Instagram comments right away.

But nothing happened and by New Year's Eve they were both feeling a bit more relaxed. Alex wanted to make a special dinner just for the two of them. So he said he'd walk into town with Ivy in her pram to get the food. It would do them both good.

She checked her Instagram page, but there were no further comments. It looked as if it might all be over. Alex had been right.

But then she saw the email.

It was in her spam folder and was from mermaid65@gmail and headed *Baltic*.

A deep breath and she opened it.

Dear Eve,

I gather you have been trying to get in touch with me about the Stella Carr exhibition. I live abroad, but will be in the UK in early January. So if you would like to meet me it should be possible.

However I would be grateful if you would not mention

that I've been in contact to anyone (even your own family).
I am a very private person and am only prepared to correspond
directly with you. If we do meet it must be alone.

I hope you'll agree because I have a lot to tell you about
your mother, most of which I'm sure you won't have heard
before. It might help to set your mind at rest.
    M. de Santis

Maggie. It was Maggie, of course. She wasn't surprised about that. Stella had no family and Maggie seemed to have been her only friend. They had been living together when she was killed, so it was likely Maggie would have *inherited* the pictures whether legally or not.

It was exactly what she had hoped for all those weeks ago. But now it felt too late.

Going back into the turmoil of her mother's life and death didn't feel safe, especially as Maggie insisted on meeting alone and didn't want Eve to tell anyone. She couldn't agree to that.

But when she reread the email it was almost as if Maggie knew of her fears and could reassure her. And then there was: 'I have a lot to tell you about your mother, most of which I'm sure you won't have heard before'. How could she turn that down?

But she had to tell Alex.

She made herself get on with filling the dishwasher, making the bed and sorting some washing. All the time running through what to say to him. She was almost sure he would want her to refuse. Or at least to insist on coming with her. But that could ruin everything.

She needed to think.

She left a note for him, bundled herself in warm clothes, and walked to the town using the steep steps down the hill. Alex would be on his way back and wouldn't be able to come up that way with the pram. She didn't want to see him until her mind was clearer.

After the muggy Christmas the weather had turned cold again and it was a sharp frosty day with the palest blue sky. It felt good to be able to stride out, light and strong, after all those months weighed down by pregnancy.

When she came to the shops she realized she had intended all along to speak to her dad. Not to tell him, but just to chat in the hopes that a decision would somehow come to her. The gallery was all lit up and as she'd hoped he was alone.

He hugged her and touched his fingers to her cheek. 'You're freezing,' he said. 'Come and sit near the heater.'

They moved to the little desk at the back of the shop. Eve loosened the buttons on her coat and unwrapped her scarf. Her dad was smiling, but as always lately she could see anxiety in his eyes.

'It's lovely to see you, darling girl,' he said. 'But Mum's having a sleep, so we'd better stay down here. She didn't get much rest last night.'

They talked about Jill for a bit. He was obviously worried and, although he tried to reassure Eve that it was *her brush with mortality* that was the root of her unhappiness, she knew it was partly her fault.

'Mum's always been such a happy person. The only time she was ever depressed was when we couldn't have children of our own. She was on tablets for a while, but they made her feel worse.' That was something Eve hadn't known before. 'She hates taking anything now, but of course there's a whole array of pills for her heart. So long as she keeps up with them the doctors say she'll be fine, but …' He rubbed his hand over his face.

Eve touched his arm. 'Give it time, Dad. It's been a big shock for her.' She began to do up her coat again and stood to go; she should never have come. But her dad's grey eyes under their pale brows looked deep into hers.

'I can see there's something bothering you. What is it, Eve?'

What could she say? To give herself time she took off her scarf, rolling it into a rough ball and putting it in her pocket.

He was waiting, eyes still on hers. 'Is it about your birth mother?'

Collapsing back into the chair she blurted it out. 'I've had an email from Maggie de Santis offering to meet me.' Even as she said it she wanted to take it back.

He steepled his fingers and pressed them hard against his lips. 'And do you want to?'

'I don't know.'

David was gazing away now, his eyes moving from picture to picture on the gallery walls, and Eve almost asked him what happened to the painting by Stella Carr that used to hang in their house, but he went on, 'Maggie would have seen a different Stella to the one we knew. And she was there at the end.'

'So you think I should agree?'

Her dad stood and walked a few paces away, looking out into the street where the coloured lights in the shops opposite were beginning to win out against the weakening sun as the street fell into shadow. 'Of course, Stella and Maggie weren't always friendly. I mean Maggie actually threw her out of the London house. I never knew her well, but I gather she could be a difficult person. And I don't think she had a reputation for being particularly trustworthy.'

'She might lie to me, you mean? Yes, I'd thought of that.'

He walked to the door and flipped the sign to *Closed*. 'And even the fact that she claimed Stella made a will just before her death with Maggie as the beneficiary always struck me as odd.'

'But didn't she send money for me?'

'Yes, but evidently she kept hold of these paintings. Paintings that seem likely to prove very valuable indeed.'

It was all true, but …

Her dad came to her and took both her hands in his. 'My advice would be to leave it alone. But if you do decide to see her, please remember what I've said. Maggie was very unpredict-able. Have Alex with you, of course. And best keep it from your mum.'

The door to the flat opened and Jill stood there, fully dressed, but her hair rumpled from sleep. Her voice wavered. Her eyes stretched wide like a child waking from a nightmare. 'You're going to meet Maggie de Santis?'

Damn. 'No, Mum, not necessarily.' *Why did she feel breathless?*

David said, 'Go back up, Jill. I'll close the shop and we'll all have a chat.'

Jill didn't move or look at him. Her eyes stayed fixed on Eve. 'What do you mean? Not necessarily?'

There was no point in lying. 'I've had a message from her offering to meet me. I came down to ask if Dad thought it was a good idea.' She stopped as she realized how that sounded. 'To ask what you and Dad thought.'

As if too tired to stand, her mother sat on the chair David had been using. Her words coming out on a gasp. 'No, Eve. It's a very bad idea. She isn't to be trusted.'

David came over to her, his hand on her shoulder, rubbing it gently. 'I already told Eve that, but we have to let her make up her own mind.'

Jill pushed his hand away as she stood and lurched towards the door to the stairs. 'I can't bear this.'

Eve found herself pressing her chest where her heart was beating so loud and fast she could almost hear it. 'Mum, don't get upset. I won't go if you're so against it.'

At the open door her mother leaned on the wall as if all the air had been pumped out of her. 'Good. Let's leave it at that then. Now come and have a drink and forget about it.' Then she turned and headed up the stairs.

David and Eve stood looking at each other. After a minute that seemed like many more, her dad rubbed his forehead and seemed to come out of shock. 'Shall we go up?'

It was almost a croak. 'No, I should get back. Ivy will need feeding. Tell Mum it's all right.'

He nodded as she put on her scarf and gloves, her fingers trembling. 'She's not herself, you know,' he said. 'I'll talk to her. Ask her to stop worrying about nothing.'

She opened the shop door to the cheerful jingle of the bell and a breath of cold air. 'I know. Just tell her I'm OK. Everything's fine.'

Another nod and a twist of smile from her dad. Although they both knew nothing at all was fine.

CHAPTER TWENTY-FOUR

Stella

Everything was different when she got to Italy. At the airport, smiling and waving, dressed in a bright blue dress and wearing an oversized white hat, there was Maggie. Straight from another life.

They took a taxi to Sestri Levante where Maggie was living. It was a small seaside town that, as they drove along beside the water, seemed to Stella like a mini version of places like Cannes and St Tropez that she'd seen in magazines. Apparently this was also part of the Riviera, but the Italian Riviera. 'A lot cheaper, but just as gorgeous,' according to Maggie, who didn't stop talking for the whole drive.

Her house was up a sloping lane some distance from the seafront. A small white bungalow with a shallow veranda fronted by a garden area that was mainly dry earth. A metal table and chairs sat under a tree that Maggie said would grow lemons later in the year.

The front door opened straight into a small room with bare walls and an open fireplace full of grey ash. The only furniture was a leather sofa with metal legs – too modern-looking for the room – and a green canvas director's chair. Leaning against the wall was a paintingshaped parcel. Stella recognized her own writing on the wrappings. It was the *Nana* picture she'd sent over.

She followed Maggie through the door at the back into a short dark corridor.

'Bathroom just here.' Maggie indicated it with a swing of her hip. 'And here's you.' She put down the bag she was carrying. 'I'm sorry it's a bit basic, but I haven't had the time or money to do much.' There was room only for a single bed with a flimsy mattress.

Stella dropped her big bag. 'It's great.'

Maggie grabbed her, holding tight and whispering, 'I'm so glad you're here. So glad you've forgiven me for being such a bitch.'

Stella returned the hug. After a moment she moved away wanting nothing more than to lie on the bed and sleep. But she knew Maggie. 'I expect you want to hit the town for a few drinks.' A short laugh. 'No, don't worry, I'll let you rest.'

She walked to the door and when she turned there was something in her face Stella had never seen before. She'd seen excitement, anger, even love – all the big emotions. But this looked like sadness. A tiny sound that could almost have been a sob.

'I've changed, Stella. I've been here ten days and apart from a trip to stock up on supplies I haven't been out. Now you unpack and I'll get us some food.' Then she was gone. One thing that hadn't changed about Maggie was how quickly she could move.

The room was a gloomy and smelled damp, but it was warmer than it had been in England, so she opened the window threw her bag onto the floor and lay down expecting to sleep. Instead a deep sense of peace crept over her. It was as if she had gone back in time. Become the girl she used to be when she and Maggie had lived together. The past year, her pregnancy, the time with David and Jill, and even the fact that she was a mother, seemed remote and unreal.

It had been torture leaving Eve behind, but somehow it took

an effort to feel that pain now. Jill had driven her to the airport and waited with her until her flight was called. Stella sat holding Eve, feeling as if they were still joined together and that when she walked away something would tear and cause terrible damage inside her. When it was time to go she kissed her baby, longing to run away with her. But Jill's hands were outstretched and there were people all around them. She couldn't back out.

On the plane she struggled to breathe, biting her lip as they sped along the runway. After that she sat frozen, forcing herself not to cry, because if she did she knew she wouldn't stop. But then she slept and when she woke felt different. More like herself. More like her old self. Before pregnancy. Before Eve. And it was a relief.

She shook her head and climbed off the bed. She'd slept too much lately. And she *was* a mother. This wasn't a holiday, but a chance to prove she was sane and stable. Capable of bringing up her child alone. And if she could get some painting done, she knew she would feel better.

Maggie shouted, 'Come on out here and stop moping,' and Stella found her sitting at the metal table, her bare feet propped on another chair. Without her hat, her hair was a messy tumble but, lightened by the sun, the messiness suited her. When she spotted Stella looking, she ran a finger through. 'Decided to go natural again. Don't trust the hairdressers over here and I need to save money.'

Maggie had dumped some food on the table. Cooked meats, a jar of olives, a lump of cheese, a half a loaf of bread. She was drinking red wine from a tumbler, and Stella couldn't help smiling at how different this picnic was from Jill's perfect meals. But then she thought of Jill sitting by her Aga feeding Eve and something sharp seemed to dig into the place where Eve had once been. She must have let out a whimper because Maggie grabbed her hand.

'Now stop that. You're going to enjoy yourself for a few days at least.'

She pointed to the wooden building over by the wall. 'Is that the studio?'

Maggie nodded. 'Yeah. Needs a bit of a clean, but feel free.'

From the outside it looked more like a garden shed than a studio, but as she walked over Maggie called, 'Used to belong to a potter.' And when she pushed open the door she could see it would be perfect. There was a clear roof mottled with smudges of green that diffused the light beautifully and one big window. It was smeared with grime, but when Stella rubbed a patch clear she could see hill upon distant hill spiked with pines, lemon trees and bushy herbs. These plants must be the source of the scent she had been aware of since she arrived. A dry rich fragrance, like Italian food. Very different from the lush damp of Jill's garden.

Despite claiming she had chosen the house for its studio, Maggie had obviously done no work in there. And when Stella came out rubbing her hands down her jeans she said, 'I've got an easel in my bedroom and some blank canvases. Use anything you want.'

Stella sat down and sipped her wine. 'What about you?'

Maggie yawned, arms stretched above her head. 'Honestly I don't know if I'll work again. I'm bored with it.' She lit a cigarette and tossed the match into the lavender bushes straggling beside the wall. 'But don't start work today. Let's talk. You can tell me all about your problems and we'll work out what to do. I've got some brilliant ideas already.'

Eve

Eve was shaken by the way her mum had behaved, and on the walk back up the hill she cursed herself for telling David. There was surely no way Maggie could find out, but it had been stupid. If she'd told anyone it should have been Alex, but for tonight she wouldn't say anything to him. He wanted them to have a lovely

New Year's Eve and so did she. If she put Maggie out of her mind until tomorrow, she might have figured out what to do.

She could smell something delicious as she came through the front door; Alex already had the slow cooker going. Ivy was with him in the kitchen still in her pram and fast asleep. The radio was on, a soprano voice very loud, and Alex joining in with his tuneless drone. It was impossible not to smile, and she crept up behind him standing on tiptoes to dot a kiss onto his neck.

He whipped round and grabbed her, kissing her hard on the lips. 'You little sneak. You can't scare me. I knew you were there all the time.'

She eased back in his arms looking up into his glowing golden eyes; loving him so much it was painful. But he was laughing down at her and she laughed too. He lowered his head and kissed her neck, then gave it a tiny bite. Her shriek must have been louder than she intended because Ivy began to cry – jolted out of sleep.

'Now look what you've done,' she said. 'And just when I was going to suggest a liedown.'

He grabbed the tea towel from over his shoulder and whipped it at her backside as she headed to the pram and Ivy.

'Sort out your child, woman, and stop trying to corrupt me.'

She carried Ivy upstairs to feed and change her. Alex came up and sat on the floor beside the rocking chair, leaning his head against her knee.

'Dinner's on. Nothing to do for a few hours. So when she's asleep again I might take you up on that offer.'

Later, they ate his special chicken and chorizo hotpot sitting on the sofa in front of the living room fire. The Christmas tree glittered in the corner and they turned off all the lamps and lit a few big candles. Eve rested her head on Alex's shoulder and he kissed the top of her head.

The phone burst into life coming from the kitchen. He jumped up. 'I'll get it.' She heard him murmuring as he walked back. 'It's your dad,' he said and headed upstairs.

For a moment she was scared that something had happened. Her parents always rang just after midnight on New Year's Eve and it was only ten o'clock, but David said, 'It's OK darling. I just don't think we'll stay awake until twelve. In fact Mum's in bed already. Just wanted to wish you a Happy New Year.'

'Is she all right?'

'Oh yes, don't worry. I'll look after her. She's a bit overwrought that's all. Best not to mention the other thing again. At least for a while.'

'I won't, but Dad, I've been meaning to ask you about the picture that used to hang in our kitchen in the old house. The one of you and Mum. Was that a Stella Carr?'

A sigh. 'Yes, it was. How strange you should remember it. You were only little when we took it down.'

'What happened to it?'

'It's in the store room at the gallery. Been there for years. I'll get it out for you if you want. Mum said I should sell it. Give you the money, but it didn't seem right.'

'Why didn't you leave it on the wall?'

'Ahh, maybe that's why you remember it. You started having nightmares when you were about four or five and Mum said that picture was one of the things that featured in them.'

After he rang off she tried to recall those night terrors, but couldn't. Were the fears she'd been having lately something similar? Then she realized how long Alex had been upstairs. Ivy must have woken again.

She went up to see them. Ivy was in her cot awake but lying happily looking up at her mobile. Alex was sitting in the rocking chair staring at her. He didn't look at Eve.

'Alex, what's wrong?'

He still didn't look at her. 'When were you planning to tell me?'

213

'What about?' She spoke softly, very aware that Ivy's lids were beginning to close.

Alex, his eyes still on the baby, stood and moved his hand slowly up and down to tell Eve to be quiet. She followed him into their bedroom. 'What on earth is the matter?'

'Your dad said you'd heard from that Maggie woman. He assumed I knew about it.' He took off his watch put it on the bedside table then sat with his back to her on his side of the bed.

Standing by the door she felt like a naughty schoolgirl. And yet there was also a boiling sense of fury with him for being so ridiculous. *What to say that wouldn't make it worse?* 'It only came today and I didn't want to spoil our New Year's Eve.'

He turned to her, his face stony. 'So you assumed I wouldn't be sympathetic. Not like dear old Dad.'

She sat next to him and put her hand on his arm, but he turned away. 'It wasn't like that. You weren't here when the email popped up and I needed to talk to someone.'

He shrugged her hand away. 'You could have phoned me. Or waited an hour.' He walked over to the wardrobe and started unbuttoning his shirt. 'The truth is you trust your dad more than me.'

This was becoming ridiculous. 'Of course not. I wanted a peaceful evening, that's all.'

He ripped off his shirt and threw it on the floor, then picked it up and put it into the laundry basket. She couldn't help smiling. He was always so tidy even when furious. But it was a mistake. 'It's not funny.'

She gave a noisy sigh as she walked over to the door. 'Oh for goodness' sake, Alex, you are being ridiculous. Come downstairs. It'll be midnight soon and we need to open that bottle of champagne. I promised myself one drink and that means you can have the rest.'

But he had taken a hanger from his wardrobe and was pulling off his trousers. 'No thanks. I'm tired.' As he climbed into bed she wondered how, although he was naked, she was the one who felt undignified.

He switched off the bedside lamp and she could only see his outline by the light from the hall. A flare of rage. 'Sometimes I can see why your first wife left you.' She whispered it, but it was a fierce whisper and something about the way his shadowy hand jerked at the covers told her he had heard.

Stupid, stupid, stupid. As she walked slowly downstairs, still hoping he would call her back or bound down after her, she cursed herself and him, but mostly herself.

In the kitchen she took the champagne from the fridge, but she didn't want a drink.

The living room fire was dying. The candles were still burning and the tree glittered just the same, but everything had gone wrong. She wished she'd done as Maggie had asked and kept it all to herself. This was her problem and no one else should be involved.

Sitting there alone, too miserable to cry, she switched on the TV to see the fireworks in London. She left the sound off, but could hear the same noises and see the same flashes through her own window. Was Alex lying in bed listening too?

Her mobile on the coffee table chirped with a message and she grabbed it. Alex saying sorry and asking her to come up. But it wasn't him.

Happy New Year. Simon XX

She sent a quick reply. For one moment she had been tempted to let him know about the contact from Maggie, but stopped herself. That would only make the situation worse. Telling her parents certainly hadn't helped.

She went to switch off her phone and hesitated suddenly realizing she was wrong. It had helped. Right from the start her parents had been against her probing into Stella's life and death, so it was no surprise they didn't want her talking to Maggie. But she hadn't agreed with them at the beginning and knew they were wrong now. She couldn't give up and only Maggie could tell her anything new.

She replied to the email:

I'd love to meet you. Just let me know when and where.

CHAPTER TWENTY-FIVE

Stella

For the first couple of days in Italy it was difficult to avoid the feeling that this was a holiday. When Maggie wasn't lounging in the sunshine she was begging Stella to play cards, have something to eat or share a bottle of wine.

This was only the second time she had been abroad. The first was a cheap package holiday to Spain with her grandmother and one of her nana's friends when she was fourteen. This felt so different and she couldn't help thinking how exciting it would all have been a year ago. Now it felt as if there was a huge gulf between that girl, Stella, and what she had become. She kept wishing she'd been able to travel here when she was first pregnant. It would have been incredibly hard, but at least Eve would be with her now.

Or would she? What if she wasn't fit to be a mother at all?

On the third evening, Maggie suggested going to the town for a drink. It was an easy walk down the unmade lane, but much further than Stella had realized when they'd arrived by taxi.

'If I'd known how far out it was, I would never have taken it,' Maggie said. 'I'm going to have to get a car if I stay.' She kicked a stone and it tumbled down the lane. 'When I can afford it that is.'

Apparently she had bought the place without visiting. Had seen photos of it at the estate agents in Milan and they had sorted everything out for her. 'It's all right now you're here, but I was really scared during the night when I was on my own.'

In town they walked to a second bay smaller than the one they'd passed in the taxi. The beach here was a slender curve with a narrow outlet to the sea. They sat at a bar right next to the sand and ordered Cinzanos. The drinks came with a few plates of snacks that were apparently called *aperitivo*. Maggie picked up a piece of cheese, her fingers glistening with oil, and waved it at her saying, 'These are just to stop people getting drunk, but I noticed in Milan that in some bars they're so generous they can stand in for a meal. Looks like this is one of those. So eat up.'

Stella had told her right from the start that she wanted to pay her own way, but she was surprised Maggie seemed to be short of cash. In the London house Stella had given her some rent from her scholarship, but Maggie wouldn't take as much as proper landlords charged. Although they never spent heavily on food then either, she was always buying new clothes or paying for drinks at the pub.

As if reading her mind Maggie said, 'You know my dad has never given me a penny. That London house used to belong to one of his maiden aunts. Making it over to me was a way to salve his conscience when he went off to Texas with his new wife, the blessed Brenda. Basically told me it was all I'd ever get out of him. But when I wrote to let him know I was planning to sell he was furious. You'd think it was the ancestral home or something. I didn't contact him at all while I was travelling and I'm pretty sure he made no effort to get in touch with me, so I shan't send him this address. He's dead as far as I'm concerned.' She stubbed out her cigarette on the low wall between the table and the beach.

It looked as if the money she always seemed to have in London must have come from her various well-heeled *conquests*. So Stella asked, 'Have you made any friends in Italy yet?'

'No. I had a couple of flings while I was mooching round Europe, but from the little I've seen of this place it doesn't look promising. Besides, to be honest I've not only gone off painting, but pretty much lost my appetite for men. Bloody Ben Houghton spoiled that for me too.'

Walking back was a lot harder than going downhill to the town and they were both getting breathless as they neared the house. But it was a lovely evening and the scents of pine and herbs made Stella feel relaxed enough to want to talk.

'Pamela Houghton told David's wife, Jill, that I was responsible for Ben's accident.'

Maggie stopped and pulled her round to face her. 'What the fuck? How did the mad bitch work that out?'

'I went to see him that evening. Begged him to get back those drawings. Stupidly I told him I was pregnant. I thought it would help to persuade him. It was no good, of course. But he must have had the fall the same night or early next morning.'

They had reached the gate and Maggie stumbled through it. She'd only had two Cinzanos in town, but had been drinking wine steadily all day. Stella grabbed her arm. Hanging around her neck, Maggie said, 'That Pamela is a cow. I told you she wouldn't let me see him when he was in hospital, didn't I?'

Stella, feeling suddenly cold, helped her into the house and to her bedroom. She collapsed on her bed and wriggled out of her skirt. Stella knelt beside her.

'Maggie?' Maggie looked at her with glassy eyes. 'Were you in London when Ben was hurt?'

Maggie turned her face into the pillow. 'Yeah, I told you.' She sounded annoyed.

'So when did you hear about the accident?'

Turning to face her, but with her eyes still closed, Maggie grabbed her hand and gave it a damp kiss. She said nothing for so long Stella thought she must be asleep. Then her lids fluttered and she gave a huge sigh. 'I've had an idea.'

'What?'

'The bitch, Pamela, probably thinks you had Ben's bastard.' Her words were slurred and she seemed to be talking more to herself than to Stella, but it still made Stella flinch and pull her hand away. Maggie's eyes, swimming with drink, focused on something over Stella's shoulder, but her words were clear. 'There's no way they can prove he isn't the dad. And if it got out, the bitch would be totally humiliated, which to her would be worse than death. So we can use it for leverage.'

Standing and rubbing her arms Stella said, 'What do you mean?'

'Use it to get some money out of them, of course,' Maggie said, then turned away and was immediately asleep.

Stella didn't wake until nearly noon. Her head was aching and she realized she must have drunk more yesterday than she'd thought. She pulled a jumper on over her nightdress, shoved her feet into sandals. She had expected Maggie to be in bed with a hangover, but her door was open, the bed rumpled.

Maggie was in the studio in shorts and a vest, her hair pulled back in a ponytail. She was cleaning the big window. 'Thought I'd make a start,' she said. 'Can never sleep properly when I've drunk too much.' Her voice sounded hoarse and Stella wasn't surprised when she said, 'Could kill for a cup of coffee though.'

When Stella brought out two cups Maggie fished in the pocket of her shorts and took out a packet of aspirin, swallowing some with a gulp of coffee. 'Already taken three or four of these, but my head's still thumping.'

Stella said, 'Come and sit down and I'll get you some breakfast.'

Maggie shuddered. 'No thanks.' But she came out, plonking herself on the ground and leaning back on the wall of the hut. Stella carried a metal chair over and sat in front of her.

It was cool outside and Maggie must have been feeling the

cold in her skimpy clothes, but she just drank down her coffee then put the cup on the ground. She reached into the front of her vest and took out a battered packet of cigarettes she must have pushed into her bra and a book of matches from her back pocket. Lighting up and sucking in the smoke, she closed her eyes and rested her head on the wall. 'Don't know what I said last night, but ignore it, will you?'

'OK.' What else could she say?

Eyes still closed, Maggie said, 'Ben's not that badly hurt, is he? I mean it was just a fall. When I tried to see him in hospital the wife made out he was half-dead. But Ben always told me what a liar she was.'

Stella could see it mattered. 'All I know is she claims he's paralyzed and will never walk again. But, like you say, we just have her word for it.' She stopped then because Maggie had pressed her half-smoked cigarette into the earth next to her and tears were squeezing out from under her closed lids. She didn't move, but Stella knelt beside her, taking her hand. It was still damp from the cleaning cloth. 'Maggie? What's wrong?'

A huge sob that made Maggie's chest heave. 'I love him, Stella. I love him, and we were going to get married.' She rubbed her face with the back of her hand, leaving a streak of dirt on her cheek. Her eyes were open now, but she was looking away from Stella. 'That was why he was playing the stock market. So he could make enough to be independent and get a divorce. It was when that went wrong that we thought of the forgery thing.'

A long silence. Stella could only stare at Maggie. A Maggie who was suddenly so different. Like someone she had never known. She dropped her hand and sat back, trying to catch her breath, to still her whirling mind. 'You did it together? Sold my drawings as fakes?'

If she'd noticed Stella's reaction, Maggie didn't show it. Just lit up another cigarette. 'It wasn't just you. Before I even met you Ben told me about these art collectors who only wanted to make

221

money. They were interested in lesser-known artists who looked like becoming fashionable. Wanting to buy in hopes the prices would rise. And there was a guy in my class who could do brilliant copies of any painting. So when Ben heard about one of these collectors looking for stuff by a particular artist, he'd tell them he might know where to locate something. Then we'd ask the guy to produce copies. They were mainly of pictures that were rumoured to exist but hadn't been traced. And Ben sold them.' She tucked a lock of hair behind her ear. 'We did it a few times.'

'Did the guy who produced the paintings know they were sold as fakes?'

A shrug as Maggie blew out a long stream of smoke. 'Probably guessed, but he needed the money and, like me, he despised idiots with more dosh than sense. But he was talented, of course, and when he started having a bit of success with his own work he wouldn't do anymore for us.'

Stella got up, her legs were damp and cold and she brushed at her shins where little stones had stuck into the skin. Walking away – she couldn't bear even to look at Maggie – she said, 'So when he stopped, you tricked me into doing it.' What a fool she was. It was Maggie who had encouraged her to do those drawings when Stella told her how much she liked the East London Group's work. She shook her head, wondering just how suggestible she had been. 'I can't remember, but did you steer me towards George Grafton, too?'

Maggie stood up, leaning back against the wall and rubbing her face again. In her shorts and ponytail, with her smudged cheek, she looked like a naughty little girl. 'I can't remember. But it worked out perfectly. A recluse. And him dying youngish. Couldn't have been better.'

That was why Maggie had encouraged her to do something original in Grafton's style. She'd probably described the portfolio where Stella kept her drawings to Ben, and when she arrived home carrying it he'd been able to grab it without her noticing. So they didn't even have to ask her.

Maggie was saying something, but her words were drowned by a buzzing in Stella's ears. 'And I was doing you a favour. I didn't think you'd agree to do it, but this way you got some extra money without the need to feel anxious or guilty. I knew you'd be all right, because no one was ever going to find out. And no one *will* find out.'

She took a long drag on her cigarette and coughed. 'Unless, of course, we decide we want them to.'

The earth shifted under her feet. 'For God's sake, Maggie. What are you saying? If people find out it'll kill any chance I've got of a career as an artist.'

Maggie came to her and grabbed her forearms. 'Not if we told the whole truth. That you were tricked. It would be great publicity for you and it would bugger that pretentious Pamela up for good.'

Stella pulled hard away. 'No. Please don't even talk about it.'

Maggie smiled at her and flopped onto a chair by the table, gesturing to Stella to sit near her. She did so only because her legs would no longer support her, but Maggie kissed her cheek, in a waft of cigarette smoke. 'Oh, Stella. You're my best friend. I would never do anything to hurt you.' She put her hands behind her head and took a deep breath. 'And anyway what we *can* do is much better.'

Stella sat frozen, unable to believe any of this, and yet Maggie's voice went on. 'You see we don't need to expose the forgeries, just threaten Pamela with it. It would be the two of us against her and Ben. We're just two gullible girls. It's obvious who'd be believed. She couldn't risk it.'

'No, Maggie.' Now it was Stella who felt like a little girl; a fierce little girl whose best friend had let her down. She clenched her fists to stop herself lashing out at Maggie, tearing at that ponytail. Instead she stood taking deep, deep breaths.

'But why not?' Maggie was saying. 'You've done nothing wrong, and they've both treated you really badly. Just like they did to me. I say they owe us. You need money and so do I. And they deserve to pay.'

Eve

On New Year's Day she woke to the bedroom bathed in the white glow that means snow. Alex was already up, and Ivy wasn't crying.

She had sat on the sofa last night for what seemed hours, staring at the TV flickering away with the sound off and the fire going cold. Then when Ivy stirred and began to whimper she had gone to her before there was any chance Alex would hear. So it was past 3 a.m. before she crawled into bed beside him.

She checked her phone, but there was nothing from Maggie. Alex came in with a tray. 'Ivy's fed and changed, so you can relax,' he said. 'And I've brought the breast pump in case you're feeling uncomfortable.'

She tried to smile, but knew it wasn't convincing. He walked over to the window and pulled the curtains. 'Look at this.' The snow was coming down fast: a drifting white veil. 'Just too late for Christmas, as usual.' Then he moved back and knelt by the bed, kissing her lightly. So lightly she didn't need to respond. 'I'm sorry about last night,' he said. 'I wanted so much for us to have a perfect New Year's Eve and what your dad said spoiled it for me.'

Gulping apple juice – she was very thirsty – she said, 'What exactly did he say?'

Alex sat back. 'Do we have to talk about it now?'

She put down her glass and nodded. 'Just tell me.'

'That you'd had an email from this Maggie and were thinking of going to meet her. He assumed you'd told me already and wondered what we'd decided. I felt like a complete idiot.' He gestured to her plate. 'Eat up before it goes cold. You hate cold toast.'

She tried a piece, but it was difficult to swallow. 'So what do you think?'

He sat on the bed. 'Well if you actually want my opinion ...' His voice had an edge and she felt her jaw tighten. 'I'd rather you didn't see her. Your dad and mum don't seem to trust her and I think you should just let the whole thing rest. Everything you've found out so far has only made you unhappy.' He squeezed her hand. 'But if you do decide to go, I'll come with you, of course.'

'She says she'll only see me on my own.'

'Well that makes it even more important to take someone with you. And meet in a public place.'

She couldn't stop a small laugh. 'I don't think she's likely to be dangerous.'

'You know nothing about her, Eve. You can't take a chance.'

Picking up her toast she tried to quash her annoyance. After all he was right to be anxious. But he obviously couldn't understand how she felt. There was no point in fighting with him. 'Well, I don't have to decide right now.'

It was a white lie, but when he jumped up with a smile she knew she had been right to tell it. 'And we'll open that champagne later on. Start the new year properly.' He bent and kissed the top of her head. 'I was very childish last night. Please forgive me.'

When he left the room she checked her phone. No email from Maggie, but a message from Simon.

I've been staying in Dorset. Driving back tomorrow so wondered if I could stop off to see you. Maybe have an introduction to your new daughter. And your husband of course. No worries if you don't want visitors. Simon XX

225

CHAPTER TWENTY-SIX

Stella

For some reason she hadn't expected rain in Italy, but today it was pouring. The studio hut was cold and water flowed down the big window like a vertical river. With the hints of green from the distant hills behind the glass, it reminded Stella of a fast-moving stream. One of those streams with waving grasses growing in the riverbed.

She was spending most of her time in the studio, painting and painting. But it wasn't going well today. So she wiped her brush, grabbed her sketchbook, and used pastels to try to capture the rain on the window.

Then she sat back on a stool to look at the half-finished painting on the easel. It was of Maggie sitting at the metal table outside the house. She had made the sketches before their argument. But everything had changed since then and the sketches no longer seemed true.

When she'd begged her not to go ahead with the plan to threaten Pamela and Ben about the forgery scam, Maggie had said, 'OK, OK, keep your hair on. It was just an idea.' But Stella couldn't forget it. Couldn't trust her.

And it wasn't the only scheme she had come up with for black-mailing them, was it? More than once she'd mentioned trying to get money out of them by pretending Eve was Ben's daughter.

And of course there was the earlier deception – the way she and Ben had conspired to steal Stella's drawings and make her into a criminal. She moved as far from the easel as she could, squinting to see it better. Why had it never crossed her mind that Maggie was in on the plan to sell those drawings as fakes? And what if Maggie had only sought out her friendship, given her a home, in order to cheat her into making money for them? She could hardly bear it.

At first she had decided to leave right away. Didn't think she could stand being in the same house as Maggie any longer. But she told herself she needed to finish the pictures she'd begun so she would have something to sell in England.

After what she'd learned about Maggie she realized there was no one she could really trust. So she had to learn to trust herself. And if she could do that maybe she could be a good mother.

She had written to Jill and David to tell them how much better she was feeling and that she planned to be back soon. Maggie had taken the post into town and the rain was a blessing because it meant she was likely to be away longer.

Something had become obvious to Stella since her mind had cleared: Jill had always wanted Eve. She probably wouldn't acknowledge it, even in her own thoughts, but the way she had behaved had been designed to shake Stella's confidence in herself as a mother. And to persuade everyone else she was unfit. And it had worked.

Since Stella had found out about Maggie she'd realized how gullible she had been in the past. It was odd, with a mother like hers, that she had been so willing to think the best of people. To think they meant well. She realized now – and in a way it was a relief to accept it – that there was no one she could rely on but herself.

She picked up her palette again. Had to keep going. Told herself not to worry about Maggie's face for now, but to try to recapture the colour of her hair. It was interesting because the sun had turned some of the strands very light.

The door flung open and Maggie stood there wearing a pale cotton raincoat, the shoulders darkened where the rain had soaked through. Her hair was dripping around her face. 'Please come and help me light the fire. The house is freezing.'

It was no good arguing, and Maggie was so chilled she looked almost ill. The rain was easing, but they had to run across the wet garden, mud splashing their legs.

It was even colder inside than out, but she soon got a blaze going. Maggie padded in on bare feet, swathed in a green blanket she must have dragged from her bed. She gave a huge shiver as she plonked down on the sofa. 'I bought a big bottle of Cinzano in town, so get us some glasses and we can really warm up.'

There was no point in going to the studio for a while. When she was interrupted like this she always needed some time to get back in the mood. Besides, she itched to do a sketch of Maggie swathed in the green blanket with her hair dripping around her pale face. Maggie as a mermaid.

When she'd poured the drinks Maggie took a huge swallow, pulling the blanket down to cover her feet. Stella grabbed a sketchbook and pencil from her bedroom and started making little drawings and notes. Maggie was used to her doing it, so she said nothing.

She wasn't sure how much time had passed, but whenever she looked up from her pad Maggie seemed to have a full glass. The bottle was going steadily down. Perhaps *The Drunken Mermaid* might be a good title if she ever turned the sketches into a painting. The thought made her smile and Maggie must have noticed. 'Thank the lord, she's finally cracked a grin. My god, Stella, you've been such a misery lately. What's the matter?'

'Just thinking about work.'

A raised glass wobbled into the air. 'Ah, yes, Stella the young artistic genius. I keep forgetting.'

Stella asked, 'Why don't you try to start something?'

'Told you, I've given up. There's no point.' She was drinking with her eyes closed. A sign she was definitely drunk. 'Do you know why I bought this house?' she said.

'I did wonder.'

Chewing her thumb, Maggie spat out a piece of nail and rubbed her nose. 'It was Ben's idea. We were going to move here together when he'd made enough money and got his divorce.'

This was the first she'd heard of it. 'Why here?'

'Ben says,' a tiny grimace. 'Ben *said* it was the perfect place to open a new gallery. Lots of artists here and more might come if someone with his reputation set up shop. It's not the south of France, but it *is* the Riviera and he says the views are incredible just along the coast.'

Stella didn't speak, and the logs crackling in the grate sounded very loud. Maggie took a drink, but it made her cough and she sat up and put her glass on the floor. When she carried on talking her voice was gruff. 'All that travelling around Europe I did was just a way to pass the time until he could join me.'

She probably should have stayed quiet but she said, 'Did he say he would?'

'When he was hurt I thought it would make him realize he mustn't waste his life. So I came here to wait for him.' Her eyes were still closed and silent tears were running down her face. Her voice had dropped so low Stella could just make it out. 'But he's not coming, is he?' she said. 'He's never coming.'

Eve

Eve told Alex very casually that Simon would be dropping by to see them. After his previous reactions she was wary about how he would take it, but he just said, 'That's nice. You can show the

229

baby off.' Then he kissed her cheek. 'I've been stupid about your friendship with him, I know, but we seemed to have grown apart and I suppose having a new baby has made me feel my age.'

For once there was a parking space outside and they saw Simon's car, a sleek black Mercedes, pull up. Eve was on the sofa holding Ivy who, fed and changed, was looking adorable. So Alex went to the door. A murmur of voices from the hall. Then Simon came in.

It was odd to see him here – he seemed to belong to a separate reality. He leaned over and kissed her cheek. 'And this is Ivy, I take it?'

She gestured to the armchair next to the fire, and when he sat she said, 'Would you like to hold her?' His face changed colour and he looked so alarmed she couldn't help laughing.

Alex came in with coffee, 'What's so funny?'

It was Simon's turn to laugh, stretching out his long legs. 'Your wife is amused because I'm terrified to hold Ivy. I'm not used to babies.'

Alex put down the tray and took Ivy over to him. Their heads almost touched: one very dark, the other gleaming pale in the flicker of the firelight. Alex gave Simon a tiny pat on the shoulder. 'Just relax. You'll soon get the hang of it.' Then he came to sit beside Eve, handing her a mug and squeezing her knee.

Looking down at the baby, black lashes fanning his cheeks, Simon smiled and took a deep breath. 'You're very lucky.'

It was the men who did most of the chatting. They had plenty in common, art in particular, and Simon offered Alex a tour of the auction house he worked for. Maybe they could be friends.

Although Alex asked him to stay for lunch, Simon said he had to be getting back. 'Work tomorrow and stuff to catch up on before then.' As he stood, he caught Eve's eye and she knew he had something private to say.

'I'll see you to the car,' she said.

She slipped on the ice as they crossed the pavement and Simon caught her arm, pulling her close. He was warm and solid and when he looked down at her she felt herself flush. A woman coming towards them glanced over with a smile. Eve moved away.

Hand on the car door, Simon said, 'I assume you've exhausted all the leads to your mother?'

She nodded. 'Looks like it.' Again she was tempted to tell him about the meeting with Maggie, but held back.

Simon came close again. 'Don't forget I'm happy to do a DNA test.'

'Thank you. If James Stone agrees to one as well that could finally clear up the mystery. And for the rest I may have to let it be.' It wasn't quite a lie.

'Do you still think it's Maggie de Santis who supplied the pictures to the Baltic?'

She answered carefully, not wanting to shut him down in case he knew something useful. 'She wrote to Mum and Dad all those years ago that she and Stella had made wills naming each other as beneficiaries.'

He barked out a sharp laugh. 'Very convenient. Although if she did get her hands on some paintings you'd think she would have tried to sell them long ago. And even now they're only in an exhibition.'

'Perhaps she thinks the publicity will raise their value.'

He nodded. 'That makes sense.' His hand was on the car door, but he didn't open it. She shivered and he said, 'It's cold out here. Let's sit in the car for a minute.'

Eve looked back into the living room. Alex must have taken Ivy upstairs or into the kitchen. When they were in the car, Simon gave a little cough and reached out as if to touch her knee, but then drew his hand back. 'I could understand if you wanted to contest the ownership of your mother's works, but if I were you I'd leave it as it is. Especially if the apparent owner turns out to be Maggie.'

Eve twisted towards him. 'I'm not interested in that. If I ever

231

got to meet Maggie it would just be to talk about what happened to Stella.'

Another small laugh. 'I very much doubt you'd get the truth.' He took a deep breath. 'Obviously I'm not her biggest fan, but that isn't just because she had an affair with my dad. She was, and probably still is, a nasty and utterly ruthless woman.'

He'd never spoken so passionately before and she had to know why. 'What do you mean?'

A pause. 'There's something you should know about her. Before Dad's accident she was involved in some kind of art scam with him.'

She moved and this time he did touch her knee, just a fleeting touch to make her listen, but she was very aware of the place where his hand had rested as he went on, 'Then, when Dad was crippled, when they were desperately trying to hang on to the gallery and we were even in danger of losing our home, Maggie tried to blackmail him.'

Another shiver went through her, nothing to do with the cold this time as he carried on.

'My mum only told me about it because I was so angry with them. They always promised the gallery would come to me eventually and I blamed Dad for losing it.'

Long brown hands relaxed on the wheel, expensive watch gleaming on his wrist, but inside she imagined that young boy, lanky and probably with spots, not knowing he would soon be handsome.

He went on, 'I was an arse and Mum must have realized I needed a dose of reality. She admitted Dad had been stupid. But it wasn't all his fault.'

He glanced towards Eve. 'She told me that even though Maggie knew how ill Dad was she threatened to expose the forgery thing unless they made it worth her while.'

Eve gasped. 'What happened?'

Another little laugh. 'What could they do? They had to pay

232

up.' He started the engine, his blue eyes locked onto hers. 'Just remember that about Maggie. Poor Stella was taken in by her, but she was utterly ruthless.'

Stella

At least the coolness with Maggie meant Stella didn't feel guilty about avoiding her. She would wake as soon as it was light. Pull on a thick jumper and wrap herself in a sleeping bag against the chill. It wasn't easy to paint like that but she needed to get maximum use of the daylight.

She stayed in the studio all day only coming out to help with the evening meal and sit having a glass of wine for an hour or so. After that, no matter how much Maggie pleaded, she went back to work.

Luckily the studio hut was fitted with electric light, so she was able to keep going as long as she needed. The finished paintings were leaning against the wall in her bedroom and she realized she might soon have to leave some in the living room. If it hadn't been for her anger with Maggie she would have felt very positive. She was so much more energetic and alive than she had been when she was living with David and Jill.

She had finished work on the Maggie as a mermaid picture and loved the way it had turned out. Although Maggie's eyes were closed in most of her sketches, she had painted them open. Green, slanted and full of secrets. More cat than fishlike. Her hair a mixture of bright red and orange floating around her face, as if submerged in clear water. The blanket became her body. Green, supple, reclining on a rock instead of the sofa, and looking almost like a snake. She had surrounded the rock with waving seaweed and considered changing the title to *Snake in the Grass*. She smiled to herself. Even if she didn't do that it was there for people to see.

She suspected Maggie would hate it.

233

The silence was broken by the sound of a car engine. She peeped out to see a taxi pulling up. Maggie must have heard it too because she was sitting at the garden table. Shutting the door quickly Stella went back to her painting. It had to be someone for Maggie. She had been talking about a guy she'd met in Milan who she hoped would visit.

Voices from the garden, fading as they moved towards the house, then a shout from Maggie. 'Just fuck off.' Things must have gone wrong very quickly if it *was* the guy from Milan. Another voice now, much quieter. Stella couldn't make out the words, but it was unmistakably a woman. She opened the door a crack. Then stopped.

It was Pamela Houghton.

Dressed immaculately in a calf-length white skirt and a blue blouse, blonde hair gleaming, she was taking something from a big white handbag. A large envelope.

They made an almost comical contrast: Maggie, schoolgirl-like in her shorts topped by an oversized green sweater, her little feet bare and dirty, and tall graceful Pamela. And Maggie looked scared.

While she was dithering over whether to interrupt – Maggie did seem very frightened – she must have moved.

Pamela turned. For the first time Stella could understand what people meant when they talked about eyes blazing. She had never seen Pamela look like this even when she had come to accuse her of pushing Ben downstairs. It was strange, because she was so involved in her work that her first thought was how well anger suited her and what a great picture her expression would make.

For a moment they all three stood without speaking. Then Pamela said, her voice low and cold, 'And I hope you're satisfied as well. The two of you have managed to ruin three people's lives.'

Stella looked at Maggie, but Maggie's eyes were fixed on Pamela Houghton, her arms folded, eyes blinking fast.

'Rubbish,' she said. 'You've got plenty. This won't even make a dent in it.' The words were strong, but one of her legs trembled furiously.

Pamela threw the envelope on the garden table so hard it bounced and fell off onto a chair. When Maggie bent to pick it up Pamela walked over to Stella. Glad to be able to hang on to the hut door she just managed to hold her ground, trying to keep her face expressionless, although she could feel the heat rising.

Pamela came so close that when she spoke flecks of spittle landed on Stella's cheek. She forced herself to stay still. 'I don't know which of you is the more despicable, but on balance I think it's probably you. What kind of mother abandons her child and then tries to profit from it?'

Stella went to speak, but Pamela was already striding away and through the gate. A door slammed, an engine started up, and the taxi moved away.

Ben

Pamela was out again. Since that bloody girl, the wretched Stella Carr's daughter, had turned up she'd been disappearing all the time. 'I'll only be gone an hour or so. Mark will look after you.' He was getting tired of hearing that.

He rolled his chair to the window, looking along the street at the all-too-familiar view. He used to love this house, but now he hated it. His prison.

Where had she got to this time?

It was strange how his feelings towards Pamela had changed. The way she'd been since the accident – well how could he not be grateful to her? But she really had no option. Of course he would never give the game away, but she wasn't to know that. And it would kill her if he did.

It worried him when she was out for any length of time these days. She was too prone to taking things into her own hands. And now that girl, the daughter, was opening up old wounds and the blasted Maggie would soon be rearing her ugly head. He was scared Pamela would do something drastic. Couldn't forget what happened in Italy.

CHAPTER TWENTY-SEVEN

Stella

They stood staring at each other. Maggie with that defiant naughty-girl expression Stella used to think so funny. She tossed her head and said, as if talking to herself, 'Stupid bitch. Coming all this way only to cave in.' Then she turned to go back in the house, the envelope full of money clutched in her hand.

'You went ahead with it? You went ahead with the blackmail? How could you?' Stella's voice sounded weak, pathetic.

Twisting fast, eyes wide and angry, Maggie said, 'Because they owe me, of course. And they owe *you*.'

'I told you not to involve me. I want nothing to do with it.'

Thrusting the envelope towards her, and waving it up and down so that some of the notes threatened to slip out, Maggie said, 'Look at it and don't tell me you couldn't use it.'

Stella was still holding on to the studio door. Didn't dare let go in case she grabbed something and threw it at Maggie. Instead she took a deep breath, trying to keep her voice under control. It was hard.

'What did you say to them? That we'd reveal something about the forgeries? Or did you say I'd claim Ben was my baby's father?'

Another head flick as a lock of hair fell across Maggie's eyes. 'Both, of course. Double whammy. My god it must really have pissed her off.' She moved closer, smiling and talking in her friendliest voice. 'But she actually managed to surprise me today. I never thought she'd turn up here. Had to let her know the address so she could send a cheque, but the last thing I expected was for her to arrive on the doorstep.'

Although she didn't want this conversation, Stella couldn't stop herself asking, 'Why did she come? If she was going to pay up, there wasn't much point.'

'Didn't want to leave a money trail I suppose. Cheques can be traced. This way no one need find out. For all I know she hasn't even told Ben, because I addressed my letter to her. After all she's the one with the money.' A mischievous little smile. 'Maybe I should try the same thing on him. See if we can get a few quid out of him too.'

'For God's sake, Maggie.' Stella wanted to shake her, to slap that silly smirk off her face.

But Maggie laughed. 'Lighten up. That was a joke.'

Stella shook her head. Her jaw was so tight. 'Was it? Was it *really*?'

'Yes. And I hate to admit it, but darling Pammy actually scared me a bit, which was obviously another reason for her coming here. She wanted to tell me this was it. Give me dire warnings about what might happen if I tried for more.'

When Stella didn't respond – she knew her face must show what she was feeling, but couldn't find any words – Maggie flapped her hand as if to say *suit yourself* and turned back to the house.

'Better put this away. It's too late to go to the bank today, but I'll do it first thing in the morning.' A chuckle. 'Don't want it getting stolen. You can't trust anyone nowadays.' At the front door she turned. 'It's £10,000 by the way. That's £5,000 for you if you want it. All you have to do is ask.'

Eve

The email from Maggie came on the fifth of January, just when she had begun to think she wouldn't hear from her again.

Dear Eve,

I shall be in Newcastle at the Baltic Gallery on 6th of January. Please let me know what time you would like to meet.

Regards

M.

That was tomorrow and in Newcastle. Eve wasn't even sure she could make it in time. The email must have been delayed. Unless it was some kind of trick, part of a plan to put her at a disadvantage from the start. That was what Alex and Simon would think.

But she looked back at the first message:

I have a lot to tell you about your mother, most of which I'm sure you won't have heard before.

Alex was working in the office, and she called up that she was going to do some shopping, taking Ivy with her. In the heated car, the blue sky made it feel almost summery, although the thermometer told her the temperature was hovering around zero. When she'd done the shopping she filled the car with petrol, telling herself she still hadn't made up her mind, but it would do no harm to have a full tank.

Still sitting on the garage forecourt, she looked at Ivy, who was wide awake, her eyes seeming suddenly very old and wise. 'You're right, baby,' Eve told her. 'I have to go. For us. For you as well as me.'

She emailed back to say she would meet Maggie outside the Stella Carr exhibition at 4 p.m..

And she wasn't going to tell anyone or ask for any opinions. This was something she had to do. And to do on her own.

Stella

As she watched Maggie saunter into the house Stella clenched her fists against the rage that boiled up from somewhere deep inside. The heat of it filled her lungs so she was gasping for breath and even the veins in her neck seemed to throb.

Maggie stopped at the door of her bedroom, looking back to smile at her, and that was it. Stella ran in and grabbed her arm, struggling to keep the bitterness out of her voice. 'OK, if half the money is for me I'll take it now.'

She could see from Maggie's face that she hadn't disguised her feelings well enough. A sly smile. 'And if I do give it to you what are you planning to do with it?'

It was no good lying. 'If you must know, I'm going to find Pamela Houghton, return it and tell her I had nothing to do with your horrible plan. Ben is not my baby's father and I won't support you with the forgery scam. I wouldn't be surprised if she comes straight here after that demanding the rest back.'

Now she'd said it a huge sense of relief came over her. She let go of Maggie's arm. 'If you don't give it to me, I'll still tell her and suggest she goes to the police.'

Maggie clutched the envelope to her chest with one hand while the other rubbed the place on the top of her arm where Stella's fingers had left red marks. 'Don't be ridiculous. She won't thank you. And if she did go to the police, do you think she'd leave you out of it?' When Stella didn't answer she came closer. 'Anyway I know you wouldn't do that to me. I was trying to help you. I'm your friend after all.'

Another of those surges of anger, this one so fierce it scared her. Maggie blinked and stepped back. 'Are you my friend?' she asked. 'Were you ever *really* my friend? I've been asking myself that over and over and I don't think so. You only ever wanted to use me. What an idiot you must have thought I was. Probably laughed about me with Ben. I can hear you saying it: "I've met this common little girl. She's stupid, but has a talent for copying. I'll take her in. Get her to trust me." And you were right. I was so gullible. I believed you liked me.' Her voice broke and when her eyes filled she wasn't sure if the tears were of misery, frustration or anger.

Maggie went to touch her. To try to get her onside again. But thought better of it and stepped quickly away and into her bedroom. When Stella tried to follow the door was locked.

It was no good trying to reason with Maggie any longer. She knew she had to find Pamela right away, because she might not be staying in town, and anyway the anger that was fuelling her probably wouldn't last. So she went into her own bedroom, grabbed her bag and a sweatshirt. As she left the house a gust of wind caught the front door making it slam behind her, and Maggie must have heard because before Stella reached the gate she had caught up with her.

This time it was Maggie who grabbed *her* arm. 'Please, Stella, don't be stupid. You're not thinking straight. Let's talk.'

The anger was still there, stronger than ever. She shook her head, 'Oh no. You're right about me being stupid, but that was before. As soon as I found out about the two of you and your forgery game I should have told the police. And whatever Pamela says I've a good mind to go straight back to England tomorrow and do just that.'

She tried to shake off Maggie's hand, but Maggie came close, her face flushed, eyes flaring. 'I don't believe you.'

Stella smiled. It was such an obvious bluff.

The smile must have infuriated Maggie because her fingers bit deeper into Stella's flesh. It hurt but she wasn't going to show it, waiting until Maggie released her to walk away.

Maggie called after her, 'Don't do it, Stella. Don't you dare do it.'

Eve

She had to go. And quickly. Before they woke up. But still Eve stood by her daughter's cradle, looking down at her in the glow of the night light, longing to stroke the warm little head once more. To run her finger down Ivy's fat cheek and across her tiny damp mouth. The baby snuffled, and shifted and Eve held her breath. It was midwinter and still dark outside, but morning was on its way. She had to go now or it would be too late.

She crept barefoot past the bedroom where Alex was sleeping, but didn't look in. She had left a note on the kitchen table.

Dearest Alex,

I'm going to meet Maggie. I'll call you later. It's better if I do this on my own. Then it will be over. I'll have found out everything I can and be able to put it behind me. Please don't tell Mum or Dad. It will only upset them. Give Ivy a kiss and tell her I'll see her soon.

I love you. Eve XX

There was nothing more to do.

In the glimmer of the street lights the pavement had a frosty glitter and she told herself to concentrate. It wouldn't do to fall.

Once, she thought she heard footsteps behind her and stopped, holding her breath. The footsteps stopped too and she looked back down the street. There was a shape, totally still, under a tree at the end. It could be a figure, but might just be a shadow. And she needed to hurry.

The car windows were thick with white and she used the de-icer and scraper as quietly as she could. The rucksack she'd packed with a few essentials was already in the boot, so all she had to do was to climb in and start the engine. But when it was humming she sat for a moment breathing heavily.

And asking herself if she really wanted to go through with this.

Stella

As she hurried into town, Stella wasn't sure what she was actually planning to do. Pamela had come to the house in a taxi and could easily have driven straight to the station and away. Even if she was still around she could be anywhere in the town. It wasn't that small. And if she *was* here … It was all very well telling Maggie what she planned, but she wondered if she would actually have the nerve to do it. And the idea of flying off to England tomorrow and going to the police herself was ridiculous. How could she persuade them of her own innocence? Still it had been satisfying to frighten Maggie, to feel as if she had the upper hand for once.

The beach and promenade were deserted and Stella guessed it was too early in the year for many tourists. And there she was, unbelievably, at a table in front of a big hotel. Sunglasses on top of her head, long brown legs crossed elegantly at the knee as she talked to a waiter. Stella froze then moved slowly into the doorway of a little shop. When the waiter had gone Pamela slipped her sunglasses down onto her nose and looked out to sea.

A breath – *come on you've got to do it* – and she strode forward trying not to think of anything. Just to focus on getting there. 'Do you mind if I sit here?'

Pamela stared and without waiting for an answer Stella took a plastic chair. Pamela looked around and glanced back at the hotel.

'It's just me,' Stella said.

Pamela adjusted her sunglasses and folded her arms tight across her blue linen blouse. 'I don't know if you've come to gloat or to get more money out of me, but if that's what you're after you're out of luck. There is no more. I tried to explain that to her, your friend.' She jerked her head to indicate the lane that led up to Maggie's house. 'Between the two of you you've ruined our lives.'

It was a relief to feel angry. Made it easier to stand up to her. 'I think most of your problems are due to Ben's behaviour. He's the one who gambled on the stock market. Then decided to get involved with forgery.'

'He certainly made some very poor decisions. Not least with the kind of company he used to keep.' Although her voice had developed a quiver her dark glasses made her unreadable.

Stella started to speak, 'I've come down here to ...' But Pamela talked over her.

'What I can't bear is not just your greed, but the ingratitude. Whatever Ben may have done he also gave you a chance to make a successful career.'

'That has nothing to do with it.' If only the woman would let her speak. Get this over with.

But Pamela carried on, her voice choked, whether with tears or fury Stella wasn't sure. 'I suppose you imagine £10,000 is nothing to people like us. And of course it is nothing compared with everything else we've lost, but it means we're likely to lose our home unless I can persuade my parents to help. It's going to cost a fortune to take care of Ben for the rest of his life. It's so humiliating for him. Can you imagine how it feels for someone like him to have to rely on other people for everything?'

'I'm very sorry for him and for you, but his accident had nothing to do with me. As I keep trying to tell you.'

A sharp crack of laughter.

Stella said, 'I came to explain that I didn't know Maggie was planning to blackmail you and I want no part of it. I've never claimed Ben was my child's father. Maggie and he used my work in the forgery scam, but I knew nothing about it and the last thing I want to do is broadcast it. I'd rather pretend it never happened.' She stopped, breathless, but glad she'd got it said.

Pamela touched her sunglasses as if she was going to take them off then seemed to think twice about it. It looked as if Stella had finally managed to surprise her. But when she spoke she didn't sound relieved. 'And how is this supposed to help?'

'You can demand the money back.'

'And that wretched girl is just going to hand it over, is she? And that will be it?'

Why did she suddenly feel so ridiculous? 'If she doesn't, you can tell the police.'

A sigh as she reached into her bag, took out a tissue and dabbed her nose. 'Oh dear. You're very young and naive, aren't you?' She raised a hand to stop Stella from speaking. 'Going to the police would expose the whole shabby business. Your dear friend knows we can't risk that.'

Although she hadn't meant to say it, Stella couldn't resist. 'Well, as I told Maggie, if you won't do anything I shall speak to them myself.'

Pamela was silent for a long moment and when she spoke her voice cracked, 'You wouldn't do that.' Then the hotel door opened and she stopped abruptly as the waiter came to the table. With a smile at him she sat back, her normally ice-cool complexion blotched pink through its delicate layer of foundation. The waiter placed a tiny cup of coffee in front of her and a bottle of Coca Cola next to Stella. Pushing her sunglasses up into her thick blonde hair again Pamela looked at him. 'No, no.' She thrust the bottle towards him. 'I don't want that.'

He glanced at the scrap of paper on his tray and held it out to her. She waved it away. 'No, I said no Coke please.' He shrugged, took the bottle, and walked back inside.

Turning those blank glasses towards Stella, Pamela said, 'Please tell me you're not seriously thinking of going to the police. If it makes you feel better, I'm willing to believe you weren't party to the blackmail, but it's best for all of us if you let it go.'

In a way it made sense. Who would benefit if she went to the police? She stood to leave, but had to say it before she went. 'I still don't understand why you told Jill I caused Ben's accident.'

Pamela shifted in her seat. 'Please go.'

'Once you explain why you blamed Ben's fall on me.'

Pamela's voice shook. 'If you hadn't come to the house, it wouldn't have happened.'

Stella gripped hard onto the back of the flimsy chair. When she could finally speak she said, 'So you admit I didn't do it?'

Pamela ignored that, her voice bitter. 'Telling him you were pregnant so he had to help you.' She went to pick up her coffee cup, but put it down again. Dark drops splashed down the side. 'When I spoke to Jill she seemed to think you were making a very poor job of trying to be a mother. And now I see you've dumped the child.'

'I haven't dumped my child. I've left her in safe hands for a few weeks. Don't tell me you never went away when your son was little.'

Pamela leaned towards her, speaking in a harsh whisper. 'If you knew anything about being a mother ...'

The urge to shake her was almost overwhelming. Instead she said, 'I wouldn't be surprised if you came back that night and had a fight with Ben yourself. That it was you who pushed him downstairs.'

Pamela stood, knocking her chair over and grabbing her bag. Stella could see her hand shaking. When she spoke her voice was too. 'You can believe what you want.'

CHAPTER TWENTY-EIGHT

Eve

It felt strange to be following the same route to Newcastle, but alone this time. She felt very anxious, wishing this was all over and asking herself again and again if she was doing the right thing.

After a couple of hours she started to worry about a silver Audi with tinted windows that seemed to be keeping pace with her. It was ridiculous, but she was so on edge she couldn't stop herself watching it, wishing she could see the driver. She had left so early the satnav told her she should be in Newcastle in plenty of time, so she pulled into the services telling herself it was nothing to do with that car. She was just so tired she needed coffee and fresh air if she was to keep going.

As she walked through the glass doors she switched on her phone. Three missed calls from Alex. She couldn't leave him worrying, but nor could she face speaking to him. Had to focus. She sent a message.

I'm meeting Maggie at the Baltic. Very public so no need to worry about me. I'll call you later and be back tomorrow. Love you both XXXX

In the Ladies she quickly used the breast pump. There wasn't time to express much, but it would hopefully be enough to stop any leaks. She must try not to think about Ivy. Just for today she needed to do that and not feel guilty.

Instead of going back to the car she sat in the café trying to force herself to eat a croissant. Her phone rang and she wondered if she should talk to Alex. But it was Simon. She didn't answer.

When she was driving again she switched on the radio. After all there was nothing to prepare. The questions had been running through her mind for months: *What was Stella Carr like? How exactly did she die? And did Maggie know who Eve's father really was?* If she could answer those, it might be enough.

But, of course, she hoped for much more. And for the first time she admitted to herself that what she desperately longed to know was if her mother had ever talked about her. And if Maggie thought Stella had loved her.

The traffic was heavy most of the way, but she made good time. Whenever she spotted a silver car she found herself dropping back or speeding up to get away from it, although she knew the one that had scared her must be miles away by now.

The satnav hadn't lied and she arrived at her hotel with a couple of hours to spare. It was the one she'd stayed in with Alex. She wished she didn't need to be away for the night, but knew she would be too tired to drive back straightaway. And she had no idea how she would feel afterwards. At least it wasn't the same room, but she kept expecting Alex to come through the door with a takeaway. She had never felt so lonely.

Then, although desperate for sleep, she rang him. There were more missed calls from him, but he didn't answer.

The first thing she needed was to use the breast pump, and as she did so, she couldn't avoid thinking of Ivy. When she tipped the wasted milk down the sink, a painful lump rose in her throat, but she whispered, 'It won't be long now, baby. I'll see you tomorrow.' It would be the first night they hadn't been together.

She stood under the shower for a long time. When she was dressed again she picked up her phone. Another missed call that must have come while she was in the bathroom, and a voicemail.

Eve, darling, I'm sorry to do it like this, but your mum has gone missing again. Your dad is frantic. She's taken the car so could be anywhere. He wanted to borrow ours to search for her, but I told him you're spending the night with your friend in Brighton. He's managed to hire a car and I'm taking Ivy out in her pram to check locally. Please be careful and get back soon. I love you.

She tried to phone him, but again there was no reply.

It was nearly time to meet Maggie, but if she set off home now she could be back before midnight. She repacked her bag and picked up her keys. But the meeting would only take an hour at most and she could leave straight after. Her mother was in the car, so not walking like before. Dad was probably just panicking.

And over there – she looked out at the Baltic, where the lights were shining brighter as the sky began to darken – over there could be answers to everything she wanted to know.

Stella

It was nearly dark as she toiled up the hill to the house, her mind racing.

Hurrying footsteps from behind. Too fast and too heavy, surely, for Pamela to be coming after her. Besides why would she? Her heart was already thumping from moving so quickly uphill, but now her breath caught and she knew she couldn't avoid whoever was approaching. Best to confront them.

The boy: Simon Houghton.

She breathed again, relieved and not altogether surprised to see him. It explained Pamela's constant looks back at the hotel and, of course, the bottle of Coke. Until now she hadn't realized that was one of the things nagging at the back of her mind. Pamela had brought her son with her, but obviously wanted to keep him out of it. He must have seen Stella from the window. Poor kid no doubt thought it was just a holiday.

At least there was no need to be scared. She slowed her steps and waited for him, smiling as he came close. 'Were you trying to catch me?'

He was panting and she could smell a hint of sweat. 'Yeah. I saw you talking to Pamela.'

She suppressed her smile at how grown-up he was trying to sound. Was sure he normally called Pamela *mum*.

'OK.' Best not say too much. No need to upset him.

He shoved his hands into the pocket of his black shorts, swaying slightly and blinking as a strand of dark hair fell across his eyes. 'I heard what you said. But I knew what was going on anyway.' One hand, fist clenched, came out of his pocket to tap his chest. 'I'm not as stupid as she thinks.'

Poor boy. She touched his forearm. It was very warm and she was surprised at how strong and sinewy it seemed. And he must be as tall as his dad already. She had been going to say she was sure no one thought he was stupid, but bit back on the words. Mustn't treat him like a child. Nothing worse than that when you're fifteen. 'So what did you want to say to me?'

'I know about the blackmail.' In the half-light she could only see the pale oval of his face.

'I'm not involved in that, as I told your mother.'

'Yes, I know you're a good person, Stella,' his voice wavered on her name. 'But you're planning to go to the police about it, aren't you?'

A breath. 'Simon, I don't think …'

His arms were crossed now. 'Please don't do that. They're

250

desperate. We've lost the gallery anyway, but my grandparents won't help us keep the house if they find out what Dad has done.'

This was awful. 'I'm so sorry. And whatever your mother has told you I didn't push your father down the stairs that night.'

A hoarse laugh as he turned away from her. 'I know *that*. Of course I do.' It was just a mutter but it suddenly all made sense.

Without intending to she found she had touched his back. 'Simon?'

And when he turned, speaking in a low gruff voice she knew she was right.

'The way he talked to you. And what he did to you. I was so angry.'

The tremor inside her and the pain in her throat were not for herself. 'I'm sure it was an accident.'

He was looking down. His hair and clothes so dark she could hardly make him out in the dusk. 'He hurt you. I saw him at the gallery that night.'

A flash in her memory of his stricken face, so young, as she left Ben's office with her dress torn and her make-up smudged. 'He upset me, but I wasn't hurt.'

A gleam of white as he raised his head. 'I heard what you said to him and how horrible he was to you. When you'd gone I had to tell him he couldn't treat you like that.'

Of course he had been in his bedroom right next to the landing where she'd spoken to Ben. She should have guessed.

'He was always upsetting my mum and that was bad enough, but you're different. You're young. You didn't have anyone on your side.'

'Oh, Simon.'

'I only wanted to stop him being so cruel to you. To get him to help you, but he just laughed at me.'

'I know.'

'And now he ... now my dad ...' This time the waver in his voice turned into a harsh sob, and she wanted to reach out to him. Tell him it was all right. But she knew it would only make things worse. 'He can't walk. He won't ever walk again. So please don't hurt him or my mum anymore.'

'Does your dad remember what happened?'

'He says he doesn't.' It was almost a whisper.

'Then why don't you tell him. It might make you feel better.'

'I can't.' This time it was low and sullen.

She felt so sorry for him, but he was fifteen and she was tired of people lying to her. She wouldn't do that to him. 'Simon, I have to tell the truth – I have to go to the police – because otherwise I couldn't live with myself. Deceiving people, deceiving yourself, never works in the end.' She shook her head. It was hopeless. She'd said it all wrong.

He moved closer and laid a big, warm hand on her forearm. His voice cracked and became a little boy's again. 'Please, Stella.'

She reached up and touched his damp hair. 'I'm sorry.' He muttered something she didn't catch before she added, 'I have to do what I think is right.'

When she turned away and headed uphill again he didn't follow. She looked back to see him going down. Hands in pockets and head bowed.

Eve

As she left her hotel a silver Audi with tinted windows drove past and she froze. Wished she'd noticed the number plate of the one she'd seen on the motorway. But, no, she was being ridiculous. The car was soon gone, and anyway there were plenty of people about.

She was five minutes early as she crossed the Blinking Eye Bridge. The walkway was separated into two sections. The lower half allowed bikes and the upper, where she was walking, was for pedestrians only. Nearing the end she heard a whizzing sound behind her and a boy skated past so fast he almost collided with

252

a small woman in a black coat. As Eve went to pass her she reached out a gloved hand.

'Hello, Eve.'

Maggie.

Eve looked at her, but she had already started walking towards the Baltic, and Eve could only call, 'Hello.'

Hurrying to catch up she heard Maggie say, 'I'm glad to see you came alone. I wasn't sure you would.' She was trying to connect this figure with the Maggie of her imagination. Or rather the two Maggies from her imagination because she sometimes saw the young woman who had befriended Stella – the vivid girl from the paintings – and at other times someone of her parents' age.

From what little she could see of her, in her heavy coat and black beanie, this woman didn't fit either image. Eve had expected she would be small, like her, because in the picture with Stella they looked to be a similar height. When they got inside and she took the bulky coat off, she also seemed to be as slim as she had been thirty years ago.

She was wearing a heavy white sweater with a roll neck, slim jeans and white trainers. Under her black beanie her hair was light brown, a short pixie cut, with paler threads that could have been natural grey or have been added by a hairdresser.

When they reached the glass lifts Maggie pointed to a set of doors to one side saying, in a slightly gruff voice, 'Let's use the stairs.' She spoke very deliberately almost as if she was unused to English, which might be the case if she'd lived abroad for years.

The stairs, with their metal steps and balustrades, looked industrial enough to have been here when the building was a flour mill, but they could equally have been designed to make visitors think they were original. The foyer area had been quiet, but as they climbed they were so completely alone they might have been the only people in the building, and Eve was glad when Maggie went on ahead. Going up surprisingly fast.

253

It was then, with a little jolt, that she realized something she must have known, but hadn't registered. Maggie was actually a similar age to Alex and years younger than Eve's parents.

It was a long way up. There were two flights of stairs between each floor and when they passed floor two Maggie stopped and leaned on the balustrade looking down. 'So what did you want to ask me?'

It was so direct she couldn't think at first how to answer. She paused. 'About my mother. What she was like when you knew her. What you thought of her.'

'Your mother was a naive young girl who made a few mistakes. And paid heavily for them.' That husky voice sounded bitter.

Eve waited for more, resisting the urge to say, 'And I was her biggest mistake, I suppose,' which was maybe what Maggie was expecting. Instead she said, 'Did you like her?'

A short sharp laugh. 'Oh God, what a question. I don't know. We were close is all I can say. And I probably knew her better than anyone else.'

This was useless. She had to ask it now. 'Did she talk much about me?'

Maggie continued on up and, without looking back at her said, 'No, she didn't.'

Eve felt the tears rise into her throat. It hurt, but she forced them down. To make sure it didn't show. Wasn't going to let this woman know how much it mattered.

She felt sick and wanted the whole thing to be over. Everyone had warned her Maggie wasn't to be trusted, wasn't likely to help her; she had been a fool to come. But she must ask her questions even if the answers weren't what she wanted.

Floor three housed the Stella Carr exhibition, but instead of going through the doors into the gallery, Maggie walked onto the landing and pointed into the stairwell. 'Look down there.'

It was disorientating. Seemed as if they had climbed endless flights of stairs rather than three or four floors. The view down went on forever and when she looked up it climbed just as far. She felt herself sway and gripped the balustrade. Maggie moved so close behind her Eve could feel warmth coming from her.

'It's an infinity mirror,' Maggie said. 'Two mirrors. One at the top and one at the bottom of the stairs giving the impression of a never-ending shaft. The artist calls it *Heaven and Hell*.' She waved her gloved hand and a tiny figure miles down waved back.

Looking down into that endless stairwell Eve shivered.

CHAPTER TWENTY-NINE

Eve

They walked into the Stella Carr exhibition gallery and Eve went straight to her favourite picture: *Maggie and Me*. They weren't quite alone now. There was a man wandering slowly round the room, so they stood looking at the painting in silence. Eve was struck again by how full of life and happiness it was. It was difficult to believe one of those girls had become the dour woman standing beside her.

Whatever she had heard about Maggie it was clear Stella had been very fond of her at this time in their lives. Without meaning to she said what she was thinking. 'I love this one. You both seem so happy.'

Eve was sure she heard Maggie give a sigh. 'We were. Thought we were starting out on a real adventure. In those days we were brave too. Something I haven't been for years.'

The man walked out of the room, and Eve knew there was unlikely to be a better time. 'Did she tell you who my father was?'

Maggie walked over to the glass case displaying the catalogues for the original Houghton exhibition. She tapped her gloved finger over the picture of all the artists together and said, 'James

Stone. They weren't together long, but they were very fond of each other. You should be happy to have him for a father. He's a wonderful artist.'

Eve's breath caught. But she told herself Maggie must have known the question would come. She'd had time to prepare her answer. And the feeling she'd had right from the start was growing stronger and stronger. Maggie might be telling the truth about this, but everyone was right. She couldn't be trusted.

'So it wasn't Ben Houghton?'

Maggie moved quickly away to stand in front of the *Madonna?* painting. The one with the faceless mother and baby on a boat. One of her hands hovered over the frame as if to wipe away a speck of dust. When Eve came close she said, that gruff voice sounding deeper than ever, 'Did your parents tell you he was?'

'No, I just wondered.'

'Well he wasn't. Stella hardly knew him.'

It was very definite and Eve believed her, but why was her first thought that it meant Simon wasn't her brother? She had the strangest feeling about it. Almost as if he was here watching them and had heard it too. She wondered what he would be thinking.

She said, 'Please tell me everything you know about the fire. About what happened to my mother.'

'I remember waking up in hospital. Much, much later. They told me the studio had burned down and Stella was inside. Apparently the fire took hold really fast because of the oil paints and rags soaked in turps.'

She spoke in a monotone, but Eve's own voice wasn't so steady. 'How did you get hurt?'

'They said I tried to help her. The roof collapsed and we were both trapped. I've hated enclosed spaces ever since. But somehow I managed to crawl out.' A pause while she pulled off one of the thick gloves she had been wearing all this time. Her hand was covered with puckered red and white scars and when she flexed her fingers she couldn't spread them completely straight. 'But she was still in there.'

Eve walked out of the room and leaned on the wall near the glass lifts trying to catch her breath.

Maggie followed still flexing her hand. 'There's something else I should tell you,' she said.

When Eve glanced at her pale profile she had a strange feeling inside. Almost as if Ivy was still kicking and squirming in there. But that had been a good feeling. 'What is it?'

'When I came out of my coma they told me the fire was likely to be arson. But the case had been solved already and nothing could be done, because the person who was responsible was already dead.' The squirm inside turned to a shudder. 'They said it was Stella.'

Stella

When she got to the house everything was quiet. There was no sign of Maggie. She tried the front door. Locked. They needed to talk, so when there was no answer, she went round to Maggie's bedroom. The shutters were closed. She circled back to her own room where she always kept the windows partly open. The shutters were fastened tight here too.

The day had been warm, but the evening was cooling fast. Hurrying up the hill had made her sweat and in her damp shirt and cotton trousers she was beginning to shiver. She pulled her sweatshirt out of her shoulder bag. There was nothing for it but to wait in the studio. At least that was unlocked and there was electric light.

The canvas where she had been trying to capture the colours of the rain was on the easel and, although she was anxious, she could see something could be made of it and was soon absorbed. Had no idea how much time had passed. After a while she checked outside, but the house was still shuttered fast. It was obvious Maggie had locked her out. Whatever happened Stella knew they had to talk in the morning and after that she wouldn't be able to stay.

She sat in the old armchair she and Maggie had dragged from Maggie's bedroom a few days ago. 'Stinky old thing. I was going to dump it, but take it if you want.' It was shabby and damp, but luckily the sleeping bag she'd taken in when she started work in the chill of this morning was still on the floor where she'd thrown it. Wrapped in it, and huddled on the chair, she flicked through her sketchbook for inspiration.

A noise from outside.

It must be Maggie, but when she looked out the garden was empty. As she closed the door she saw a flicker of movement through the big glass window. Switching off the light she stood staring into the darkness. It was probably a fox, a bird or even just the breeze, but all the same she was unnerved. She left the light off, waited until everything was still, then made her way slowly back to the armchair, for once sorry about that huge uncurtained window.

Everything was completely silent and after a while she could see fairly well in the dark. There was no one out there.

She was too tired to work anymore so she left the light off, put her head back and tried to relax.

Hot, she was so hot. She threw off the sleeping bag. She'd been dreaming about sunbathing and when she opened her eyes she thought she was still on a beach and a thick sea mist had come up.

But it wasn't mist.

Scrambling from the chair made her gulp in a huge breath that filled her lungs with choking smoke. Pain in her chest so sharp she didn't dare breathe again. And stinging eyes. Boiling tears on her cheeks. A salty taste in her mouth.

As she turned towards the door her foot caught in something. A fold of sleeping bag or a cushion from the armchair. She fell to her knees. *Up, get up, get out.* She tried to run but tripped again and her flailing hand hit something hard. It crashed down on her. The easel.

Falling on one knee this time, her back screeching with pain, she pushed away the easel. Didn't try to stand again. Just began to crawl through the clutter on the floor. Sharp things piercing her knees. Screws, bits of metal or glass. It didn't matter. *Never mind, keep going.*

Crawling through smoke and darkness.

Her head bumped hard against something.

The door.

Oh thank God. Reach up. Reach for the door handle.

Her hand flinched back. The metal was scorching. Pulling down the sleeve of her sweatshirt to cover her fingers, she took hold of the handle again and jerked at it. Nothing. There was no lock so what was it? Another push and a slide of movement. But not enough. Something was in front of the door.

Shoulder against it, she shoved. Shoved as hard as she could. Heard whatever was blocking it scraping the ground as it moved. But then the door stuck again. Still not even a narrow gap to squeeze through. Push again. Push hard.

It was no good. There was a small window along the wall and, *thank God*, she managed to get to it and force it open a crack to suck in some cool air.

Her watering eyes could just make out the grey night time garden. So peaceful.

Then a light. A light from the house. And Maggie. *Thank God.*

But Maggie wasn't moving, and when Stella tried to call out her voice wouldn't work. The words, *help me, help*, were only in her head.

A crash. Something fell from above. A fierce crack of pain in her leg. One of the ceiling joists had collapsed. She tried to move, to pull herself to the door, but her leg was trapped under the wooden beam. She forced out a scream, 'Maggie. Help. Please help me, Maggie.'

Too late.

The blinding pain that struck her head told her it was too late. Even as the blackness swallowed her.

Eve

She had to get away. To think about what Maggie had told her. For some reason she ran up the stairs not down. And found her way out onto a balcony. Night came early at this time of year and the grey twilight was already deepening to black, the windows of the buildings opposite standing out as bright rectangles in the gathering dark. The curves of the Blinking Eye were lit up. It was still busy with people crossing back and forth.

She wanted to cry. She'd left her baby and Alex, wasn't there when her mum and dad needed her. And all for this.

The balcony door swung open. Maggie. She was breathing heavily from running up the stairs, but probably also from the biting cold. No one else was likely to brave the place.

For a moment, looking down the stairwell, Eve had been frightened and maybe that was the point. To intimidate her. But Maggie was over twenty years older. She surely couldn't be a physical threat. Still it was good to see the clear panels stretching above the actual barrier.

Maggie went to the front of the balcony pressing herself against it. Eve couldn't see her expression and her voice was emotionless. 'It wasn't true, Stella didn't kill herself, but it's what you might be told, by other people.' A little noise that could have been a laugh or a sob. 'They tell so many lies about Stella.'

'Will you tell me the truth then? About the fire?'

Maggie pointed to the side of the building. 'In spring and summer those ledges are full of little seabirds' nests. The kittiwakes treat the place as a cliff edge and come back year after year to lay eggs and raise their chicks. Nature is amazing, isn't it?'

She mustn't allow herself to be distracted. 'Please tell me.'

A headshake. 'I only have sketchy memories of it. I was injured and spent a long time in hospital afterwards. Haven't wanted to think about it since.'

Looking at Maggie's back as she stood so calmly staring out over the Tyne, Eve knew she had to try to jolt her into being more forthcoming. The closest she had come to a normal response was when Eve asked her if she liked Stella. Something she probably wasn't prepared for. So she said, 'When you blackmailed the Houghtons was my mother involved as well?'

Maggie half-turned towards her. Eve could see the white plumes of her breath. She waited, forcing herself to keep quiet. Finally Maggie said, 'Who told you about that?'

'Does it matter?' She could be cagey too.

'It had to be the Houghtons. Who did you talk to? Pamela or Ben?'

'I spoke very briefly to Pamela.' It seemed best not to mention Simon. 'And I just want you to tell me if Stella was involved.'

Maggie shivered and squeezed her gloved hands together. 'She wasn't. In fact she tried to stop it.' The hint of a laugh and a mumble under her breath. 'What a fool.'

Eve clenched her fists. 'You thought she was a fool for trying to do the right thing?'

'She was. Pamela called her young and naive and that was one thing she was right about.'

'I've been wondering if the money you sent my parents was what you got from the blackmail.'

Maggie walked to the other side of the balcony, stamping her feet and pushing her hands deep into her pockets. 'After the fire it felt tainted. I offered to return it, but Ben, naturally enough I suppose, thought it was a trick. So I decided to do some good with it.'

If she was expecting a thank you Eve was going to disappoint her. 'Then Stella didn't inherit it, like you told my parents? Did she actually make a will?'

'Why would she? At twenty-one you don't think about things like that. And she had nothing except her paintings, which as far as she knew might turn out to be worthless.' A long pause during which Eve could hear her breathing harder, as if the climb up the stairs had suddenly caught up with her. 'The only thing she had in the world was you.'

Eve almost blurted out, *and I was something she didn't even want*. But she stopped herself. Instead she said, 'In case you're thinking I might want to claim her work, you needn't worry. I'll never be able to get to know my real mother, but you were her friend and the only thing I want from you is to learn as much about her as I can.'

Maggie turned away again, gazing down towards the Tyne Bridge and the other bridges crowding the river. A train was passing over one of them. She spoke so quietly Eve could only just hear. 'What did your parents tell you?'

'That she was young and alone and couldn't support a child.' If Maggie didn't know about Stella almost killing them both, she wasn't going to reveal it.

A long silence. Eve could hear Maggie breathing hard and fast, but she fought to stifle the sound of her own breath. Something important was coming. She knew that. Finally. 'You mentioned the pictures. Well, they belong to you. Stella wanted you to have them. They were painted for you.'

Eve forced back the exclamation she had almost let out, sure there was more to come. But Maggie seemed to freeze, staring over the river, remembering something or perhaps seeing something that Eve was too far back to spot.

Then, in one swift movement, Maggie was in front of her grabbing hold of her forearms. Her grip was incredibly strong despite those scarred hands, and Eve heard a gasp of fear. It had come from her own throat.

Maggie's eyes were twin slivers of pale brown glass and she spoke in a gush of chilled breath. 'You wanted to know if your mother ever talked about you and I told you the truth. But the reason she didn't talk about you was because it was too painful. And I know, I absolutely know, that not a moment went by when she wasn't thinking of you.'

It was so surprising Eve felt almost as disorientated as when she'd looked down the stairwell into the infinity mirror. As quickly as she'd done it, Maggie let go, talking even faster. 'Wait here. I'll be back.'

And she was gone. Through the balcony door and away.

Eve rubbed her hands over her forearms. Feeling a tingle where Maggie had gripped her. What had just happened? The words and that touch had been so surprising. Even Maggie's accent seemed subtly different. It was as if she had suddenly become another person.

But no.

No. It wasn't possible.

Her mind went back over the last hour. Over everything Maggie had said, everything she had done. The way she had looked. The way she'd avoided looking at Eve.

She ran down to the Stella Carr exhibition. To the *Maggie and Me* picture. In her mind they had always come as a pair: Stella and Maggie.

The catalogue in the glass case. Just now when they stood together looking at the group photo Maggie had been pointing at James Stone. Her thickly gloved left hand was flat on the glass so it covered the opposite page. The photo of Stella and Maggie together.

Stella and Maggie. Maggie and Stella.

CHAPTER THIRTY

Ben

Didn't drink like he used to. Couldn't imagine anything less dignified than falling out of a wheelchair because he was soused. Scrub that, there were plenty of things less dignified, but falling out of the wheelchair drunk would be just the excuse Pamela needed to deliver one of her lectures. But he needed a Scotch now.

These past weeks had been a nightmare. Having to manage without Mark while he kept an eye on that wretched girl was bad enough, but Pamela was no use to him either. All she did was talk about it. How to stop the interfering little cow from going any further.

The mother, Stella, had been a big enough nuisance, but Pamela thought she'd dealt with that.

It wasn't until the other night that she told him the truth. 'What were you thinking?' he shouted at her. 'It was bound to come back and bite you.'

Of course that gave her the chance to go on her usual rant about how it was all his fault. He started it. And he couldn't disagree.

But why, oh why, had Simon got himself involved with the daughter? He had always been a bloody idiot, but this beggared belief. Ben had asked him over and over what he thought he was playing at. 'I'm trying to help her, Dad. She's suffering and she's a complete innocent in all this.'

Sentimental rubbish. Ben knew he'd been besotted with the girl, but that was when he was a kid. He was a grown man now and thanks to inheriting his father's looks he could probably have any woman he wanted.

Ben said they should tell him the truth, but Pamela, wanting to protect her darling boy as usual, begged him to go along with her story. The less Simon knew the better.

But then Pamela heard from that silly woman Jill – just as well they'd kept in touch. Apparently the daughter was planning to meet Maggie (or so she thought). Jill had tried to persuade her not to go, but wasn't sure it had worked.

Mark was watching her movements, but what could he actually do?

So finally Pamela agreed they needed to tell Simon everything. It had taken days to get in touch with him. At one point Ben nearly said it in a voicemail, but stopped himself just in time. Wouldn't do to let that go on record.

When Simon finally picked up Ben had launched right in. 'You're still seeing this Stella Carr's daughter, aren't you?' No answer, but he could just imagine the mulish expression on Simon's face. 'Well she's been in contact with Maggie de Santis and they may be going to meet.'

'So what?'

'You need to try to persuade her out of it.'

'I couldn't even if I wanted to.'

'You're not still convinced she's your sister, are you?'

'If you say she isn't, I have to believe you. And I'm fine with that because it means I can be her friend.'

Ben took a deep breath. 'There's something I have to tell you.

It's something your mother should never have kept from us. At the very least she should have told us about it when that girl turned up asking about Stella.'

'What are you saying?' Simon's voice had changed and Ben wondered if he'd guessed what was coming.

When he told him, Simon had said nothing and rang off without a word.

Ben poured another drink wondering if he'd made a serious mistake.

Stella

Light. A window. Red flowers in a vase, the clear water around their stems glinting in the sunlight.

Thirsty. She was so thirsty.

A voice said. 'Maggie?'

She squinted. Too bright. Her eyes hurt. She blinked the tears away and the man came into focus. Grey hair, smiling face.

'Hello, Maggie. It's all right. You're quite safe. You were in an accident. A fire. Do you remember?'

A bolt of panic. 'No.' *Help me.* She stared at the man. White coat: a doctor. Italian accent. For some reason she was pleased she had recognized that. He told her to relax. Called her Maggie and, yes, thank God, the name meant something to her. Maggie.

She must have slept because there was a lit lamp beside her bed and the window was dark. A woman was holding a cup to her sore lips. The water cool and soothing. 'Thank you.' It was a croak. The woman said something she didn't understand, but the kindly tone made tears run down her cheeks. The woman dabbed them with a tissue, then smoothed her bedclothes.

The man with grey hair again. 'Do you know where you are, Maggie?'

A tiny thrill of pleasure at knowing the answer. 'Italy. Hospital.'

'That's right. Well done.'

267

'How long?'

He touched her shoulder. 'Quite some time, but don't worry about it now.'

'What happened?' The words came out more easily and clearer this time.

'There was a fire.' A flash of a room with a big window, but her mind flinched. Didn't want to see that.

'But you'll be all right. And your friend, Pamela, will be here to see you soon. Just rest now.'

Rest, yes. She closed her eyes, giving in to the huge weariness that swept through her and slipped back into the lovely dark.

Eve

She had to catch up. Had to find out if she was right. If this woman calling herself Maggie was really Stella. Her mother. No time to think why she had deceived everyone all these years or to wonder why she would want to meet Eve now.

A pause at the lifts. Trying to look through the glass partitions to see if Maggie – Stella – had reached the foyer. It was no good; she couldn't see. But the lift was here and if Maggie was using the stairs again Eve might beat her. Inside she pressed the button. Still looking down.

Her phone rang from her pocket. *Dad.* She had to answer. 'Have you found Mum?'

'No. Oh Eve, I'm so scared.'

'But it's not like last time. She's in the car. She'll be all right.'

Out of the lift, phone still to her ear, she ran outside. Scanned the bridge. The walkways. Even the other side of the river. No small black-coated figure.

David was still talking. 'She left a letter,' he said.

A sickening realization. She walked slowly back inside. 'What are you talking about?'

His voice was so choked she was sure he was crying. 'She's

terrified at the thought of you meeting Maggie. Says she'll tell you all kinds of lies and you'll end up hating Mum.'

She'd come to a few steps just before the lifts and the doors to the stairway and her legs were so weak she had to sit on them. It was hard to catch her breath, let alone speak. 'What kind of lies?'

'About what happened when Stella was living with us.' A choked gasp.

'Dad?'

'She's afraid Maggie will say that the story about Stella trying to hurt you wasn't true.'

What had Maggie – Stella – said? *They tell so many lies about Stella.* Eve forced herself to stand and head for the stairs. 'Tell me the rest, Dad. Everything.'

She started walking up again. Phone still tight against her ear. The stairs seemed to have grown steeper.

'She admits she gave Stella some of her own tranquillizers and sleeping pills. Put them in her food or drink because Stella refused to take the ones the doctor prescribed.'

Oh God! She paused to breathe, leaning against the wall, as he carried on.

'They did advise her to take something, Eve, that's true. But of course it was wrong to do it without her knowledge.'

She had to ask. 'And the other thing? Do *you* think Mum was lying about Stella trying to kill me?'

Another gasp. 'I don't know. Don't know what to think. But Jill loved you so much, Eve. Wanted you so much. And really believed we were the best parents for you.'

It was all the answer she needed.

After a minute she began to trudge up the stairs again. It was probably too late to catch Stella if she'd run away, but maybe she'd really gone back to the balcony. 'When you find Mum …' she just stopped herself from saying, *if* instead of *when*, 'don't say you've told me about the letter. We can sort that out later.'

'Yes, you're right, but I had to tell you. There've been too many lies.'

There was nothing to say to that. 'I'll get home as soon as I can. And it'll be all right. Mum wouldn't do anything silly.'

She stopped on the landing of the third floor. The same spot as on the way up – so long ago. And looked down into the infinity mirror. A tiny movement flickered in its depths. In Hell. But of course the flicker wasn't really coming from below, but from high up. She craned her neck.

Two people were standing on a landing above her. And she recognized them both.

Stella

Looking out from the balcony and seeing Simon Houghton walking across the bridge to the Baltic had been such a shock she could only think about getting away before he spotted her. She ran down the stairs telling herself it should be all right. He'd probably come up in the lift and go to the Stella Carr room. She couldn't let him see her. She might have been able to fool Eve for a while, but she couldn't hope to fool him. And she mustn't let him tell Eve. Had to do it herself. Explain properly.

She'd made a complete mess of it so far. Should have come out with it right away, but she'd been so scared. Wanted to know what Eve had heard about her, what they'd told her, first.

Eve must have met Simon when she talked to Pamela. He could have no idea she was alive and Maggie dead, but she knew he would recognize her immediately.

Footsteps below her on the stairs. She stopped. Peeped over the side. Someone tall with dark hair. It had to be him. *Go back up.* Her shoes had soft soles and she was small enough that he might not spot her if she kept close to the wall.

Up, up and a pause to listen. The footsteps had stopped. A moment to breathe and then on again. As far as she could. To the top landing. Floor five. One flight above the balcony floor where she'd asked Eve to wait. She came round the last corner.

And there he was. Leaning on the balustrade.

He must have glimpsed her when she looked down at him, then left the stairs and taken the lift the rest of the way. At least Eve wasn't likely to come up here.

He was taller and even more handsome than Ben had been. But his smile and bright eyes were still those of the boy she remembered.

'Hello, Stella,' he said. He didn't sound at all surprised.

She carried on up, her legs suddenly heavy. 'Hello, Simon.'

When she got to him he bent to kiss her cheek just as if this was an ordinary meeting. He smelled fresh, of shampoo and washing powder.

'How long have you known?' she asked.

He laughed. 'Just a few hours. Can you believe that? My dad finally told me what my mother did. All this time I thought you were dead. Do you know I cried for you night after night for months afterwards?' He tapped his knuckles against his mouth. 'You were my first love.'

'I'm sure there have been plenty more since.'

His voice was suddenly different – hard. 'I'm not my father. Nothing like him.'

'I didn't mean that.'

Then he said, 'Your daughter is just as lovely as you were, you know.'

Take care. Something was wrong.

'It's just a shame about the husband,' he said. 'You wouldn't like him.'

She moved slightly away. Best not to respond to that. But he wasn't paying attention anyway. He was looking down the stairs.

'And here she comes. The beautiful Eve.'

When Eve was a few steps from the landing she stopped. 'Simon? What are you doing here?'

'Can you believe it? My dad has had someone following you. And I followed *him* today. Had to make sure you were safe.'

The footsteps. The silver Audi. Ben must have posted the Instagram comments as well.

Before she could say anything he waved his hand in an introductory flourish. 'Have you met your mother?'

So he knew as well. His tone was odd. Didn't sound like him. But he didn't matter for now. She could only look at Stella.

Their eyes met for a long, long, moment and Eve whispered, 'I know.' Even in the low light of the stairway she could see Stella's eyes were glassy. With tears? She wanted to ask so many questions, but this wasn't the place for them. She focused on her mother's face. *Her mother. This was her mother.* 'Shall we go back to my hotel and talk it through properly?' Her voice wobbled. 'You owe me that at least.'

Stella stepped forward as if to come to her. 'Yes, let's do that.'

But she stopped because Simon had taken her arm. 'I hope I'm invited.'

Eve could see Stella trying to pull away, but Simon didn't let go. What was wrong with him?

'I think my mother and I need some time alone first,' she said. She took a step up.

But Simon put his head to one side, looking almost like the young boy he must have been. 'That's hardly fair. After all I've known you both much longer than you've known each other.'

A shout and a teenage lad ran up behind Eve and into the gallery spaces on this floor. He was chased by another, calling in some language she couldn't identify.

When it was quiet again Simon laughed and carried on as if

nothing had happened. 'In fact, I haven't just known you both. I've loved you both.'

This must be some kind of weird joke. Eve said, 'Simon?' But he either didn't hear or ignored her.

'And I need to be there to protect you. Because I know how Stella treats people who love her. What she makes them do.'

Stella said, the tiniest tremor in her voice, 'You go on, Eve. I'll meet you in the café in a few minutes.'

Simon was still holding her arm, and Eve felt a slow curdling in her stomach. This was all wrong. 'No, I'll wait for you.'

Stella made to move again, but Simon pulled her back.

Eve swallowed hard. 'What's the matter, Simon? Why are you being like this?'

A headshake. 'You know why. She must have told you by now.'

Stella's voice was very quiet. 'I haven't told her anything about you.'

He ignored her. Sky-blue eyes gleaming behind those black lashes as he stared down at Eve. 'What she won't have told you is that everything I did was because of her. She made me do it.' Now he sounded like a teenager too.

Stella spoke fast. 'It's all in the past, Simon. It doesn't matter.'

But he was only talking to Eve. 'What I did to my dad was because I couldn't let him treat her like that. I wanted to help her, but she was going to tell him I pushed him downstairs. There was no need for that. To make my dad hate me.'

Eve's heart stumbled as he turned back to Stella, grabbing her other arm and twisting her towards him. She ran up the final steps, but Stella said, 'It's all right, Eve. Go down.' Then very quietly to Simon. 'I would never have told Ben it was you. It wasn't my place to do that.'

He bent to talk into her face. So close he might have been about to kiss her. But his voice was harsh. 'You're lying. In Italy you said you were going to tell about everything. Didn't care what harm it did.'

273

Eve was frightened now. She touched his arm. 'Simon, you're hurting her.'

He shrugged her hand away, swinging Stella round so that her back was against the balustrade. 'And all these years I thought you were dead. That I killed you. I never wanted to do that. Just to scare you. Destroy your paintings. Never wanted to hurt either of you.'

Eve froze. *Oh God.*

But Stella sounded icy calm. 'All right. All right. Let's go somewhere and talk. You were just a young boy. I understand.'

He shook his head so that a lock of black hair fell across his eyes, and with a sudden thrust Stella was in the air. For one unreal moment it looked to Eve as if they were dancing. He lifted Stella so high her feet dangled helplessly and her head was over the stairwell.

'Simon, don't, for God's sake.' Eve scrabbled at his jacket trying to find something to grab on to, as Stella shouted, 'Get away, Eve.'

A thunder of footsteps behind them and the two boys from earlier rushed back and then down. One cried out as they stopped, 'Jeez, man.'

Simon wasn't moving. Still holding Stella aloft so they seemed like some terrible statue. Eve couldn't see the boys, but she heard them breathing. One of them said, 'No, man, no.' It was enough to make Simon look at him and for Eve to reach out and grasp her mother's leg with one hand and Simon's arm with the other.

Her face pressed into his back, nose and mouth smothered in the rough cloth of his jacket, she yanked so hard she heard Stella scream, but didn't dare let go.

For long nightmare moments the three of them swayed back and forth gasping and grunting. Then a brutal kick to her knee. Searing pain. Her hands dropped and she stumbled to the edge of the landing.

Unable to turn, she was toppling backwards down the metal

stairs. She clutched the balustrade. *Thank God.* But her hand slipped and she was falling, falling. Slamming into something.

Too warm and cushioned to be the landing. She'd collided with the boys. She fell to her knees, pain shooting through her body.

Stella. Had to get up to her. Jerking the boys' hands away she was half running, half clambering back up. Saw Stella kicking out wildly. Simon struggling to hold her.

An agonized moan.

He doubled over. Hands on his knees. And Stella was on the ground crawling away.

Eve reached out for her, dragging her close. *Thank God. Oh thank God.* They clung together reeling back and almost falling. Managed to stagger down to where the boys were standing. One of them kept saying, 'Jeez, man, jeez.'

She looked up at Simon. He was upright again but wasn't moving. Panting and staring ahead as if in a trance. 'Simon, come down. It's all right.' Her voice trembled and she could feel Stella shaking too.

Stella said, 'Don't, please don't.'

For a moment Eve wondered what she meant. Until she saw Simon hoist himself to sit on the balustrade.

One long look towards them, blue eyes glinting. A little smile playing on his lips. Then he stretched out his arms. Like a bird. Or an angel.

And was gone.

The crash came almost at once. Although the infinity mirrors made it appear to be an endless drop, it wasn't that far after all.

But it was far enough.

CHAPTER THIRTY-ONE

Stella

One of the boys shouted, 'Don't look. You don't wanna look.' But Stella made herself go back up, her knees trembling, and stare down. The mirror had cracked. One huge jagged crack. He was face down. So far away. And so many of him repeated into infinity. The beautiful red pool of his blood surrounding each image, over and over down into Hell.

Eve had come up beside her. Her voice quivered. 'I trusted him. This is my fault.'

Stella took her daughter's hand. In spite of everything she wanted to bring it to her mouth and kiss it. But she just squeezed and said, 'No, it isn't. You're the only innocent one.'

'Why did he do it?' Eve must have heard Simon's words, but when she looked at Stella her face was a little girl's asking her mother why bad things have to happen.

Stella's heart shuddered. She swallowed down on what felt like shards of glass, as if splinters of the mirror had flown up and lodged there. Then whispered, 'In Italy he more or less told me he'd caused his father's accident. He started the fire to try to stop me revealing that and reporting the forgery scam.'

'Did you know it was him? The fire I mean?' Eve choked on a sob, and Stella touched a finger to her soft cheek to wipe away a glistening tear.

'No. He obviously thought I saw him that night, but I didn't. I always imagined it was Maggie in one of her fits of anger. Regretting what she'd done when she realized how bad it was.' Now tears filled her own eyes. Hot painful tears. *Poor, poor Maggie.* 'She tried to save me. Must have dragged away whatever he'd put in front of the door. Got into the hut. My leg was stuck under something, so she must have moved it, and somehow I crawled out.' A flash of Maggie in her shorts and vest, a smudge of dirt on her face, smiling that naughty-girl grin. It hurt. 'But she got trapped.'

She pulled Eve closer. 'Let's go down. We'll have to talk to the police. But keep it simple for now. Don't tell them what he said yet. I need to explain a lot of things to you first.'

Eve

Someone had locked the doors into the gallery on their floor and as they went down they saw all doors on the successive floors were closed. The boys ran on ahead chattering wildly together, but the stairs swayed under her and she had to catch hold of the metal balustrade. *How was any of this possible?*

Stella put her arm round her waist holding her close. 'We'll talk. Make sense of it.' There was a crack in her voice.

At the bottom of the stairs three people were crouching on the lowest mirror. Looking at what had been Simon. Trying to help him, although it was too late. His blood, so bright, spread out over the shining surface. She had an urge to go to him. Brush back his dark hair and tell him to get up. He was all right.

Stella pulled her towards the door. Her voice only just audible. 'Poor unhappy boy.'

Then Eve thought of what he'd done, what he'd tried to do,

and shook her head. 'But he hurt you so much. And tried to do it again. And Maggie. What about Maggie?'

Her mother said, 'I know. But it's over now.' She took Eve's hand, 'Let's go.'

The foyer, which had been almost empty earlier, was full. People milling about trying to see into the stairwell. Lights flashed outside. Police and ambulance.

Without knowing how she got there she realized they were in the café and someone had put a cup in front of her. Her hand shook so much she couldn't pick it up.

She closed her eyes, leaning back. Holding tight to her mother's hand.

CHAPTER THIRTY-TWO

Eve

They had to talk separately to the police. The officer who interviewed her was very kind. Said they would do this as quickly as possible. It was difficult to get through it, but in one cynical part of her brain she realized her obvious distress meant she would only be expected to stick to basics. She said she knew Simon, although not well. 'Simon met Stella Carr and her friend, Maggie, years ago, as did my parents. On the landing he had seemed distraught, was saying all sorts of wild things, before he jumped.'

The officer said, 'Sometimes there is no obvious explanation.'

So she'd accepted it as suicide. Which of course it was. And if her mother wanted her to leave it at that for now, she had to trust her.

They met in the foyer; their hands coming together as naturally as if they had always been connected. Eve could feel the ridges of puckered scars on her mother's skin and fresh tears came to her eyes. Stella already looked different to her. How had she not seen it from the start?

Pushing through the crowds still milling outside, past the

emergency vehicles, they walked across the bridge. The winter night was bitterly cold and they headed to Eve's hotel.

In her room Eve sat on the bed and Stella on a chair facing her. She threaded her scarred fingers together. 'There's a lot I need to explain, I know. That's why I couldn't find a way to get round to it earlier on. I suppose I hoped you'd guess and make it easier for me.' A deep sigh. 'The first and most important thing is that I always wanted to be your mother and to bring you up. But everyone seemed to think you were better without me. So I went to Italy. To clear my head, because when I was with Jill and David I couldn't think straight.'

Eve now understood why that was, but she said nothing because Stella went on, 'I felt so much better once I was out there and I thought it would be all right. And it might have been if Maggie hadn't decided to blackmail the Houghtons.' Her mouth twisted and she looked towards the ceiling. 'After the fire I was in a coma for months. And I woke with no memory, so when they told me I was Maggie I believed it.'

'But why did they think you were Maggie?'

'Pamela came to the hospital right after the fire claiming to be our friend and found out only one of us had survived. They'd already made the assumption I was Maggie because they found her papers in the house. Her passport was pretty old and we looked similar. And nobody knew anything about me. All my stuff was in my bag in the hut, so it was destroyed. Pamela just confirmed the identification. I imagine the temptation was too much for her. She told them neither of us had any family, which was more or less true, so her word was all that mattered.'

'But why did she do it?'

'One thing I've always known is that she wanted to stop me carrying out my threat to go to the police in England and tell them about the forgery scam. But now I realize she knew Simon had started the fire. So that made it far more important to keep me quiet.'

Stella pulled a bottle of water from her bag and took a long drink. 'He must have confessed to her. Probably thought I'd seen him through the hut window or when I looked out of the door before he barricaded it. So she made sure the fire was blamed on me – Stella – instead. And somebody died. If I came round and said who I was, I'd be in big trouble. She hoped that fear would keep me quiet. Stop me from talking about the forgery, but especially about the fire.'

So it was all about Simon. Pamela had to protect him whatever he'd done and whatever the cost.

'I was in a coma and she asked them to contact her immediately if I showed signs of waking. And when I did she was there.' Another gulp of water. 'She was there and I thought she was my friend.'

'When did you remember who you really were?'

'I started to have dreams. Dreams that told me something wasn't right.'

Stella rubbed her forehead as if it hurt and her eyes narrowed as she squinted into the past.

Stella

Crawling. She was crawling through the dark. Sharp things piercing her knees. Pain in her chest. Something weighing on her leg so she couldn't go forward. Heaviness pressing on her chest.

A figure in the mist. She tried to cry out, but no words came. The figure had no face, but she knew who it was. 'Maggie, Maggie, help me.'

Her own voice: a guttural groan straining her throat. Fighting to scream. Fighting to get out of the deep, deep darkness.

And she was out.

In the light surrounded by softness. In a place she seemed to remember. Hospital. That was it. She was in hospital.

A rustle nearby. 'Bad dreams?' English accent. Blonde and smiling. And, yes, she knew her. It was her friend, Pamela.

She nodded, pulled herself up in the bed. 'Fire. I dreamed of the fire.'

'OK. Don't think about that now. Dr Rossi says we can go out for a walk.'

They put her in a wheelchair. She felt sick as it began to move. But then they were outside. Grass. Fresh air. Sunshine. She put her hand up to shield her eyes. And saw the bandages. She began to cry.

Pamela kneeling in front of her, rubbing her knee. 'It's all right, Maggie. The doctor says your emotions will be in turmoil for a while.' That sweet voice, as familiar as anything in this strange world. This was her friend, Pamela. And she would remember her tomorrow. It was something to cling to. Like Dr Rossi and Nurse Gina. She knew them too. And her own name. Her name was Maggie.

Maggie, Maggie. Snatches of recent dreams came back. And with them the fear. That she was lost in the dark and didn't know who she was. She jerked her head. It hurt, but she had to clear it. *She* was Maggie. But in the dream Maggie was far away in the white mist and she was someone else. She groped for the name.

A gentle touch to her head. 'Try to keep calm, Maggie.' Pamela pulled the wheelchair up to a bench and sat next to her.

She closed her eyes and reached into the dark and the mist. *Stella.* That was the name. Her name. *Say it.* 'I'm Stella.'

A glitter of blue before the lids came down to hide Pamela's eyes. Her voice very patient. 'No, darling. You're Maggie and poor Stella is dead.' Pat, pat, on her bandaged arm.

'No.' She pulled away.

Pamela leaned close. 'If you're starting to believe that then I need to tell you something important, *Maggie.*' Stress on the word and a glance around. 'It was lucky I was still in town the day after the fire because, otherwise, they wouldn't have been able to identify either of you. Especially Stella. She was so badly burned they had no way of telling who she was.'

She tried to speak, but it was just a croak.

'I'm afraid the police suspect it was arson. That Stella did it deliberately. I told them that the two of you argued that day. So she wanted to get back at you by destroying the place or even by killing you.'

Think, think. Try to remember.

'You've been out of it for quite a while you know, Maggie, so you're bound to be confused. But poor Stella is dead and that may be for the best. If she was alive, the police would prosecute her, and not just for arson but for murder. She would end up in prison for a very long time.'

It was too hard to think. None of it made sense.

'And soon I'm going to get you released. You can go home. Your house is absolutely fine. You're very lucky to have somewhere to go and money enough to last a while.'

The blue eyes gleamed in the sunlight, 'It's terribly sad, but in a way it's best for everyone that Stella's gone.' She leaned close. 'I'm on your side, you know that, don't you?'

Yes, Pamela was her friend.

'So please don't say anything for now. You'll be out of hospital soon. And we can talk about it then.'

Eve

Her phone rang. Alex. Stella nodded at her, 'Please, answer it.' Then she sat back and closed her eyes, looking grateful to stop.

Alex said, 'First of all, Ivy's great, missing you, of course. Like me. But, Eve, they found your mum.' It didn't sound good. She kept quiet. His voice was soft. 'She was at Beachy Head.'

A cold hand gripped her throat. 'Oh, Alex.'

Very quickly. 'No, no, it's not that. She wasn't near the cliffs. They found her in the car park. Just sitting in the car with some music on.'

A deep breath, but the way Alex had spoken told her it wasn't all right. He said, 'She's in Eastbourne Hospital now. Your dad's with her.' A pause. 'I'm sorry, Eve, but she's had a stroke.'

That icy grip tightened again. 'Is it bad?'

'I'm afraid so. You should get back as early as you can tomorrow.'

'I'm coming now.'

'But you can't be in a fit state to drive.' She was so close to Stella that she must have heard every word because she gave Eve a steady look, and Eve just said, 'I'll be all right. Something's happened here, but I'm fine.'

When she rang off Stella said, 'Where do you need to go?'

'Eastbourne. My mu …' she stopped herself and turned away to grab her bag. 'Jill has been taken ill. It's serious.'

'Well, let me share the driving. I flew in to Newcastle, but I can easily get a plane to Italy from Gatwick. It means we can keep talking.' She looked down, threading her fingers again. 'If that's what you want.'

Eve moved to hug her, breathing in the scent that already seemed familiar. 'Of course I do. Thank you.'

It was easier to listen while Stella drove, although she sometimes spoke so softly Eve could only just hear her over the engine and road noises. 'I didn't remember you. Can't imagine how I could forget you, but it all took so long to come back. And I was medicated the whole time.'

'How did you manage?'

'When they let me leave hospital Pamela took me to Maggie's house. Organized carers.' The tiniest laugh and she looked over at Eve, the oncoming headlights making her eyes glisten. 'I was so grateful to her.'

They were silent for a few minutes, watching the road whizz by. It was a clear cold night; the sky glinting with stars. 'The doctors gave me plenty of pills, so the time passed in a haze. It made it easier. And I was never alone. Pamela came occasionally, but the rest of the time there were nurses. Sometimes Italian, sometimes other nationalities. Never able to speak English.'

Eve saw her flex her scarred hand on the gear stick. 'For a long time I didn't remember you and then I began to. And of course I told Pamela. At first she tried to persuade me I'd imagined you, but then she admitted you'd been adopted and that it could never be overturned, even if I proved I wasn't dead. And I remember her saying this oh so clearly, "Besides you wouldn't want to spoil things for Eve. She's happy and settled with a wonderful family. The family you chose for her yourself." And she showed me a photo of you with Jill and David.' A real tremble in her voice now. 'You did look happy.'

It was difficult to speak. 'And after that?'

'One day I took extra medication – a lot extra – but I survived. And eventually I came back to some semblance of myself. Realized Pamela was no friend of mine and sent the latest nurse away. Told Pamela what I would do if she ever came near me again.' Another tiny laugh. 'And she hasn't.'

Then Eve asked the question that had been bothering her all the long sleepless night. 'But why have you kept quiet all these years?'

'For a long time I didn't want to be Stella. Pamela gave in to my threats, but she'd made sure Stella was blamed for the fire. So I'd have to face that.' She reached out and squeezed Eve's hand, her words choked. 'But mainly it was because I hated the mess I'd made of everything when I was Stella. And there seemed no point in being me again if you were gone.'

It was hard, but Eve knew she had to keep on. She swallowed, trying to steady her voice. 'Did you never want to see me?'

'I did see you.' Eve turned to look at her and Stella's mouth wobbled. 'When I got properly better, I came over. Maggie's passport had run out, but the picture was old and I'd cut my hair and dyed it. So I was able to replace it. I wasn't too worried because I could say I actually believed I was Maggie. But no one queried it anyway. And by then I'd met enough people – ex-pats and British people with holiday homes – who knew me as Maggie, so I had no problem getting the new photo endorsed.'

Eve sat back in her seat, staring out at the road. A breath from Stella. 'I've seen you quite often. The first time you were on the beach with your parents and another little girl. You looked so happy.'

That hurt. The thought that Stella had been so close. Why hadn't she sensed it? 'But when I grew up? Why didn't you tell me then?' This time she knew there was bitterness in her voice.

'I wanted to. Wanted to so much. But the longer it went on the more difficult it became. I was a coward. And if I became Stella again I'd have to face the charge of starting that fire. You would learn about that and I knew you'd have heard other horrible things about me.'

This wasn't the moment to tell her she hadn't been told anything at all. 'Then why now?'

'I couldn't paint for ages. Apart from the confusion I needed skin grafts and so on. Eventually I started doing some little things for a few local craft shops. I was terrified even to try my own stuff. But one day I did try. And it began to work.' Eve's phone rang. 'Go on. Please answer it.'

It was her dad. 'How is she?'

'Not good I'm afraid. When can you get here?'

A glance at the satnav. 'A couple of hours.'

Afterwards Stella said, 'Don't blame your parents. David was kind to me. And Jill – well – you've been happy with them, haven't you?'

'Yes, I have.' It was the simple truth.

They stopped at the services just to swap seats. Eve hadn't slept, but she felt wide awake. The road was very quiet now and it was soothing to simply put her foot down.

As if the conversation had never paused Stella went on, 'Finally I was tired of all the lies. All the little lies I was so keen to fight when I was Stella. I needed to be her again. And I hoped ... I hoped the exhibition might make you want to find out about me.'

Eve laughed. 'Well that worked anyway.'

Stella's voice softened, 'I met someone I trusted and I told him the truth. He's a lawyer and wants to try and help me become my real self again. We knew it would be difficult because of the fire.'

Eve said, 'But now we know who did that. We can tell the police that Simon confessed. Those boys might even have heard what he said.'

A shuddering breath. 'If I'd known he was responsible for Maggie's death, I would never have stayed quiet.'

In the long silence afterwards Eve thought, not just about Stella, but about Pamela and Jill and the way motherhood could be so good, but also so cruel.

All the lies Pamela had told had been for Simon. To keep him safe. And all Jill's lies had been for her. Just to keep her.

Ben

He knew what had happened when he heard Pamela's moans from the hall. Didn't get in the lift and go down. She wouldn't want him. So the police came up to tell him. One of them put his hand on Ben's shoulder. 'I'm so sorry.' When Ben didn't speak he said, 'Is there anything we can do?'

He turned his wheelchair away to hide his face, but managed to control his voice enough to say, 'You can pour me a whisky if you like and then fuck off.'

The idiot made a little sound. Probably about to say he shouldn't have a drink, but thought better of it. Another of those maddening pats on the shoulder forcing Ben to repeat, 'I said *fuck* off now.' And at last he was alone.

Thank God he'd managed to hold it back, but when the door

closed great wrenching sobs tore up from somewhere deep in his gut. As he choked and coughed a flood of tears and drool – his nose was running too – he kept seeing images of Simon. As a baby – Ben had been so proud to have a son. A good-looking little boy always trying to be like his dad, even if Ben had to admit he was a bit of a wimp. Then the lanky, awkward teenager who irritated him. That was where it all went wrong.

Pamela would blame him, of course, and he wouldn't bother to argue. After all, as Simon often said to him, it was his fault in the end. He started the whole thing with his cheating and lies. But it was her too. If she'd loved Simon a bit less and other people a bit more ...

Maybe if Ben had admitted he knew it was his son who pushed him, paralyzed him, he could have said he'd forgiven him and the boy wouldn't have thought he needed to do what he did. Get rid of that bloody Stella Carr.

He wiped his nose and pushed himself over to the lift. Better go down to her. Get it over with. And of course it was all Stella Carr's fault. Maggie he could forgive. She'd got her punishment. But the sainted Stella, who was never prepared to bend the truth even when it was to her benefit, stupid bitch.

It was her fault his son was dead.

CHAPTER THIRTY-THREE

Stella

As they approached Eastbourne Stella began to get anxious. She couldn't face meeting David or even being near Jill. They were off the motorway so there were no services. She checked her phone. 'I see there's an all-night supermarket on our route. If you drop me there I can take a taxi to the station.'

Eve looked over at her. Her voice sounding suddenly very young. 'Can't you stay a day or so? Meet my husband and baby? Get to know your granddaughter from the start.'

A thrill ran through her. It was more than she'd dared hope for. They agreed Eve would come back for her after she'd been to the hospital.

In the café she sat by the window with a coffee she didn't want. She kept telling herself it was true. She had finally done it. Found her daughter and explained it all. And Eve still wanted to know her.

It was dark outside and the winter dawn was some way off. But the headlights of the traffic passing by sparkled. Some emotion she found difficult to identify flooded through her. She was nervous, yes, and excited, but it wasn't that. Then she thought of Eve and the granddaughter she was soon going to meet and realized what it was.

It was happiness. For the first time in so many years she was happy. Completely happy.

Eve

Her mother was in a private room. David came to her at the door and put his arms round her. His breath smelled sour, as he whispered, 'Oh, Eve.'

'How is she?' she spoke softly too.

His face told her everything, but he raised his voice, making it too hearty. 'Well here you are. It's a lot of fuss about nothing, but your mum will be glad to see you.'

Jill was almost as pale as the sheets. When Eve came close one of her hands twitched. Eve took it as she sat on the plastic chair by the bed. 'Hello Mum.' Jill's face was contorted, one eye opened completely, but the other stayed half shut. She seemed to be trying to say something, but it was just a gurgle.

'Wait until you're feeling better.' But that one eye focused so hard on her that Eve knew she was trying to tell her something. And she remembered that Pamela and Jill used to talk to each other. If Pamela was carrying a huge secret for all those years – a secret that affected Eve and Jill so deeply – did she let it slip? Did Jill know Stella was still alive?

They sat, eyes locked, for long moments. But it was too late now and finally Eve sighed and nodded. 'It's fine, Mum.' That seemed to give Jill permission to relax, and Eve sat watching until her breathing slowed and she slept.

David came to the other side of the bed. 'She hasn't been conscious much. Must have heard me say your name.'

After a while Eve moved her hand and Jill's fell from her grasp. She walked over to the door. Her father followed gesturing for her to step into the corridor.

'What do they think?' she said.

'There isn't a great deal of hope, darling. Apparently she's had a series of small strokes over the last few days, possibly weeks, before this big one.' He pressed his palm to his mouth, not quite stifling a sob. 'It's my fault. Should have known she wasn't taking her tablets. Realized how unhappy she was.'

'If anyone's to blame it's me.' She thought but didn't say that Jill had made the decision to stop the medication herself. Knowing what it might mean. When he turned to look into the room she rubbed his back.

'You must be exhausted,' he said. 'You should go home. I'll call if anything happens.'

She went to the bed and touched her mother's hair. 'Goodbye, Mum. See you soon.' Somehow she knew she wouldn't. At the door again she turned. Jill's face was pulled down on one side even in her sleep.

It was so strange. One half was the plump apple-cheeked Mum she knew. The other some grim stranger.

There was a rare parking space in front of the house and Alex must have heard her draw up because he was out of the door and gathering her into his warm familiar arms in moments. She felt as if she had been away from him for weeks rather than hours.

When they broke apart she saw him look at the car as Stella climbed out. 'Alex, it's going to take a lot of explaining and I'm too tired to do it all right now, but let me introduce you to my mother. This is Stella Carr.'

He must have been astounded, but he coped well. After an initial, 'Well. This is quite some surprise,' he shook Stella's outstretched hand. 'Come in, come in.'

Eve smiled at her mother. 'Yes, please come in and meet your granddaughter.'

Minutes later Stella was sitting at the kitchen table with Ivy in her arms smiling and smiling. And it looked as if Ivy was smiling back at her. Alex had put drinks in front of them and was making breakfast as Eve explained the basics of Stella's story.

He said, 'When you told me something had happened at the Baltic I didn't expect this. Thought it was something bad.'

She exchanged a tiny nod with Stella. The news about Simon could wait.

Instead she said to Stella, 'I've been in touch with James Stone.'

Still looking down at Ivy, Stella said, 'I never told him I was pregnant. I've often wished I had.'

'He seemed quite happy with the thought that he might be my father. Said very nice things about you.'

Stella looked up and smiled. 'You should try to meet him. We did care for each other, you know. But we were young.'

'That's what he said. And he hopes to come to the exhibition before it closes. Maybe we can go together to see him.' She held out her phone to Stella. 'He showed me the painting he did of you.'

'Oh my. I loved that picture and those gold earrings. And of course I was pregnant at the time, although he didn't know it.'

Eve laughed. 'So I was there too. I thought I might be.'

Alex brought some toast over. 'Stella, I expect you to persuade your daughter to go back to her own painting now she knows both her parents are so talented.'

Stella smiled at him. 'I will.'

He held out his arms. 'Shall I put Ivy in her carrycot while you eat? I'll leave her near so you can keep looking at her.'

Stella laughed. 'Is it that obvious?'

Kissing the top of Eve's head he laughed too. 'Only to equally besotted people like us.'

Eve smiled up at him, and his answering smile told her how glad he was for her.

With Ivy on the floor beside her Stella took out her own phone scrolled through and put it on the table in front of Eve. 'While we're on the subject of you appearing in paintings,' she said.

At Eve's gasp Alex came to sit close to her, peering at the screen as she clicked through.

'Oh, Stella, these are beautiful,' he said.

And it was just as well he could speak because Eve could only stare down at the paintings. There were five of them from different stages of her life. The earliest on the beach from what must have been Stella's first visit back to see her. With her arms above her head and one foot raised she looked like a young angel about to take flight. The sun turning her hair to fire and her face to gold.

She reached out and clutched her mother's hand. Alex put his arm round her waist, and they sat hardly breathing, while she looked and looked, and Ivy gurgled at their feet.

ACKNOWLEDGEMENTS

My love and thanks to the Curran clan – original and newly forged. Likewise to the Farmers in all their guises. You are not (much) like my fictional families!

Heaps and heaps of gratitude to my first readers, especially Sue and Jack, Sheila, Trisha, Claire and Liza. To my brilliant editor Finn Cotton. To Sarah Hodgson, Janette Currie, Emilie Chambeyron and the whole team at Killer Reads for your support, skill and dedication.

Above all I thank my readers past present and future – there's no point without you. A big virtual hug to anyone who takes the time to post a review and particularly those wonderful bloggers who, for no reward but the love of books, work so hard to spread the word.

And, always and forever, thank you, Paul.

KILLER READS

DISCOVER THE BEST
IN CRIME AND THRILLER

Follow us on social media to get to know the team behind the books, enter exclusive giveaways, learn about the latest competitions, hear from our authors, and lots more:

/KillerReads    /KillerReads